For Ozzy, Ali, Pete and Shirley
– the people who make me feel safe.

Day Zero

Kath

It used to be more of a community round here. When these flats were built at the end of the Sixties there were a lot of young families. The kids played out. We all looked out for them, kept our doors open in the summer, left them on the latch in the winter. It's not like that now. People come and go. You don't know your neighbours. There's gangs and drugs and whatnot. I don't know why I stayed here so long, except that it's home. Where else would I go? So I keep my front door shut and put the chain on and sometimes I don't talk to anybody from one day to the next.

I was going to say something like this wouldn't have happened then, but it would, wouldn't it? Things like this did happen. Maybe they didn't hit the headlines in the same way. Maybe a lot of it was kept quiet. But was it really any safer? Is anywhere safe?

Of course, I blame myself for the way things turned out, even though I was looking out for her, Mina, the little girl next door. We had a system. She walked home on her own, see, let herself into an empty flat where she'd knock on the wall three times. Three-forty every weekday. Knock, knock, knock. *I'm home safe*

1

and sound. And I'd knock back. Knock, knock, knock. *I hear you.* It was our little secret.

It all started quite soon after she and her mum moved in, eight or nine months ago. One day *Countdown* had finished and I'd switched over to *Tenable* and I heard this noise, at least I thought I did. I grabbed the remote and turned the volume down and there it was. Knock, knock, knock. Somebody banging on the wall just behind my chair. I didn't know what to do. It didn't sound like DIY or anything. I'd heard the door go a couple of minutes before, so I supposed it must be her. Her mum was out all hours – I know from experience it's not easy being a single parent – so I reckoned she was there on her own, like me. I hadn't spoken to anyone all day, hadn't been out.

So I got up, went over to the wall and I knocked back and then I shouted, 'You all right?' These walls are as thin as paper. I was pretty sure she'd have heard me, but I didn't catch a reply. I didn't have my hearing aids in – I don't bother if I'm not going out anywhere. I carried on anyway, 'You knock tomorrow, love. Then I'll know you're home safe. I'll be listening out for you.'

And I did. The next day I kept the volume on the telly low and I put my hearing aids in and at three-forty precisely there it was again. Knock, knock, knock. And I got up, walked over to the wall and I knocked back. And that was it.

I moved a chair from the little table in the kitchen and I set it by the wall, ready. Every day, when *Countdown* finished, I went and sat there, waiting for her. Monday to Friday, she always knocked, and sometimes that was the best bit of my day. Knock, knock, knock. *I'm home safe and sound*. Knock, knock, knock. *I hear you.*

For a while, that was enough, but then I got curious. So one day, instead of settling down in my armchair and giving my attention to Warwick and his *Tenable* tower, I grabbed my walking stick and went into the hall. I undid the chain and opened my front door, checking I'd got my keys. I went out onto the walkway and shuffled in my slippers to the next one. I rapped the metal knocker – one, two, three – but she didn't come to the door. Bracing myself on my stick, I leaned down and prised the letter box open. I couldn't quite get my face level, but I wasn't far off. 'Hello? It's only me from next door.' I waited. I thought I heard movement, but I couldn't see anything, couldn't get low enough. 'My name's Kath. I'm the one knocking on the wall.' Still nothing. 'If you ever need anything, I'm always there. Or if you want a chat . . .' I felt awkward now, like I shouldn't have started this. 'Anyway, I'm glad you're home.'

I was about to go when I heard a sound, a scuffling noise, and I got the sense that she was very close to the door. And then I heard her voice, almost a whisper.

'My mum says you're a witch.'

I was taken aback. It was such an odd thing. I felt like I'd been stung. I tried to keep calm.

'Goodness, that's a funny thing to say. No, darlin', I'm not a witch. I'm just an old crock living on my own with bad feet, creaky knees and going a bit deaf.'

'Definitely not a witch?'

'Definitely not.'

'I'm not allowed to open the door. Not to anyone.'

'Very sensible.' My back was starting to hurt doubled over like that. 'I'd better go now anyway. I've left Warwick on pause. He won't like that for long. I just wanted to say hello. I'm Kath. Did I say?'

'Yes. I'm Mina.'

'Hello, Mina. That's a nice name. Knock tomorrow, Mina. Let me know you're home safe and sound.'

And she did. The next day and the next, and although we didn't speak again, it felt like I spent my afternoons with someone, that I was checking in with her and she was checking in with me. One time, just on impulse, I bought a Freddo frog in the corner shop – you know, one of those chocolate ones in their own wrapper – and posted it through her letter box. In the morning I never heard my letter box go, but when I went to the kitchen to put the kettle on for a second cup of tea, just before nine, there was a single piece of paper on the mat and a drawing of a rainbow and 'Thank You' in beautifully neat handwriting. I stuck it up on my fridge door. I've still got it. Get a lump in my throat every time I see it.

Then one afternoon, Wednesday 14th November, I'll never forget it, she didn't knock on the wall. I keep going over and over it, even now. If I'd done things differently, right there and then, none of what came after would have happened, and that little girl would still be safe at home.

Day One

Den

The rain had been lashing against the front window of the café for two days. People kept bursting in, puffing and blowing, dripping onto the floor, trailing wet, dirty footprints all over the place. From the kitchen, Dad was constantly on at him to mop up, keep it dry. 'We don't need any lawsuits, Den. All it takes is for one of the buggers to slip over and we'll be overrun with fucking lawyers. No win, no fee! That's all we need!'

Den sighed as the bell rang again and the door flew open. He looked up from wiping down the table but when he recognised who it was, he raced over and held the door open. He didn't know her name but the old woman was one of his regulars, one of the nice ones. She was all wrapped up in a big black raincoat a bit like a cape, hood up, water glistening on its plastic surface. Her walking stick made a clicking sound on the lino and her trolley left two wet parallel lines as she dragged it behind her.

'You all right?' he said, as she peered out from under her hood. 'This weather, eh? Nasty.'

She reached up and took her hood down. The front of her

hair was all wet, thin grey strands plastered to her head, and her glasses were spattered with raindrops and starting to fog up. It wasn't a good look and she seemed bothered, very flustered. This weather would get anyone down, especially if you're not too steady on your legs. 'Nice weather for ducks, eh?' He was trying to cheer her up, but she squinted at him.

'What?'

'That's what they say, isn't it? Nice weather for ducks, although I'm guessing most ducks would be as pissed off as the rest of us with this lot.' He heard himself give out that nervous laugh, the one that seemed to come out at the end of nearly every sentence whether he wanted it to or not.

She looked at him blankly and he wondered if she'd even heard – she didn't sometimes – then her expression darkened and he thought, *Shut up, Den, there's something really wrong with her.* 'Are you okay? Do you need to sit down?'

She put her hand on his arm, her grip surprisingly strong through the material of his sweatshirt. 'It's not me,' she said, 'at least it might be me. I might just be a stupid old fool, but I'm worried about my neighbour.'

'Okay, sit here and you can tell me about it.'

He pulled the nearest chair out and steadied her a little as she sat down. She let out a grunting sort of sigh and he wondered how difficult it would be to get her up again. She took her glasses off and started wiping them on the bottom of her sodden coat. He sprinted over to the counter, put his wet cloth down, and fetched her a clean tissue. 'So, who's your neighbour and why are you worried?'

'I only know her first name. It's a little girl. She lives with her mum. I know this is going to sound silly, but I haven't seen her since yesterday.'

She scrubbed at both lenses and then crumpled the tissue and put it in her pocket and her glasses back on.

'The girl?'

'Yes.'

She frowned and he could see this had been eating away at her.

'What does her mum say?'

'I haven't seen her either.'

'They're both away? Like, on holiday or something?'

'No, I don't think so. It's not half-term.'

'So maybe they've moved? I mean, are you close? Would they have told you?'

'We're not close, not like that. I've barely spoken to the woman, but the little girl and I are . . . well, sort of friends.'

He was tempted to put a reassuring hand on her shoulder but reticence held him back. 'Mrs . . . ?' He raised his eyebrows, inviting her to tell him her name.

'Cartright. Kath. Everyone calls me Kath.'

It didn't feel right, somehow. Felt disrespectful with her being so old, so he came out with something else. 'Mrs C, it doesn't sound like there's any cause for alarm. I'm sure there's a perfectly rational explanation.' His laugh was there again.

'No, something's not right,' she said. 'You see, we'd got into the habit of knocking on the wall. When Mina got back from school, she'd knock three times and I'd knock back. It was our little thing. She went off to school like normal yesterday, but she didn't come home. Not today either.'

His stomach gave a little lurch. 'Mina, did you say? Mina's your neighbour?'

'Yes, do you know her?'

'Just started secondary school? Really small for her age? Brown hair tied in two plaits?' She nodded. 'She comes in here sometimes. Has a doughnut or some chips.'

There were a few kids like Mina. Stragglers and strays, making their own way home to an empty house. Most of them were okay, but he worried about the others. The pinched faces, the shadows under their eyes. When there was mud on their sleeves or the knees of their trousers were torn. Sometimes they ran into the café

7

like it was some kind of sanctuary. They didn't buy anything, just dawdled in a corner, letting time pass, hoping whoever was outside would have got bored and gone away. Dad would chase them out, but Den, knowing a bit about being picked on, let them stay.

Mina was one of the ones he worried about. She was always on her own, never with a friend. She never had much money either, sometimes none at all. She'd come in and linger by the counter where there was a box of lollipops, some chewing gum and little bars of chocolate. She'd pocketed a lolly once when she thought he wasn't looking. After that he'd taken to turning away sometimes, pretending to clean round the coffee machine when she was in, so she could do a bit of foraging in peace. Other times he'd slide a chocolate bar across the counter towards her, then wink and hold his finger up to his mouth. Their little secret.

She never said much. He'd try, 'Good day at school?' but she'd shrug or mumble something. He only knew she was called Mina because she had dropped her bag one day and her books had spilled out. He had helped her pick them up and her name was on the front of her planner in beautifully neat, clear handwriting. 'There you go, Mina,' he'd said, as he handed it back.

She'd flashed a look at him then, like the sound of her own name stung her. She stayed looking, just for a moment, a deer in the headlights, then looked away. He'd made a mental note not to use her name out loud again. He'd never meant to worry her.

'—her today or yesterday?' Mrs C was looking at him, expecting an answer. He realised he'd been miles away. 'Have you seen her?' she repeated.

'No. No, not today. Not yesterday, I don't think. I can't remember. But if her mum's not home either . . .'

'Her mum sometimes isn't there for days.' Her mouth formed a straight, disapproving line.

They looked at each other. It wasn't exactly a surprise to Den, but it was still shocking, that someone would leave a child that young on their own.

'I'll keep my eyes peeled, Mrs C,' he said.

'Should I report it?' She was blinking at him through her thick lenses, her eyes distorted, almost cartoon-like. But this wasn't funny, thought Den – she was worried, and so was he now.

'I'm not sure. I mean, if they're both not there, there's not really anything to report, is there?'

'Maybe not. I'm going to walk up to the school. See if I can find any clues on the way.' She started to gather herself in order to get up from the chair, then frowned.

'What's that?' She leaned sideways, stretching her arm down the side of the chair, and scrabbled about on the floor under the table. When she sat up, she had something pink in her hand, like a scrap of cloth or something. 'It's one of those scrunchies that they do their hair with these days,' she said. 'It was rubber bands and ribbons in my day.'

'Someone must have dropped it,' Den said. 'I'll keep it behind the counter, shall I, in case they're looking for it?' He held his hand out. She hesitated, then handed it over. 'Don't suppose they'll ask. Kids lose things all the time, don't they?'

Den offered her his arm to brace against and helped her up. The rain spattered against the window as another gust blew in from the west.

'It's dark and it's coming down in stair rods, Mrs C. You're best off going home.'

'I can't bear just sitting there waiting,' she said. 'I want to do something.'

She started walking slowly towards the door. Her swollen feet looked like they were trying to escape from her saturated Velcro shoes.

'Do you want me to come with you?' He hadn't thought this through. Mum wasn't in to help out. Dad would go nuts if he had to cover front of house as well as the kitchen. But it was quiet now and besides, there was something about her. He could see she needed help.

'Oh, no, it's all right,' she said, and he felt a surge of relief. No need to risk the wrath of his father this time. 'But thank you . . . ?' It was her turn to enquire.

'Den,' he said. The laugh was there again, almost like he was apologising for his own name.

'I might as well treat myself now I'm here. Can you wrap up a couple of those iced buns for me, please?' she said.

'Sure,' he said and went round the back of the counter, selecting the two biggest buns for her and placing them in a paper bag. Mrs C tugged at the top of her trolley and started digging about inside. 'On the house.'

She frowned. 'It's all right. I'm not a charity case. I can pay my way.'

She handed over the money.

'Okay. Let me know how you get on, yeah?'

'Thanks, love. I will.'

She put the paper bag in her trolley and fastened the top shut. As she headed for the door, the trolley kept banging into the tables and chairs. Hearing the noise, Dad bustled out of the kitchen. 'Is everything all right? Has there been an accident? I told the boy to keep the floor dry. I mean, how difficult is it?'

'Everything's fine, Dad,' Den said. He held the door for Mrs C and she hobbled out into the filthy evening. There was an umbrella lying in a puddle near the bin, a dark colour with lighter spots on. Some of the spokes were at odd angles, clearly broken. Dad was a stickler for keeping the pavement outside their café clean, so Den stepped across, picked it up and put it in the bin. Then he took shelter again in the doorway and watched, with a creeping sense of unease, as Mrs C headed up the road. He wasn't sure everything *was* all right. He wasn't sure at all.

10

Day One

Sandy

Sandy hadn't meant to stay out overnight, but there'd been a lock-in at the Flamingo Bar. Brett had said that he'd bung her a few extra quid and with things being the way they were, she couldn't really turn down extra money. The party had gone on until the early hours and one thing had led to another – she and Brett had been circling round each other for ages, not quite getting it together – and it just felt . . . okay. Better than that, it felt right.

Mina would be fine. She was always asleep by the time Sandy got home after work so it wouldn't make any difference to her. She usually let Sandy sleep in, too – she was eleven now and could get herself up and off to school no problem. No harm done. Just this once.

Brett was as good in bed as she'd thought he'd be. They were both a bit pissed; maybe that helped. But, if anything, it was even better the next morning. Waking up together, feeling so comfortable and relaxed with each other. They both said a sleepy, 'Good morning,' and then smiled. She snuggled up to him and he held her in his arms and, for the first time in ages – years? – she felt safe. She traced the shapes of the ink on his chest and neck. He had a little scar on his bottom lip. She ran her finger over it gently.

'How did you get this?' she said. She wanted to know everything about him.

'I'll tell you later,' he said, and kissed the tip of her finger, then pulled her even closer.

They got up at about ten and she helped him clear up the bar and get everything set up for lunchtime opening. There was a steady flow of customers, regulars and passing trade. Brett had a good little business here. She started wondering about the life they could have together. Living here, working side by side. The flat above the pub was a hundred times nicer than the shithole in Nelson House that she shared with Mina.

Mina! Jesus, she'd almost forgotten about her. She must get back before she got home from school. She checked her phone for the time. There was a missed call from a number she didn't recognise, probably just a call centre, and a text, too. The text was from the school.

'*Mina Dimitriou has been absent on the following day 15/11/2018 9.15am. Please respond by specifying the reason for absence.*' Shit, it had come through when she was still in bed with Brett. Damn.

'I'd better go,' she said. 'I think Mina's off sick.'

Brett was busy with some customers. 'Okay, babe. See you tomorrow.' He hardly looked at her, before going back to pulling the next pint. She felt a surge of disappointment but knew she was being unreasonable. She went to collect her coat from the hallway behind the bar. As she was doing up the zip, a shadow darkened the doorway. Brett was there, watching her.

'Hey,' he said. 'Come here, you.'

He folded her into his arms and kissed her.

'Take care, okay? Let me know how Mina is. Text me, yeah?'

'Okay.' Her face was glowing with pleasure. He was the real deal.

It was dark as she rode the bus home. The rain spattered against the window. She wondered what was wrong with Mina, felt a pang of anxiety at the thought of her being ill on her own. Typical it was the one night she wasn't there. She must get her a mobile phone. They couldn't afford it, but perhaps she could pick up a cheap pay as you go one somewhere. She'd ask Brett. Someone in the bar could probably get her one.

She got off at the stop at the edge of the estate, and a gust of wind blew rain into her face. She put her hood up and ran for it, along the parade of shops and into the square. A young guy on a bicycle was coming the other way, with a dog running along beside him. The guy was dressed all in black – hoodie, joggers, trainers – and rode too fast, too close to her for comfort, the wheels of his bike sending spray up from a puddle as he passed, soaking the bottoms of Sandy's legs.

'Hey!' she called out, but he was away. She didn't even know if he'd heard her.

She was glad to get through the door to the stairwell, puffing a little with the exertion and the weather. She pulled her hood down and checked the lift. Still broken. With the familiar smell of urine and cigarette smoke catching at the back of her throat, she set off up the stairs.

The flat felt wrong as soon as she opened the door. It was dark and quiet, just the muffled sound of next door's telly coming through the wall. It wasn't like Mina was a noisy kid but she would always have the lights on and the TV going. Perhaps she was in bed. Oh God, how bad was she?

Sandy flicked on the hall light and called out, 'Mina? I'm home.' She walked along to Mina's bedroom. The door was open. She knew it was empty before she put the light on and looked in. In a way, it was a relief. She hadn't been there all day, being sick or shivering with a temperature, but where was she?

Sandy frowned. She knew she shouldn't have left her overnight, but Mina knew the rules, straight to school, straight home again, but she hadn't been at school, so what on earth was she playing at? Maybe she was proving a point. If Sandy could stay out, so

13

could she. That's not how it worked, though, and she'd have to have words with her. God, why was everything so difficult? She had to work – Mina knew that. Why couldn't she have behaved just for one night? Anger was starting to replace her relief.

Day One

Kath

I didn't find anything between the flats and the school, of course. Not sure what I was thinking might be there – her schoolbag, her coat? Anyway, it was cold and dark by the time I got back and my feet were sopping wet and killing me. I looked up at Nelson House and contemplated the broken lift and the three flights of stairs between me and home and a hot bath and bed. I was pretty much done in and I didn't actually know how I was going to get my trolley up there.

There was a soft light in the kitchen window of my flat – I leave the hall light on and the telly, so it's nice to come back to, but that wasn't what caught my eye. The lights were on in the flat next door! That was all the incentive I needed to tackle the stairs. I didn't even notice the pain in my knees – I was up there like a jack rabbit.

I stopped at number seven and knocked on the door. Almost straight away I heard a voice, 'If you've lost your key, I'm going to fucking kill you—' The door opened and I was looking at the angry face of Mina's mum. She still had her coat on, an oversize khaki parka with a pink fake fur collar, so I guessed she hadn't been home for long.

'What do you want?' she said, in the nice, neighbourly manner I'd come to expect.

'I'm sorry to knock.' I wasn't. I was actually bursting with curiosity. 'Is your daughter home?'

Her scowl grew deeper. 'Mina? No, she's not. What's it to you?'

'I've been worried about her. She didn't come home from school yesterday. I listen out for her, you see, and I didn't hear her yesterday or today.'

I was expecting another volley of hostility, something about minding my own business, but it didn't come. Instead, her face softened a little. 'She hasn't been home?'

'No. I don't think so. I usually hear the door, and—' I stopped. Mina knocking on the wall might not be allowed and I didn't want to get her into trouble.

'Shit,' Mina's mum said. 'Wait there.'

Leaving the front door open, she retreated into the flat. She went into one of the bedrooms and I could hear her swearing.

She came back to me and this time she was wide-eyed with panic. 'Her bag's not here. Her coat's not here. What should I do?'

'Could she be staying with a friend?'

She was chewing at the inside of her mouth now, eyes darting here, there and everywhere. 'No. No. She hasn't got any friends.'

'She might have made friends at school and not told you . . .'

The fierceness was back. 'She wouldn't go off with anyone. Not Mina. She knows the rules. Straight to school. Straight back. No messing. Something's happened. Someone's got her.' And then she crumbled, disintegrated before my eyes. Her face seemed to collapse in on itself and her knees gave way and she crouched in the doorway and let out a heart-rending scream. 'Where is she? Oh, my baby! My baby!'

As she fell apart, I somehow became calmer. Someone needed

to take charge. I bent down and rubbed her back. 'It'll be all right. She won't have gone far. We'll ring the police. They'll find her.'

'The police?' She looked up at me, tear-stained face a sallow yellow in the harsh light of the walkway.

'Yes,' I said. 'We need to report her missing. The sooner the better.'

Day One

Sandy

She was dog-tired and a bit hungover but she needed to stay awake for when Mina came back. She got some music going and put the kettle on for some coffee. She'd have to read her the riot act, of course, but then maybe she'd cook them both something nice. They could sit and eat together, watch some crap on the telly. Mina was obviously pissed off with her; fair enough, but she couldn't act up like this. Sandy had to work, so they needed to find a way to deal with it. They'd work it out, find a way through, like they had been doing for eleven years. It wasn't perfect, never had been, but they were both still here, weren't they?

She wandered over to the fridge, but it was almost bare. She'd been going to do a Lidl shop on Monday when Frank's lackey had called round, demanding the latest payment. She didn't have it all, so she'd given him what cash she had. Which included the food money. She had last night's wages from the bar, now, though. Perhaps they'd get a takeaway. Payday treat.

She was going to run a bath, then remembered that the immersion heater wasn't working. She needed to ring the bastard landlords again. Where had she put that number? The time flashed up when she switched on her phone – just gone five. For fuck's sake, they'd all have gone home. She felt a flash of temper at the thought of another night with no hot water. Jesus, this was a dump. What the hell had she done to deserve this?

Gone five, though . . . where was Mina? This was getting beyond a joke.

And then she heard the door knocker. She charged towards the door, ready to tear into Mina, but when she opened the door, it wasn't her. It was the old bag from next door, standing there looking like a drowned rat. It took Sandy a while to take in what she was saying. Yes, she knew Mina wasn't home yet. What about it? Then she twigged that the woman was telling her that she hadn't heard Mina yesterday either.

Her mind started to race. She checked Mina's bedroom again, even though she knew she wasn't there. And it started to sink in. Mina was missing. She'd been missing for at least twenty-four hours. Her baby was gone.

Day One

Kath

It seemed to take an age for the police to come, but I suppose it was only ten minutes or so. Mina's mum rang them from her mobile, crouched down in the doorway, and when she'd answered all their questions, I helped her inside and sat her down in the lounge. I made us both a cup of sweet tea. I don't normally have sugar because of my diabetes but I needed it. I needed something. We had to have it black because the milk in the fridge was so far gone it made me gag when I sniffed it.

Mina's mum sat on the threadbare sofa and nursed her mug with both hands. The cigarette she'd started was lying on the rim of a saucer full of fag ends, on the upturned crate they were using as a coffee table. Tears were still running down her face, dripping onto her lap, but she didn't make any effort to wipe her eyes. Her lips were moving but I couldn't hear what she was saying, even with both hearing aids in. She was muttering and mumbling to herself.

Eventually her speech became slower and clearer, although it still sounded like she was talking to herself not to me. 'I'm not a bad person. I never meant this to happen. Oh my God. Oh my God.'

She might not have meant it to happen, but a good mum doesn't leave their child overnight, do they? I've been there – single parent on this estate, trying to make ends meet – but I never left my Evie alone. This wasn't the time to say it, so I kept quiet.

The place was an absolute state, so depressing – wallpaper peeling off, stains on the carpet. The sofa faced a massive TV set on a low stand, and apart from that there was a ratty-looking beanbag on the floor and the upturned crate. No bookshelves or books. No pictures on the walls. No ornaments.

'You on your own with her here?' I said, knowing what the answer was. 'I would've helped, you know, if you'd asked. Given her some tea. I'd have been happy to.'

Mina's mum looked blankly at me. 'We were doing all right, thanks, doing the best we could, anyway. We *are*, I mean. She's sensible. She knows the rules and she follows them. The more I think about it, the more I think that something's happened. She wouldn't just go off.'

'Should we ring the hospital? Perhaps she's been in an—' I didn't want to say the word out loud. Silly, isn't it? Saying words, putting a name to things, doesn't actually make them worse, or jinx things, but it feels like they might.

'They'd have rung me, wouldn't they? She's got her name on her schoolbag. They'd have found me or . . . do you think we should?' She glanced up at me and I could see real fear in her eyes. I felt it too, a sense of responsibility for this little girl I hardly knew.

'The police are coming now. I imagine they'll do all that. Let's sit tight, shall we?'

I looked round the room and tried to think of Mina here every afternoon on her own, knocking on the wall. It made me so sad. She could've been with me.

'Where were you last night, love?'

She seemed to see me for the first time since we'd come

indoors. I wondered if she'd ask me not to tell, beg me, maybe, but she didn't do that. Instead, her face darkened and she sort of hissed at me. 'What's it got to do with you? Who do you think you are?'

I'm the witch next door, I thought, as far as you're concerned, but this wasn't the time to wade in.

'I'm Kath,' I said. 'Just Kath. I should have introduced myself properly when you moved in.'

To be honest, I'd tried. I'd seen them going in and out, carrying their stuff in black bin bags, so of course I said hello. Mina's mum had ushered her daughter into the flat, closed the door in my face and that was that. I didn't try again.

Now there was a loud rat-a-tat-tat from the front. She looked at me, startled, but didn't make a move.

'That'll be the police,' I said. 'Shall I let them in?'

I thought for a moment she was going to say no, but instead she said, 'The police. Is this real? Is this happening?' She looked utterly lost, and young, like a girl herself.

'Yes, love. I'm sorry, it is. I'll go, shall I?'

She nodded and I went into the hall and opened the door. There were two uniformed officers outside, a man and a woman.

'Miss Dimitriou?'

'No, she's in the lounge. Do you want to go through?'

'And you are?'

'Just a neighbour. I'm next door.' I followed them back to the lounge and hovered in the doorway. 'I'll leave you to it, shall I?'

The officers introduced themselves as Naz and Jodie, the use of first names a nice touch, I thought.

'Is there someone else we can call? A relative? A friend?' Jodie asked, sitting next to her on the sofa.

Mina's mum shook her head. 'There isn't anyone. Can you stay, Kath?'

The officers nodded at me and I said, 'Okay, love,' and looked for somewhere to sit. There was no way I was tackling the beanbag, not with my knees, but Naz was ahead of me. He fetched two chairs from the kitchen and set one down for me near the door, while he took the other one.

They started by asking her name. 'Sandy. Alexandra.' You learn something every day, I thought. Then Jodie asked for basic details about Mina and when she had gone missing.

Sandy was hesitant.

'I'm not sure exactly. Kath here said Mina didn't come home yesterday.' Naz glanced at me. I nodded but didn't say anything. 'I was working last night. I always work late. Mina puts herself to bed. I know it's not ideal, but she was sensible. Is sensible. I stayed out last night. Before you say anything, I've never done it before. This was the first time.'

Was sensible.

'Did you check in with her by phone or text?' Jodie was asking the questions and Naz was taking notes in an old-fashioned notebook.

'No. She doesn't have a phone. There's no one to call apart from me, and it's difficult, taking personal calls at work, you know.'

'What is it that you do, Sandy?'

We all caught her hesitation. 'I do all sorts, anything I can to make ends meet. Bar work. Waitressing. I'm trying to get extra hours at the moment.'

'So where were you last night?'

'I was working in a bar.'

'All night?'

'It was open till three last night. The boss let me stay over.'

The officers exchanged glances. 'You'll have to give us the details, Sandy.'

'Yeah, all right. It's not about me, though, is it? You should be out looking for Mina. Every minute you're here, you're not looking for her. It's another minute she's with whoever's got her.' Her voice was getting louder, shriller as she spoke. She was working herself up again. 'Is anyone even out looking for her now?'

'We just need to check a few details. So when did you last see her or have contact with her?'

Sandy held her forehead with her hand and closed her eyes. 'Yesterday. I last saw her yesterday morning.' Her jaw was tensing. 'She went off to school like normal. Half past eight. It only takes ten minutes to walk to school.'

'And she walks there on her own?'

'Yes. She's fine. Like I said, she's sensible.'

'And do you know if she got to school?'

'There was a text. Looks like she didn't turn up today, so she must have been there yesterday.'

'You've only just seen it?'

'I just saw it this afternoon. I came home straight away,' she snapped. This time she noticed the glances exchanged. 'Look, I'm not gonna win Mother of the Year, okay? I know that. And I know you're gonna hang me out to dry but I'm doing my best, okay? I made one mistake, that's all. One mistake and I'm being punished for it. It's not about me. It's about Mina. Where is she? Where is she? Kath, you tell them, please? Tell them that Mina's a good kid. That she wouldn't just go off.'

Now everyone was looking at me, and I could feel myself getting hot and bothered. 'She is a good girl,' I said. 'She comes home on her own every day, good as gold. I hear her getting in, you see, round about three-forty every day, regular as clockwork. That's why I started worrying yesterday. I didn't hear her. Sandy's right. This isn't normal, officer. Something's happened.'

Day One

Sandy

The woman officer, Jodie, asked Sandy for a description of Mina. She found herself at a bit of a loss what to say. She was a young girl. Small for her age, slight, like a little bird – she'd been six weeks premature and somehow she'd never caught up. Long brown hair, school uniform. That's all there was.

'We'll need a recent photograph.'

She could see all three of them scanning round the room. She hadn't got round to putting any photos up. No one said anything, but she could feel them judging her.

'I haven't got one, not printed out,' she said. 'There's one from her primary school somewhere, but it's ancient.'

'Maybe on your phone. Can I have a look?' Jodie reached her hand out towards Sandy.

Jesus, the thought of them going through the pictures on her phone! She tightened her grip.

'I'll do it,' she said. She turned away from Jodie and started scrolling through. There was nothing bad on here, just selfies from the bar, but it wasn't a good look in the circumstances. Maybe

25

she'd delete them later. She was sweating now, could feel little beads of it coming out on her forehead. Her pits were getting sticky and smelly. At last she found one – a selfie of Mina and her they'd taken on her birthday. 'Here. This one. It was in April.'

She twisted round and showed the screen to Jodie and then Naz.

'Great,' said Jodie. 'Can you send it to me? We need to get this out as quickly as possible.'

Her hands were shaking as she entered Jodie's details and messaged her the photo. She was willing it to send, so they wouldn't take her phone off her. As they waited, she stared at the picture. Two faces grinning at the camera. *Me and my girl.* That had been a good day. A burger and a milkshake and then sitting in the park on a bench overlooking a little pond. It had one of those brass plaques on the back – 'Elizabeth's bench – she loved this place'. It was soon after they had moved here. New place, fresh start and all that. She'd been worried about money, tired from dealing with all the admin and extra expense that goes with moving, but Mina had been all right. They're adaptable, aren't they, kids?

She didn't care what these pigs and her snotty neighbour thought. She was a good mum. She did her best. Looking at the picture, it showed. Mina was happy. Wasn't she?

'Okay,' said Jodie, 'I've got it. I'll send it through to the office. Now, can you tell me what she was wearing yesterday morning?'

'I dunno, school uniform – not like in the photo, her new one for Fincham Park School. She's in Year Seven. Polo shirt, green jumper, black trousers.' She tried to picture her leaving that morning. 'She had a black quilted coat and she'd done her hair in plaits with pink scrunchies.'

Kath squawked as she spilled her tea. It slopped down the edge onto her hand and then dripped on the carpet.

'What?' said Sandy.

'I found a pink scrunchie,' Kath said. 'When I went out looking for Mina just now. It might not be anything. I mean, lots of girls have them, don't they?'

Sandy was on her feet now. 'Show me it!'

Kath looked startled.

'I don't have it,' she said. 'I found it on the floor of the café on the corner. I gave it to the young lad there. Den, his name is. Den's got it.'

Day One

Kath

'The café?' Sandy screeched. 'That's where that photo was taken! That's where I took her for her birthday!' She was heading for the door, but Naz stood up now and blocked her way. 'What are you doing?' Sandy screamed. 'Get out of my way!'

Naz stayed where he was. In fact, he put his arm out to stop her pushing past. 'Calm down, please, Sandy,' he said. 'We'll send officers round there, get them to talk to him. For the time being, we need you here, in case she turns up.'

'Bullshit! If she was gonna turn up, she'd be here! Someone's got her. It sounds like it's this guy, Den or whatever. You can't stop me!'

'Sandy, think about it, please. The scrunchie could be anybody's. You won't help find Mina by rushing round accusing people. Let us do our job, okay? Jodie's already sending Mina's picture through and it will be circulating soon. We'll have all our officers looking out for her. Let's sit back down and have some more tea.' Sandy let herself be led back to the sofa by Jodie. Naz turned to me. 'Do you know where things are, Kath? Helping hand?'

I eased myself onto my feet, puffing a little. My ankles were really swollen and my knees were sore. I'd pay for all this tomorrow, but I wouldn't care if little Mina was safe and sound. Once in the kitchen, Naz started pumping me for information. He wasn't even subtle about it.

'I'll need to take a statement from you, but to start with, can I just check, you heard Mina setting off for school yesterday but she didn't come home?'

'Yes, that's right,' I said, lining up three mugs and dropping teabags into them. I didn't want another one. I needed a wee as it was, and there was no way I was going to use Sandy's bathroom. I could just imagine the state it was in. 'I definitely heard her leaving in the morning, but then nothing yesterday or this morning.'

'Is that your TV playing?' He tipped his head towards the wall.

'Yes, I leave it on to deter burglars. Is that wrong, officer?'

'Call me Naz, please, and no, it's just . . . it's quite loud. I'm wondering if you'd actually hear the door. You might have missed something.'

'Oh, I see. I do have it up loud if I haven't got my hearing aids in, but I have the sound off and the subtitles on in the afternoons, because I listen out for her. For Mina. We have an arrangement you see. She knocks on the wall when she gets home and I knock back. It's our little thing.' Naz raised his eyebrows. 'I was worried yesterday, but, you know, I told myself she could've been at an after-school club or something. And now I just think I should have done something then. Well, seeing this place, I feel like I should have done something a long time ago. Rung the NSPCC or something. I mean, look at it . . . I had no idea.'

The kitchen had the same layout as mine, but it was very different. My cupboards were full of tins and cereal packets, bags of porridge and biscuits, and there's always the basics in my fridge – milk, spread, a packet of ham and whatnot – there was hardly anything here. I suddenly felt so sad for the life that Mina had been living in this flat, with only a wall between us.

My bottom lip began to tremble. I blinked hard, then fished in my sleeve to find my tissue and pressed it under my glasses and against my eyes before the tears could leak out.

Naz put his hand on my shoulder. 'It's all right, Kath. We'll find her.'

I sniffed, hard, tucked my tissue up my sleeve and turned to the kettle, which had finished boiling. As I poured steaming water into each of the mugs, he said, 'Did you hear anything else, Kath? Did Mina and her mum argue at all? Did they argue yesterday morning?'

My hand wavered and some of the water spilled onto the worktop. 'I don't like to tell tales . . .'

'Kath, it's not telling tales. This is a missing girl we're talking about. Anything, any little detail, could be useful.'

'Well, they did have a row yesterday. I heard voices, shouting, and the door slamming.'

'Yeah? What time was that, Kath?'

'Normal setting-off time, twenty-five to nine.'

'And the voices? It was Mina and her mum?'

'Yes. I couldn't hear what they were saying, but she – Sandy – was angry and I could tell Mina was upset.'

It felt bad telling him, like I was pointing a finger. I was getting flustered, blinking hard and starting to feel all hot.

'It's okay, Kath. Anything you say will be treated in confidence. We just want to find Mina.'

'I know. So do I. That's why I went looking for her when she didn't knock this afternoon. I walked right up to the school, called into the café, asked around a bit. The thought of her being out there somewhere in this filthy weather. She's only little . . .'

'Someone's checking out the school now,' he said. 'Let's talk about the café. Had they seen her there?'

'Not today. They knew who she was, though. The lad there, Den, was worried when I told him, offered to come looking with me.'

'And did he go with you?'

'No, I said I was all right walking there and back on my own. I asked him if I should ring you, the police, but he told me not to.'

'Wait a minute. He told you not to ring us?'

I hadn't thought anything of it at the time, but now I was starting to wonder. I could see that Naz was too.

'Yeah. Said there was nothing to report. He actually suggested that I stopped looking and came home . . . and then I found that scrunchie.'

'Where exactly was that?'

'I was sat on a chair by one of the tables and it caught my eye, lying near my feet. I bent down and picked it up. We agreed he'd keep it, in case someone came looking for it. He was quite insistent on keeping it. Was that wrong? Should I have kept it?'

The word 'evidence' kept crossing my mind. That's what it was, wasn't it? I'd found a piece of evidence.

'No, no, it's fine. We'll check everything out. Try not to worry. You've done everything you could. It's up to us now. We've got the resources. We'll find her. Let's get these teas sorted.'

'Okay. How do you like your tea? Milk and sugar?'

'Just milk, no sugar for both of us, please.'

'Ha! Julie Andrews, that's what my Ray used to call it.'

'Julie Andrews?'

'White nun. Milk, no sugar! *The Sound of Music*?' He was looking blankly at me and I didn't know whether he'd never heard of Julie Andrews (was that possible?) or there was something un-PC about joking about nuns. Maybe he was shocked I was joking at all at a time like this and I was wishing now that I hadn't said anything. I changed the subject.

'There's no milk,' I said. 'It's gone off. Wait a minute, though. I've got some in my bag outside. I'll fetch it.'

'Thanks, Kath,' he said and he gave me a reassuring smile that let me know that whatever the problem was with Julie Andrews, we were over that now. I could hear Jodie on her radio in the

31

lounge and I stopped in the kitchen doorway and then went back to Naz.

'She'd done it before, you know,' I said.

He was mopping up the spilled water from the kettle with a drying-up cloth. Lovely to see a man pitching in like that. Now he looked up at me. 'Done what, Kath?'

'Left Mina on her own overnight. I'm sorry I never rang the NSPCC. I should have done. Being a parent is a privilege, isn't it?' I sighed, close to tears again. 'There are some people who should never have kids . . .'

Day One

Den

It wasn't unusual to have blue lights and sirens round the estate. When he was a kid there had been community coppers and Den had known them by name. Dad would call them in for vandalism or antisocial behaviour in the car park outside the shop. They'd often stop by for a bacon sandwich and a cuppa – Dad offered an unofficial discount to anyone in uniform. 'It's like protection, innit? Keep the people who matter on your side.' Den didn't recognise the officer who came in just after six, though, and walked straight up to the till.

'Evening, mate,' he said. 'We're looking for a missing girl. Have you seen her?' He held his phone out. The little girl in the photograph was only just recognisable. The photo, cropped and blown up, had obviously been a bit blurry to start with. And the girl's hair was down instead of tied back. But it was still Mina, and the pang of concern that had been gnawing away at Den's stomach since Mrs C had been in got sharper.

'I haven't seen her today,' he said.

'Do you recognise her?'

33

'Yes, she comes in here sometimes. I'd know if I'd seen her. She definitely hasn't been in today.' The staccato laugh at the end of his sentence – there, whether he wanted it or not.

'How about yesterday?'

'No. I don't think so. Maybe.'

Dad came bustling out of the kitchen, wiping his hands on his apron. 'What's going on? Another stabbing, is it? I blame the parents. These fucking kids need a bit of discipline. It's like the Wild West out there.'

'No, Dad, it's the girl Mrs C was looking for earlier. You'll know her.' Den tipped his head at the copper, who took the hint and held his phone out across the counter towards Dad, who grew quiet as he studied the photograph.

'There are so many kids in and out of here, mate. I'm in the back most of the time. I don't know about this one, but that's a bad do, for a child to go missing. Have you got posters we can put up? We need to get people looking.'

'We haven't got posters yet, but we will have if this goes on tomorrow.'

'Tomorrow? Tomorrow might be too late! We need to get this out there now!' Dad had come out from behind the counter. He was gesticulating wildly, invading the copper's personal space.

'Dad! It's okay. They know what they're doing, right? It's their job.'

'To be honest, sir, social media is the place to start these days. The force will be tweeting about it. We'll send this picture to all the news sites. It goes straight to people's phones. That's what everyone uses these days.'

Dad shook his head. 'Social media! People need to get off their phones and start looking in the garages and sheds and anywhere else. We need a search party! People can meet here if you like.'

'Trust me, sir, we have this in hand. We'll be doing house-to-house inquiries. If you think she might have been here yesterday, what time would that have been?' He was talking to Den now

34

and Dad stopped his grandstanding for a moment and looked at his son.

'I don't know. I can't be sure. It might have been the day before. She sometimes comes in on her way home from school. It would have been around half past three.'

'Do you have CCTV?' He was scanning around now. Dad told him that there was one camera in the café and one outside. 'Okay. I've got to get along this row of shops, but either myself or someone else will be back to look at the footage. I've noted it all down. Someone will be back.' He checked his phone and frowned. 'Hang on. I'm being told that you're holding a pink hair scrunchie here? It was found on the floor?'

Den felt his face flush, like he'd been caught out. 'Yes, it's behind the till. Here—' He laughed again, an automatic defence mechanism.

The scrunchie was drier but still grubby from the floor and now he noticed there was a dark hair caught up on it. He felt almost weak at the sight. It could be Mina's – this could be the last trace of her. Irrationally he wanted to keep it, but of course he handed it over, dropping it into the plastic bag the officer held open.

'And where exactly did you find it?'

He pointed to the spot on the floor, next to where Mrs C's chair had been. 'It was this afternoon.'

The officer sealed the bag, put it in his pocket and with a quick, 'Cheers, mate,' turned to leave. Dad saw him out, then stood in the open doorway watching him go.

'It's a bad business,' he said. 'Bad for the estate. Bad for us, maybe.'

'How could it be bad for us?'

He tapped the side of his head. 'Use your loaf, boy! What if she did come in here yesterday? What if that is her hair thing? What if you were the last person to see her? How many cop shows have you watched on TV? The last person to see her is the prime suspect! We don't want people poking around into our lives – *your* life – do we?'

Dad's words stirred the anxiety that was already swirling in the pit of Den's stomach. His guts twisted with the sort of low pain that made him want to run to the toilet. 'That's TV, Dad, not real life,' he said, trying to ignore his body. 'If she's on our CCTV it will help them narrow it down. Shall I look through the footage?'

'No, no. I'll do it. You stay out here.'

'But you just said you didn't recognise her. At least I know who I'm looking for.'

There was no arguing with Dad when he was like that. Logic didn't come into it. Den watched him march back into the kitchen and through into the tiny office behind. Then he got out his phone, went onto Twitter and searched 'missing girl, Fincham'. There was an official post from the Metropolitan Police, with the same grainy photo attached. It had already been retweeted seventy-five times. Den retweeted it himself and then took a screenshot of the photo and studied it.

Mina was smiling. When she was in the café after school, she was quiet, reserved, serious. It was nice to think of her more carefree like this. Except that the smile in the photograph bothered him. When you looked, it didn't reach her eyes. The reserve was still there, the wariness. Was that really the best photo her family could come up with? What sort of life did she have?

He looked away from her face at the rest of the photo. It was cropped quite close, but it looked like it had been taken in a café. He could see the chairback and the edge of a plate. He held the screen closer. It was *their* chair, *their* plate. The photo had been taken here.

Day One

Sandy

Kath and Naz came back in with more bloody tea. Honestly, they meant well but she really needed a proper drink. She ignored the mug they put near her and took out another fag.

'Everyone will be looking now,' said Jodie. 'Just a few more questions – I need to be clear where you were last night.'

Sandy sighed. 'Like I said, I was working at the bar, the Flamingo Bar, and then I slept over.'

'So if we contact the owner, they'll confirm that, will they?'

'Sure.' Brett wouldn't thank her if the police went sniffing round. Her hands were shaking a little, but she managed to light the cigarette and took a long drag. Kath was looking at her, flapping her hand in front of her face. *For Christ's sake,* thought Sandy, *I can smoke in my own flat, can't I?* 'I don't see what that's got to do with anything, though,' she said. 'Can't you just drop it?'

'I'm afraid we can't. We need a full picture of Mina and her family.'

'Well, her family's just me. Love me or hate me, I'm all she's got.'

'And her father?'

Sandy sent her daggers.

'Sorry, Sandy, I've got to ask.'

'Jason? He's nobody. A deadbeat. He hasn't seen her for six years.'

'Is there a chance that Mina could be with him? That he picked her up from school yesterday?'

Sandy laughed. 'No. Like I said, he doesn't want to know. No child support. Not even a birthday present. He's out of the picture.'

'I'm going to need his details.'

'Yeah, whatever.'

Jodie took down the contact details that Sandy had for him.

'Could you text him anyway, please? Tell him what's happening? On the off-chance that Mina's looking for him.'

Sandy pulled a face. 'I'd rather not. Could you do it? I really don't want him messaging me.'

'Sure,' said Jodie, calmly. 'What about other family? Are there grandparents she might go to?'

'No, I told you. I'm her family. End of. I don't have anything to do with my parents, and I don't want Mina to either. Don't want them doing to her what they did to me.'

'What was that, Sandy?'

Sandy's expression darkened. 'What's this? Therapy?' She put on a plummy voice. '"How does that make you feel, Sandy?" No thanks, Jodie. Been there, done that. That's one of the things they tried – my parents – to fix me. Make me normal like them.'

On her chair by the door, Sandy could see that Kath was riveted. Sandy cringed inside at the thought of her neighbour knowing all about her. Now she was sending her a sympathetic look, which was even worse.

'When's the last time you saw them?' Kath said.

'I don't know. Mina was about four. We went for Christmas. It didn't go well.'

That face again. Seriously, it wasn't judgemental – not the tangible, tight-lipped disapproval that was her mum's default expression – but sympathy was almost worse. The thought of people feeling sorry for you.

Jodie cleared her throat and Kath sat back in her chair and mimed zipping up her mouth. 'Going back to Mina,' Jodie said. 'It sounded earlier like you don't always get on?'

'Not always, no, but that's normal, isn't it? She's almost a teenager. We've been through a lot together. I can't lie and pretend it's always great.'

'So, yesterday morning, was that one of those days when you weren't getting on? Did you have a row before she went to school?'

Yesterday seemed like a long time ago. Sandy couldn't remember much about it at all. She certainly couldn't remember a row.

'No, it was just . . . normal. I could hear her moving about getting ready. I got up cos I needed to use the bathroom and then I made a coffee. She'd had her breakfast by then and was packing her schoolbag. I asked her if she'd done her homework and she said yes, cos she always does it. That was it.'

'Are you sure?'

'Yes.'

The cigarette was calming her down a bit. She took another drag and saw Kath and Naz exchange a quick glance.

'What did she take with her?'

'Just the normal stuff – her bag, her coat. She put a little fold-up umbrella in the outside pocket of her bag. That's all.'

It was clearer now in her mind's eye. She could see Mina stuffing that brolly into the side of her backpack, her plaits falling forward as she bent over, bright pink scrunchies at the ends, keeping them done up. Shit, the scrunchie. If that bastard at the shop had hurt her, so help her she'd . . .

'Sandy?'

She realised that Jodie was looking at her.

'What?'

'You were telling me about yesterday morning.'

39

'Yeah, okay. I told her I'd be back late. I gave her a few quid to get something for tea. She was fine; she's so sensible. She just said, "Bye, Mum," and set off.'

Not strictly true. She had pretty much ignored Sandy that morning, just carried on with getting ready when she had walked into the kitchen. It was only when she had said she'd be back late that Mina had looked at her. She hadn't said anything, just looked and her eyes were sort of dull and closed off.

'No arguments, then?'

'No.'

Again, another look between Kath and Naz. What was it with those two?

'And is anything else missing? Has she taken anything else with her?'

'I haven't checked properly. I mean, she wouldn't run away – she's not that sort of girl.'

'Let's have a look at her bedroom together, shall we?' said Jodie.

'Okay.'

She stubbed the cigarette out and got up off the sofa. Everything felt unreal, except it was suddenly too real at the same time. She stumbled a bit as she walked into the bedroom. There was that feeling again, the one she'd had when she first came back to the flat, that absence, that emptiness. It was starting to hit home. Mina. Her Mina. She was really gone.

She looked around the room. There was a mattress on the floor, like the one she had, but Mina's was neat – the duvet all squared up. The chest of drawers on one side of the room had a selection of Mina's things on top, all set out in order – her hairbrush, a box of tissues, some little toys that came with Happy Meals. Mina's drawings were up on the wall, loads of them, stuck up with Blu-tack, like a little art gallery.

She opened each drawer in turn. Everything was folded up neatly. She couldn't really tell if any clothes were missing. If they were, it would just be one or two things.

'I don't know,' she said. 'There could be some pants and socks gone. I'm not sure.'

She glanced round again and it struck her then, with a tightening feeling in her guts, how her little girl had tried to make the best of this room, to make it homely. She hadn't really noticed before. She hadn't noticed much at all.

'What about her toothbrush? Has she taken that?'

They both went into the little bathroom. Two brushes were standing in a mug on the shelf above the sink.

'The pink one's hers,' said Sandy. 'She hasn't taken it. I'm telling you, she wouldn't run away. Not my Mina. Someone's taken her.'

Day One

Den

Den's mind was going nineteen to the dozen. When had the photo of Mina been taken? He was about to go and talk to Dad about it when he saw a couple of young guys outside the front. One of them leaned a bike against the café window, then the door pinged and they came in, a stumpy-legged dog in their wake. He recognised the lads. They were part of the gang that hung around the estate. He knew them from school, too. They'd been in Year Seven when he was in sixth form.

'All right, Dennis,' one of them said. This was Danno – just under six foot, pale skin and a slick of dark hair. He wasn't the biggest of the gang, but he was the one they all seemed to look up to. Den cringed inside at the use of his full name – something he hated, which had followed him right through school – but tried not to show it.

'You can't bring the dog in here. You know that.'

Danno raised his eyebrows. 'Looks like I can, doesn't it?'

Den knew he should insist. He also knew how ugly this could turn. If they got a takeaway, maybe it wouldn't matter. It would only be a couple of minutes.

'Okay, just quickly. What can I get you?'

Danno studied the menu on the board behind Den, even though it never changed and he'd been in here a hundred times. He rubbed his hands together.

'Double cheeseburger, mate,' he said. Den added it into the till. 'With bacon.' A pause while Den added that. 'And fries.' Another pause. 'Hang on, scrap the bacon. Just the double cheeseburger.'

Den could feel the colour seeping into his face. Why did he get like this? They were customers; he was behind the till. This was his job. Somehow, though, it felt like they were taking the piss.

'Eating in?' he said.

'Yeah.'

'And I'll have the same,' Danno's mate said. Den couldn't remember his name but he was a stocky lad who always seemed to be at Danno's side. His wingman. 'But just one burger, cheeseburger, and I'll have bacon on mine. But no tomato.'

'Lettuce?'

The guy looked at him like he's said something stupid. 'Yeah, lettuce but no tomato.' He looked at Danno and they both pulled faces to indicate their amusement at Den's slowness. Den was full-on blushing now.

'Do you guys want drinks?'

'I'll have a Coke.'

'Yeah, make it two.'

Den read their order back to them. He was sure he'd written it down correctly, but they both rolled their eyes as he was reading.

'No, I was a double bacon cheeseburger with no mayo and Vince here is a double cheeseburger, no bacon, lettuce but no tomato. Got it this time?' Danno twisted his fingers into the side of his head.

Den tried again.

'That's it,' said Danno. 'Simples.' He paid in cash. Den noticed he pulled a couple of tenners from quite a fistful of notes. He gave them their drinks and told them he'd bring their food over when it was ready. They sat down at a table near the wall, away from the window. Den couldn't hear what they were saying but they kept looking over in his direction and laughing. He just knew they were going to eat half their food and then complain he'd got the order wrong and demand their money back or more burgers for free.

Den took the ticket for the food through to the kitchen. Dad wasn't there, so he continued into the office. Dad was leaning forward in his chair, his face illuminated by the light of his PC.

'There's a food order, burgers and chips,' Den said.

'You deal with it. I'm busy.'

Den frowned. Whenever he tried his hand in the kitchen, the results were always disparaged by Dad. Nothing was ever good enough, even a bacon sarnie. It was unlike him to trust Den with the grill and fryer.

'Dad, it's those kids again. If I cook it wrong, they'll kick up a fuss.'

Dad looked at him disparagingly. 'So don't cook it wrong, son. You took their order. You know what they want.'

The screen in front of him showed a static image from a CCTV camera.

'Have you found something?' Den said.

'I'm not sure. Maybe.'

'Let me look.'

Den peered over Dad's shoulder. The footage was from the camera that covered the counter and the till. The timer in the bottom of the screen read, '14/11 15:32:05'. The image wasn't pin-sharp – you had to pay extra for good quality – but he could see two figures on screen. One of them was behind the counter. The camera angle caught the person's shoulders and the top of their head. Den did a double-take. Was he really starting to thin on top? That much? Because, of course, the server at the till was him. On the other side of the desk a small girl was reaching across, placing a coin on the counter. The hood was down; the

44

shoulders of her coat were glistening from the soaking she'd had outside. Her hair was tied into two pigtails.

'I think it's her, Dad. I'm not one hundred per cent. Is that all we've got?'

Dad played the footage backwards and forwards. They tried the camera outside the shop, but it hadn't been working – there was nothing at all from that one. So there was just the one sequence. It lasted one minute and thirty-five seconds. As Den watched it again, his gut spasmed and he felt a shiver run up and down his spine. He remembered what Dad had said before. *What if you were the last person to see her?*

Day One

Kath

As Jodie asked the questions and Naz wrote down the answers, Sandy's cigarette smoke caught in the back of my throat and made my chest go tight. I badly wanted to go home, but part of me – the worst part of me, I suppose – wanted to hear more of whatever Sandy had to say. I know it's not nice to be nosy, but you can't really blame me. I was learning so much about what had gone on here, next door. I'm no expert, but even I could tell she was being a bit shifty about where she'd been and what she'd been up to.

Jodie may not have been judgemental but, God forgive me, I certainly was. I don't care how difficult things are, how much you need the money, you don't leave a young girl like that overnight. Not without a babysitter there. That poor little girl. On her own in this bleak flat. And cutting off her parents like that, too, denying them all the fun of seeing Mina growing up. That's not right. I tried not to show my disgust, though. The way I saw it, the thing was to get Sandy talking. If being there, making her feel she had someone on her side, helped then I was happy to do my bit. The more she could tell the police, the better. And, of course, you get the best view from a ringside seat.

As they stood up to go and look in Mina's bedroom, I got to my feet too.

'I'd better be getting home,' I said. They all looked up at me. 'I'm only next door if you need me. Please let me know if she turns up. When. When she turns up.' I was at it now. You can't let yourself think negatively, can you?

Naz walked me to the door. He stepped onto the walkway with me, where my trolley was still parked. It was gone six now. I'd missed *The Chase*, but I might be able to catch the end of *Richard Osman's House of Games*, although I didn't think I'd be able to concentrate. The telly didn't seem so important now.

The rain was finding its way under the parapet and I gathered my coat round me. Even though Naz had pulled the door to after us, he still spoke in a low voice. 'I won't keep you now, but I'll need to take a statement from you, Kath. Whatever's gone on here, we've clearly got child protection issues.'

I couldn't help letting out a sigh. I was done in and needed to put my feet up.

'Do you really need it? You've just heard it from the horse's mouth, Naz. She stayed out all night and she's hardly ever here in the evenings.'

'It's part of building up a picture. Neutral, reliable witnesses like you are important.'

I was well aware he was trying to butter me up, but it worked. 'Of course,' I said. 'I'm happy to help. I only wish I'd known how bad it was next door. I just hope it's not all too late.'

He shook his head sadly. 'Hindsight is a wonderful thing, Kath, but we are where we are. Do you want to have a bit of a rest and maybe I could come round for that statement in an hour or two?'

'Yes, love, that'd be fine. Maybe Mina'll be back before then anyway.'

'Let's hope so. Do you need a hand with your shopping?'

'No, I think I can manage from here,' I said, looking at the door a few feet away. We both grinned. It felt lovely to share a tiny moment of warmth, but then immediately I was hit with a sense of guilt, like it was wrong to feel anything other than worried.

'I'll see you in a little while, Kath. You take care, okay?'

I let myself in, shut my front door and parked my trolley in the hall, before heading for my nice, clean familiar bathroom. Bugger the diabetes, I was going to have another cup of sweet tea, skip my beans on toast and go straight to one of the iced buns I'd got from the café. I couldn't take my bra off yet, not if Naz was coming round in an hour, but I could at least take off my shoes, put my slippers on, and have the fire on for a little bit. As I pottered around the kitchen, the rain was still battering at the window and there was a cold draught through the gap in the frame. It wasn't a night to be outside.

I ate my bun in front of the telly. My feet and legs were killing me, so I put them up on the pouffe. My brain was working overtime. When you live on your own like I do, the worst thing is not having someone to talk to, to share the little things. If my Ray had still been with me, I'd have had some tales to tell him today! I'd spoken to more people in one afternoon than I had for the whole of last week, longer probably, and I'd learned more about next door than I really wanted to. It's true what they say about closed doors, isn't it?

There was something really odd about how Sandy was reacting to everything. I mean, she should be completely beside herself, shouldn't she? We'd had tears when she'd first realised Mina was missing, flinging herself to the floor and all that malarkey. But was that just a little bit over the top? And since then, she'd been pretty calm, chain-smoking those awful cigarettes and getting lippy with the police. I don't know. It all felt a bit off.

And then there was the scrunchie at the corner shop – if it was Mina's then what did that mean? Had it come off during a struggle? Had Den stopped me ringing the police because he had something to hide? He'd always seemed like a nice lad, but was he? Was he really? It was awful that Mina was missing, but it was also awfully *interesting*.

All my favourite TV detectives had a sidekick – Morse and Lewis, Holmes and Watson, Inspector Gently and that lad, John whatsisname – but I was on my own with this one. I'd kind of made my peace with that; after all, Ray had been gone such a long time, but every now and then I felt a pang of nostalgia, remembered what I was missing.

Maybe it was okay, though. Miss Marple figured things out on her own. I might be old and past it in most people's eyes but, like her, I still had all my marbles and I knew this estate inside out. I may have let Mina down for the past few months, but I could do my very best to help sort this all out now that she'd gone missing.

Day One

Den

'We need to call this in,' said Den.

'Sure,' Dad said but didn't reach for his phone.

'Are you going to do it, or shall I?'

'All right, all right! You're worse than your mother! I'll do it. Haven't you got an order to cook?'

Den had a sinking feeling. 'Can you do it now? I'll only mess it up.'

'Why don't I watch you?'

God, that was even worse, having the old man breathing down his neck.

'Umm . . .'

'Come on! Shift your arse!'

Dad scraped his chair back and started ushering Den out of the office and into the kitchen. He leaned on the doorway and watched as Den stood in the middle of the room, gripped by indecision.

'Get the burgers on, get the chips in, let's go!' Dad clapped his hands, the noise ringing in Den's ears. He didn't need geeing up, he needed calming down, reassurance, but Dad had never understood that. Den fetched four burgers out of the freezer – it was two doubles, wasn't it? – and put them on the griddle, added a couple of strips of bacon, then shook some chips into the fryer. The fat bubbled and hissed as they went in.

'Check the burgers. Flip them over if they're ready and start toasting the buns and get your garnishes ready.'

Griddle, fryer, buns, garnishes. Den's head was starting to spin. Then something else was there. Mina. The footage.

'Did you ring the police?'

Dad looked at him, irritated at the reminder. 'No. I'll do it. Check the temperature of that fryer. There's more lettuce in the fridge. Keep on it, Den.' He retreated into the office, leaving Den on his own in the kitchen.

'Okay, okay, I've got this.' He didn't, though. He was thinking about too many things at once, trying to remember what order those wankers had finally settled on. It was much too hot in the kitchen. The noise and the heat and the smell got right inside your head. The smell. There was an edge to it, a hint of bitterness that caught in the back of his throat. The burgers! He flipped them over to reveal four black crusty surfaces. God, he'd have to start again. Maybe he could get them into the bin and another lot going before Dad came back.

He started again, nursing the new set of patties until they were cooked to perfection. He was sweating so much, drips of it were hitting the hot metal of the griddle, evaporating instantly. By the time Dad reappeared he was laying the burgers onto toasted buns and putting on the sauces and garnishes. Everything except mayo on one of them, no tomato on the other.

He studied Den's efforts.

'Yeah?' said Den, seeking his approval. Dad pursed his lips, nodded, but then walked to the bin wordlessly and pressed the pedal.

'There's my profit margin,' he said. 'We might as well just throw money away. Did you think I wouldn't notice?'

Den took the food through to the café. The dog was lying on the floor next to Danno, with its back legs splayed out. Danno and Vince were opening little sachets and writing on the table with trails of sugar, laughing. They sat there with smirks on their faces as Den approached. He looked at the result of their efforts, 'Dennis Sucks Cock', and placed the two plates on top without saying a word, feeling the grittiness beneath the plates as he did so.

'Can I have some ketchup?' Danno asked.

'All the sauces are over on the table.' Danno stared at him. Already dripping with sweat, Den felt himself getting hotter. He willed himself not to give in to the pressure, but, of course, he caved and walked over to the table by the counter, hating himself every step of the way. He brought a bottle of ketchup back to Danno and Vince.

'And some vinegar.'

He wished he could manage a sarcastic, 'Bon appétit,' but he didn't have it in him, so he fetched the vinegar then left them to it and retreated behind the counter. Dad was already there, watching him.

'You shouldn't let them get to you, Den,' he said. 'They're just being arseholes. You need to man up a bit, have some cojones.' He puffed his chest out like a prize rooster.

'Thanks, Dad,' Den said. 'I'll remember that next time.'

'And what's with the dog?' He stabbed a finger towards a sign on the wall: *No dogs except guide dogs*.

'I know. I know. It's pissing outside, though. And there's no one else in here.'

Dad looked at him. The disappointment in his eyes was familiar. Growing up, he'd borne the full brunt of Dad's hopes and expectations – child genius, athlete, football player, Jack-the-lad – and had failed to live up to them, one by one. The only time he had ever seen his dad really glowing with pride was when he got his university place, the first person in their family to do so. And now here he was, back in the café, that little adventure well and truly over.

Dad turned to go back into the kitchen, then stopped and beckoned Den to come close to him.

'This missing girl,' he said. His voice was so quiet Den could hardly hear him. He was used to him booming and ranting. This had him rattled.

'What about her?'

'The CCTV.'

'Yeah?'

'Would it be better for you, better for all of us, if that camera wasn't working?' He glanced at Den, shiftily.

'It was working, Dad. We've got her on screen. It could be important.'

Dad brushed some imaginary dust from the counter with the flat of his hand. 'What if we didn't? Things happen. Files get wiped by accident.'

Den couldn't believe what he was hearing.

'No! We've got to keep it and show it to the police. It's evidence. You haven't wiped it already, have you?' He started to push past his father, but he stopped him.

'No, I haven't, but I could. I meant what I said about it bringing trouble here, to you. After all that business in Hull. If you're seen on CCTV talking to a girl who's gone missing, people are going to start asking questions about you. I don't want your mum getting upset again.'

Sometimes, just for an hour or two, Den could almost forget how much he'd messed up his only attempt to live away from home. His student career, which had lasted all of seven months. He felt his face growing warm, knew he was going red again.

'Dad, that was completely different – you know it was. It was just . . . a misunderstanding.'

'That's not how everyone will see it if they're raking over our lives. Your mum's nerves aren't in a good way, anyway. It's all tears and hot flushes. I don't want anything making her worse.'

Den was pretty sure that Mum's 'nerves' were due to her time of life, but this wasn't the moment to have a man-to-man chat about the menopause. Besides, if anyone was on edge, it was Dad. He was the one with insomnia, pacing around the flat taking handfuls of antacids morning, noon and night.

'Dad, please! That's got nothing to do with this. You've got nothing to worry about.'

'Nothing to worry about . . .' Dad echoed him and sighed audibly.

They both looked up as Danno approached the counter.

'Scuse me,' he said, presenting his plate on which there was a half-eaten burger and a few chips. 'This isn't what I ordered. I asked for a double cheeseburger, and this has got bacon in.'

Dad looked at the food, then took a teaspoon from a pot near the till and carefully flipped the top bun off the burger. 'You've eaten it, son. Or most of it.'

'Yeah, but it's not what I ordered. So, are you going to cook me another one?'

Dad prodded the open burger with the end of the spoon and carefully peeled off the sole remaining fragment of bacon and placed it on the side of the plate.

'Fixed it, mate,' he said, then put the spoon down and folded his arms.

Danno seemed undecided for a split second, then went back to his table.

'Come on, let's go,' he said to Vince.

'And don't bring your dog next time, mate. We won't serve you,' Dad shouted.

Danno stuffed the chips into his mouth, then picked up the end of the burger and headed for the door, Vince scuttling in his wake.

'That's how you deal with little toerags like that,' Dad said. 'And next time, get the fucking order right.'

The doorbell pinged as the door swung open. The police officer who'd been in before was back.

'I'm back for the CCTV?' he said.

'Yes, sir,' Dad said and showed him to the office. Den stayed at the front, but they soon called him through. He didn't want to leave the front unsupervised again, so he messaged Mum in the flat upstairs who he'd heard coming home half an hour ago. She came downstairs quickly and sent Den a questioning look when she saw the uniformed officer in the doorway of the office.

'I'll tell you later,' Den said, as he went to join them.

'Do you think this is her?' said the copper.

'Yes. I'm sure.'

'Can you remember what she said, how she seemed?'

'I don't think she said much.' He stared at the screen, frozen on a frame where Mina was at the counter. The light was shining on the shoulders of her coat. 'Hey, no, it was raining, wasn't it? She was drenched, actually. Her coat wasn't all that waterproof. I guess it had soaked through. She was shivering, so I said something like, "You're soaked."'

'And she said?'

'"Yeah, my umbrella broke. I'm frozen." Something like that. So I said, "Soon be home." She'd got some money – she didn't always – and she was buying a chocolate bar, a Kit Kat, I think. I—' He looked towards Dad, who was listening intently. 'I slipped her a sachet of hot chocolate powder, so she'd have a warm drink when she got in.'

'You gave it to her?' the officer asked. Dad's face was a picture. His eyebrows had shot up to meet his hairline and he was blinking very rapidly.

'Yes. Sorry, Dad.'

'My own son stealing from the café,' he said.

'Dad! It's not—'

'No wonder I can't make a bloody living and my stock control is down the shitter.' The volume was turning up now, almost unbearable in the confined space of the office.

'Mister Hammond, please! Please, sir, this needs to wait until later. There's a missing girl, remember? Now I need a copy of this. I've got a USB stick. Can you help me do it? Please, sit down, sir.'

Dad sat down and Den retreated a few steps to the doorway. 'It's only now and again, Dad. Just little things. You know some of our customers are skint.'

Dad was concentrating on copying the video, but he still fired at him: 'They're not the only ones. We're not a bloody foodbank, you big lump!' Den heard the front door ping again and soon after he saw Mum going into the kitchen and start cooking. He went out to help, muttering, 'Saved by the bell,' under his breath.

'Just a bacon sandwich,' Mum said. 'What's going on?'

Den told her as the bacon sizzled on the griddle. Mum's face creased with concern and she stayed with Den in the café when the food was ready. He showed her Mina's picture on his phone. The official tweet had now been shared eight hundred times, and the hashtag #findMina was trending. There was a Facebook page now, too, with people sharing her picture and posting up where they were searching.

Before long, the officer came out. 'I need to take a quick statement from you too, Den.'

'Sure.'

He more or less repeated the questions he'd asked when they were looking at the video, this time taking notes. When they were finished, he left with a quick, 'Cheers, mate.'

Another customer came in, a tall guy in a high-vis jacket and very muddy boots. He grabbed an energy drink from the fridge, brought it to the counter and asked for a sandwich.

Den showed him the picture on his phone, asked if he'd seen Mina. 'No, but that's why I'm here. She's in my daughter's class at school. We've got to find her. There's a group of us knocking off work now. We're going to join the search. Everyone's gathering at the bottom of the flats at seven, if you want to join us.'

'Okay. I will, thanks.'

When he'd gone, Den walked through to the office again to

ask if Dad would mind the café while he joined the search. His father hadn't moved. Now he was slumped on his desk, head on his arms. For a terrible moment, Den thought there was something wrong with him. He raced across the kitchen, muttering, 'No, no, please no.' Before he reached the office door, though, Dad stirred and sat up rubbing his eyes.

'Jeez, Dad, are you okay?'

He looked at Den in a way that spoke more of disappointment than words ever could.

'I'm sorry, Dad. I've let you down. I'll make it up to you, I promise. I'll pay you back for stuff I've given away.'

Dad waved a hand in the air dismissively. 'A packet of hot chocolate isn't going to bankrupt us. A part of me – a very small part – is a little bit proud of your kind, foolish heart, but you've got to stop doing that.'

'Okay, thanks, Dad.'

He frowned. 'You're not off the hook!' he barked, but Den suspected that he actually was.

'There's a search party getting up. They're meeting at seven by the flats. Is it okay if I join them? Are you all right to mind the café?'

Dad sat back in his chair and drew his hand across his forehead. 'You're not going, Den. You need to keep your head down.'

'Dad, I haven't done anything.'

'I know, but that won't stop people throwing mud. Especially if they find out about Hull. Stay at home, son.'

'Then it looks like I'm not worried about her, like I don't care. Dad, we're part of this community. I *should* be seen there. It's the right thing to do.'

'I don't think it would do any harm. The more ears and eyes searching, the better. Nobody knows about Hull; that's all in the past. It doesn't help to keep dragging it up,' said Mum, who had come to join them.

Dad shot her an irritated look and seemed about to bite back, then rubbed his hand over the top of his head and sighed. 'Maybe you're right. You go, then, do what you can. Actually, we'll stay open while the search is going on. Give a free drink for anyone joining in, eh? Make sure you tell people, yeah? Make sure people know we're here for everybody.'

'I thought you were against giving stuff away.' Den couldn't help getting the dig in.

'This is different. It's PR, innit?' Dad tapped the side of his head. 'Plus some people will want a bacon sarnie or a bag of chips with their free drink. It's brass monkeys out there, cold enough to freeze your—'

'Yeah, all right, Dad.'

Dad was right about one thing, Den thought, as he set off later to join the search. It was freezing, a terrible night to be out, especially if you were as little as Mina.

Day One

Kath

I turned the telly down low so I could hear the comings and goings next door but I still had the subtitles working. I got a bit of a shock to see our flats on the local news at half-six. It was just a tiny item, less than a minute, saying that police were appealing for information about a missing girl and showing Mina's picture and then our block. Then the presenter said, 'There'll be more on this on our late bulletin after the ten o'clock news.'

I couldn't relax, not knowing that Naz was coming round to take a statement. I pottered about, tidying up, putting things away. I was just wondering if I should run the hoover round when there was a knock on the door. It was him.

'Hello, Kath. Is now a good time to come in?'

I held the door open and ushered him into the hall. 'Yes, 'course. Is there any news?'

'Nothing concrete. She made it into school yesterday and we think there's a confirmed sighting yesterday afternoon at around half past three, so that narrows it down. If we can be sure that she didn't come back into the flat, then we're really looking at a very small timeframe. Shall we sit down?'

He looked tired. I expect shifts go out the window on a case like this.

'Do you want a cuppa?' I said.

'No. No, thank you. I'll just take the statement if that's okay. You have one, if you want one.'

'Oh no, love. I'm awash. Let's sit in the lounge.'

We sat down, him in the armchair and me on the sofa. I tried to get comfortable, although to tell the truth I felt a little nervous. Making a formal statement like this was rather intimidating. Naz seemed to sense my reticence.

'Lovely room,' he said. He'd got a file with him and opened it up, resting it on his knee. 'You've got it really nice in here. Cosy.'

'Thank you. I do love all my bits. Some people would call it clutter, I suppose, but you gather a lot of stuff over a lifetime and I couldn't bear to throw any of my knick-knacks away. They all mean something. Sorry, I'm going on. Ask me what you need to.'

He started by confirming my name and address, then moved on to what I'd heard or hadn't heard yesterday. I just repeated what I'd told him earlier. About hearing the row in the morning and the door slamming, but after that, nothing. About getting worried and going out looking this afternoon.

He asked me some questions about the shop and finding the scrunchie.

'Have you got it back?' I said. 'Cos if it was hers and he'd got rid of it, I'd never forgive myself.'

'I shouldn't really discuss this, but just to reassure you we have collected the item. Sandy's confirmed that it looks like Mina's, but it's going for testing. Lucky you spotted it.'

'These varifocals are a marvel. They were a devil to get used to but I wouldn't be without them now.'

He didn't seem very interested in my eyewear.

'Would you say you know Den well?'

'I've seen him grow up over the years. He's a nice polite boy, although, no . . .'

'Kath?'

'I'm really not one to gossip.'

'Of course not, and I'm not asking you to, but I do need as much information as possible about anyone who saw Mina in the last couple of days. Do you know something about Den?'

'He went away to uni, but he came home after a few months. Under a cloud. Think he had some sort of breakdown. He wasn't in the café for ages after that, but I never got to the bottom of what was behind it.'

'Okay, that's very helpful. Thank you, Kath.'

He pressed his lips together and made some more notes, then looked up again.

'When we talked earlier, you said Sandy had stayed out all night before, Kath?'

I was warming to this now. If you thought of it as information rather than gossip, it actually felt like a public duty, and it turned out I had a lot of help to give.

'Couple of times a month? Maybe more? I'm so ashamed, Naz. I should've reported it.' I couldn't look him in the eye. Instead, I kept pulling at a loose thread on one of the buttons on my cardi. It was starting to unravel, but I couldn't stop.

'Kath, it's not you who should feel ashamed. You're really helping us now.'

I glanced up at him. He had a kind face, made me think that I could tell him anything.

'I'm not a hundred per cent sure,' I said, 'but a couple of times, I've seen Mina out on the walkway and I've wondered if she's got bruises. On her legs. I couldn't swear to it, though.'

A little crease appeared in between his brows. He made another note on his clipboard. 'Thank you, Kath,' he said. 'I know this isn't easy.'

The stray thread came away from the cardigan and the button fell onto the carpet. Naz reached forward and picked it up. He passed it to me. 'There you go. Don't want to lose it,' he said. His hand closed on mine for a moment. 'We'll find her, Kath. Don't worry.'

'And send her back next door?'

My chin was wobbling now. I was on the edge of tears.

He shook his head. 'I can't say, obviously, but there's a whole team involved now, social workers and everyone. We'll find her and we'll make sure she's safe.'

'What if it's too late?' A tear trickled out of the corner of my eye and I reached behind my glasses to wipe it away with my finger.

'We can't think like that, Kath.' He gave my other hand a squeeze. 'Kath, you're in a unique position here. You know Sandy. You know the local area like the back of your hand. If you think of anything, anything at all, which might help us, just come and have a word, or give me a buzz. In cases like this, we rely on the community; we need people like you.'

I couldn't help glowing a little. I was so used to be ignored and overlooked. When you get to my age, people like that dragon on reception at the doctor's and those snotty council workers at the One Stop Shop make you feel more like a nuisance than anything else. It was wonderful to be appreciated.

'There was something,' I said. I'd been thinking back over the week, trying to remember if there was anything different. 'Sandy doesn't seem to have many friends round or anything, but she did have a caller on Monday. A man.'

'Yeah? The boyfriend, was it?'

'No. Well, I don't think so.' If he was, he had girlfriends all over the estate because I'd seen him for a few years, knocking on doors in our block and the others. 'Not a boyfriend, no. He's a debt collector.'

Naz stopped writing and leaned forward, his attention fully on me. He asked for a description and I did my best. Thirtyish, close-cropped hair, black bomber jacket and jeans, a big man. My Ray would have used the words 'brick shithouse' but I'd never say that to a policeman.

'Thank you,' Naz said. 'That's exactly the sort of information we need.'

After he'd read my statement out to me and I'd agreed it was a fair record, I showed him out. I stood in the doorway and listened to the noise drifting up from the courtyard below. It had stopped raining, but there was still a stiff breeze. I shuffled across the walkway and peered over the concrete balustrade. There were quite a lot of people gathered there – not the normal crowd: youngsters up to no good, wheeling around on bikes or skateboards, although I noticed there was one little group of them off to one side, keeping their distance – but adults in thick coats and hats, waiting for something. Soon enough, a couple of men stood on a little wall and spoke to them. Their words were carried away on the breeze, but I got the picture. They were organising a search.

I felt a swell of pride. Sometimes it felt like this place had gone so far down there was no hope for it, but by the time they got started there must have been sixty or seventy people involved. For a fleeting moment I wondered if I should join in, but my feet and ankles were properly swollen up and my knees were killing me. Time to call it quits.

I took a last look and saw someone in the crowd raising a hand. The lamplight picked out his face and I could see it was Den. I wondered if his ears had been burning earlier, but I waved back, and then another gust rattled along the walkway. I wrapped my cardi around me and turned to head into the flat when I heard a voice, a man shouting out, 'Mina!' He repeated it a couple of times and then others joined in, until it seemed like the whole crowd was shouting, their voices echoing off the concrete walls so that her name seemed to come at me from all directions. It was the most eerie thing, chilling me far more than the wind whistling along the walkway.

Just as soon as the noise built up, somebody started shushing and the shouting faded away, leaving just the echoes and the memory of it. I shivered and hurried inside.

Day One

Den

There were about thirty people in the courtyard by the time he got there. It was a sombre gathering. A guy in a tracksuit moved through the crowd handing out flyers. He gave Den a clump of them – there was the now familiar picture of Mina and a number to ring if you had any information. 'We're looking anywhere we can, round the garages, in the park, and posting these through letter boxes, putting them up on lampposts, okay?'

'Cool. Hey, I'm from the Corner Café. We're offering a free hot drink to anyone who joins the search. Perhaps you can tell people?'

'Wow, that's great.' The guy high-fived him and then disappeared into the crowd.

There was a mixture of 'civilians' and police, with some press and photographers hanging round the edge of things. More people were joining all the time, swelling the search party to seventy or more. There was a group of teenagers to one side, hoods up, shoulders hunched, half of them on bikes, just watching. Danno and Vince were among them. Danno's dog was snuffling about at some rubbish under a bench. At five past seven, the guy in the high-vis jacket who had been in the café earlier climbed up on a small wall. He fumbled in his pocket, took out a whistle and blew it hard. The low hubbub that had been building up stopped and everyone turned to look at him. He spoke with authority and assurance.

'Thank you to everyone for coming this evening. Fantastic response from our community. We're just volunteers, right, and we all want to find Mina as quickly as possible. So I'm gonna hand over to Sergeant Taylor who will tell us how we can help.'

He gave way to a uniformed officer who joined him standing on the wall. 'Thank you, Marlon. It's great to see everyone. Children go missing all the time for all sorts of reasons. There is absolutely no need for anyone in this community to panic. However, Mina is only eleven, she's small for her age and she's been missing since yesterday afternoon—' a ripple of concern went through the crowd '—so we do need to find her. Let's get her back home. I'd like you to concentrate on posting the flyers through people's doors. We need to get Mina's face seen. Obviously, keep your eyes peeled as you're walking round. If you see anything suspicious, call one of the officers over. We'll be walking with you. We won't be far away. Okay, we're aiming to be out until ten. Thanks again, everyone.'

There was a man with a film camera perched on his shoulder a few metres behind Den, recording the talks, and a woman next to him, in a smart coat and bright scarf. Den thought he vaguely recognised her from the local news. Now, as everyone milled around, waiting to set off, the pair approached Den, who felt a twinge of discomfort as he realised he was being filmed.

'Hi there,' she said, 'BBC News, can I have a few words?'

Den could hear Dad's voice in his head: *Keep your head down.* Was there a polite way to say no?

'Um, sure.' His nervous laugh was there. He was painfully aware it had been caught on camera now. He mustn't do it again.

'So, you're helping to look for little Mina this evening. Can you tell us why you're here?'

It was kind of a dumb question. Was it a trick?

'I just . . . well, obviously, if a kid goes missing everyone wants to find them as quickly as possible and I want to do my bit. I work in the café round the corner from here. It feels very close to home.' He could feel a smile twitching on his lips, even though he was willing himself not to.

'So, do you know Mina?'

'Well, um, yes. She comes in, like everybody. We serve the community here.'

'What's she like?'

'She's just, you know, just a young girl. Kind of quiet. I really hope she's home soon.'

'Thank you very much.' Interview over, she turned to the cameraman and made a twirling gesture with her finger. 'Can I just take your name, sir?'

'Den. Den Hammond, from the Corner Café.'

'Brilliant. Thank you, Den.'

She moved on through the crowd, looking for her next victim. Despite the cold wind funnelling between the tower blocks, Den found that he was sweating. He wiped his forehead with his sleeve. He wondered if he should go after the reporter, ask her not to use his interview, but it was too late now. He hadn't said anything wrong anyway, had he? The gang of youths had turned their backs on the gathering and started moving away. Everyone else was starting to form groups. Den joined a cluster of half a dozen people, who seemed to have their own assigned officer. Marlon was part of it. He recognised Den and shook his hand.

'Hi, Den, good to see you.'

The police officer explained to the group that they would be leafleting in the nearest block of flats. Den looked up. It was only three storeys tall, but quite long and sprawling, with two wings extending from a central staircase. Recessed lamps created pools of light dotted along the walkways. Here and there you could see people leaning on the concrete ledges, looking down. As he scanned the third floor, he saw a silhouette – Mrs C, the woman who'd done a search of her own a couple of hours ago. Turned out she'd been right to be worried. Would any of this have been different if they had raised the alarm when she was in the café earlier? They say every minute counts, don't they?

She was standing quite still, taking it all in. Den thought he caught her looking his way and raised his hand. She waved back and he wondered whether it would be weird to call in on her sometime, check that she was okay. He didn't like to think of her fretting all on her own. She turned away and retreated into her flat and he realised that the group had moved off and was nearly at the entrance to the stairway. He ran to catch up.

Day One

Sandy

She heard them shouting Mina's name. One of the coppers was coming through the door and the sound came with them, drifting in on the cold November air. Stupid calling out, she thought. Treating her Mina like a lost dog, although part of her wanted to stand on the balcony and yell her name too, scream it out and keep screaming until she came back.

She'd been told to stay put. Better to be in the flat in case they found her. Besides, she was knackered – lack of sleep, for all the right reasons, although that seemed a million years ago, and now the worry.

Brett kept texting. She had messaged him that M was missing so she wouldn't be at work for the foreseeable future and warned him that the cops would be round to talk to him. She kept reading his messages over and over. He was so *nice*. That, more than anything, made her want to cry. She'd finally found a man who wasn't a complete arsehole, unlike Mina's dad, and now this was happening. Like a punishment or something. Like she wasn't allowed to be happy. It was so *unfair*.

69

She wondered if she should ask him to the flat, so she could have someone to wait with. The thought of him being there was almost too much. She literally ached for him – even while the search party started looking through the bins and in the stairwells. Did that make her a bad person? She just wanted someone to wrap their arms round her and tell her everything was going to be all right.

She couldn't ask him, though, could she? They'd had one night together, that's all. It's not like he was her boyfriend. Not yet. If she did ask, he'd think she was too needy and that would be that.

So, here she was, stuck in the flat with two cops and nothing to do but wait. No, she didn't want another bleeding cup of tea. No, she couldn't think of anywhere Mina might have gone. No, they didn't row yesterday morning. No, she'd never left her overnight before – IT WAS THE FIRST TIME, FOR CHRIST'S SAKE! How many times did she have to tell them before they believed her?

Unable to take much more of it, she went into her bedroom. The police said they'd stay in the flat all night, and she didn't have the strength to argue. It was better in a room on her own, but there was no way she could sleep. She scrolled through her phone, read Brett's texts again and forced herself to resist texting him, turning instead to social media.

The #findMina hashtag was trending on Twitter, but there was no news. The original tweet had been retweeted thirty-two thousand times. There was a Facebook page with hundreds of comments and shares. People were posting up where they had looked. Others were offering thoughts and prayers. Sandy frowned as she read one post: 'Check out the Our Fincham page – reports of a white van hanging around the school gates and a man talking to Year Seven girls in the past three weeks.' Sandy clicked the link. Sure enough, there were several posts about girls saying they'd been followed along the street. Girls as young as eleven.

Eleven. Just like Mina.

What sort of pervert would pick on an eleven-year-old child?

It was too awful to think about. The incidents had been reported to the police but no one had been arrested. Sandy wasn't in any parents' WhatsApp groups, hadn't known about the Our Fincham page before. If she'd known, she could have warned Mina, maybe found someone for her to walk home with.

That's when it hit her again. Mina was gone.

She curled up in a little ball and her tears soaked into her pillow. There was no shouting outside now, just the wind against the window. She wondered if people were still out there, looking. She missed Mina so much it hurt. Who would have thought? It felt like everything had been a struggle for the last eleven years. It wasn't easy when you were on your own. It wasn't just figuring out how to bring up a kid, you had to juggle all the rest of it – finding somewhere to live, taking any job you could to pay the bills, borrowing money when you needed to, cooking, washing, putting the bins out, changing bloody light bulbs. You had to do everything. It was too much. How many times had she wished for a break? A couple of weeks off from being a mum – just a bit of breathing space.

She didn't have any backup, not like other people. Those bridges were all burned a long time ago and there was no going back. No, just like everything else, she'd have to face this on her own. She got up and padded across the hall to Mina's room. The room was dark but she didn't put the light on. She bent down by the bed, peeled back the duvet and climbed in. Mina's pyjamas were folded up nicely on the smooth sheet. She turned onto her side and held them against her face, breathing in and out through the cloth, the mother in her responding to the scent of her child. She couldn't have put it into words – it was just Mina. Parenting hadn't come easily but there was an animal connection – it had been there from the beginning. Her tears had stopped and now she just breathed in the darkness, wide-eyed.

After a long time, she felt her body relaxing, her eyelids starting to close. In her woozy state, she moved her hand around the mattress and under the pillow. The anxiety that had started to slip away stabbed her again. She sat up and put on the torch on her phone, sending the light under the covers, along both sides of the mattress. Since she was a baby Mina had kept a square of soft cloth with a knot in one corner. It was a disgusting thing really, but she called it her cuggy and took it to bed every night, even now. Except that it wasn't there, where it should be.

She jumped up and put the overhead light on. She started hunting round the room, rummaging through the drawers. She pulled the top drawer off its runners and dumped the contents – little socks and pants – on the floor.

Jodie appeared in the doorway. 'Sandy? Everything all right?'

'Her cuggy's gone. It's her toy. She always has it in bed with her.'

'Okay, calm down. Let's look together.'

But there was no soothing Sandy. 'She wouldn't take it out of here. Wouldn't risk it at school. Where is it? *Where is she?*' She pulled the next drawer out and tipped it over.

'Sandy, please, it's okay. We'll find her.'

She didn't want to hear it. She just wanted them to do something, to stop this nightmare. She wanted this over and done with.

And most of all she wanted Mina.

Day One

Den

Just before ten, the café was packed. People were stamping their feet and blowing on their hands when they first came in, but soon began opening their coats and loosening scarves as they acclimatised to the muggy atmosphere. Condensation was running down the front window, even though the extractor fan in the kitchen was going full pelt.

Den had been freezing when he got back to the café, but he'd warmed up taking orders and making hot drinks. Dad was frying sausages, bacon and burgers and toasting buns as fast as he could. When Den went into the kitchen to collect another order, Dad broke off from the cooker to slap him on the back. 'Hey, how about this, then?' he said, eyes gleaming, sweat glistening on his brow.

Den couldn't bring himself to say anything. It seemed in bad taste to be so triumphant about a busy café in such circumstances. He picked up two plates that were ready and took them through to the café. It was strangely hushed given the number of people crammed in. A feeling of defeat and disappointment hung in the greasy air.

'Great effort, everyone!' Marlon, the seemingly self-appointed community leader, turned to face the room and raised his tea mug in salute to the other volunteers. Those with drinks already raised them back in a half-hearted way.

'We didn't find her, though,' a man near to him said, shaking his head.

'No, but we've been all over that estate, so we know she's not hiding outside or had an accident or something.'

'So someone's got her?'

'We don't know that for sure, do we? She could have run away somewhere. The thing is, we've done as much as we can. We done it together. Searched the whole estate.'

There were murmurs of agreement.

'What about tomorrow?'

'Let's see what happens overnight. Perhaps there'll be good news.'

Den was in and out for another half an hour or so, listening to fragments of conversation. Marlon was talking to the man next to him.

'Why do you think she wasn't reported missing yesterday? Where was the mum?'

'Yeah, it's fishy, innit? You don't just leave a child that age alone overnight.'

'You shouldn't. People always going on that a kid needs their mum, but some of them, man—' Marlon shook his head. 'No one talks about fathers, do they? Fathers like us.'

'No, mate. It's like we don't matter.'

'That's it, bro. It takes two to raise a kid. They need a mum and a dad. Some people just don't see it that way.'

'Do you think her mum's got something to hide? Do you know her?'

Den, picking up a pile of dirty plates from the counter, suddenly realised that Marlon was talking directly to him.

'Sorry?' Den said.

'Do you know the girl's mum? Does she come in here?'

There was a pile of flyers on the counter. Mina looked at Den from the top of the heap. Now, her eyes didn't seem sad, so much as accusing, her face going in and out of focus, but the eyes boring into him.

'Yeah. No. I don't know.'

Marlon picked up a flyer. 'That was taken here, wasn't it?' It felt like he was being accused of something, put on the spot. The top of that chair – it's the same as yours.' He showed it to the man next to him, who nodded. 'So they come in here. What's her mum like?'

Den could feel the palms of his hands getting clammy. 'I honestly don't know. I can't remember them coming in together. Just Mina on her own.' The laugh was back – stuttering, traitorous, inappropriate.

Marlon looked at him, held his eyes for longer than was comfortable. 'Okay, man. It's cool. Just thought you'd know.'

Den scurried into the kitchen. He dumped the plates on the top next to the dishwasher and leaned against the side.

'Not there! What have I told you? Get them straight in the dishwasher.'

It was even hotter in the kitchen. Den felt a wave of nausea sweeping upwards towards the back of his throat. He gripped onto the edge of the surface and tried to control his breathing.

'It's not the time to slack off, Den!'

'Dad . . . I don't feel very—'

Dad turned round. 'You okay?'

Den swallowed hard. 'I think I'm just tired.'

Den expected his dad to give him a bollocking, tell him to get on with it, but instead he put two thick rashers of bacon onto a slice of bread, then topped them with another slice and said, 'We'll call it day. Take this out. No more orders. Chucking-out time.'

Den took a deep breath and stood upright. 'Okay.' He took the plate into the café and shouted the order number. The crowd was thinning now anyway and the door kept pinging as more people left. On his way out, Marlon raised a hand and called out, 'Thanks for staying open, mate. Good to bring everyone together.'

Den managed a feeble hand raise in return. Before too long, the café was empty and Den made his way wearily around the tables, somehow finding the strength to gather up crockery and wipe down tables. Dad came out to join him when the kitchen was clean, holding two open bottles of beer.

'Here, sit down a minute. You've earned this.'

'I just need to do the floor.'

'Do it in the morning, son. Come on. Sit down.'

The beer was icy cold as it travelled down into Den's stomach. He rolled the bottle across his forehead. They sat in silence, taking slugs of beer, enjoying the quiet of the empty café.

'We did a good thing today. People need places like this, to come together. That's what we are. A place for this community.'

Den was too tired to pop his bubble. 'Yeah,' he said.

'You look shattered. I'll finish up down here. You go to bed.'

Den didn't need to be told twice. Too tired to even finish his beer, he left it in the kitchen and walked wearily upstairs. He stripped off his clothes and climbed into bed, expecting to go straight to sleep. Instead, he lay awake, eyes open, going over the events of the day. Below him, he heard the faint clattering of the mop and bucket as Dad finished the cleaning. Somehow this made him relax and his racing thoughts started to slow.

He was finally drifting off when he heard the back door go – on rainy days the wood swelled a little and you had to pull it really hard to shut it – and then the sound of an engine starting up, the low growl of the café van. He was asleep before it came back.

Day Two

Den

The first thing he did when he woke up was check his phone. Half past five. The #findMina hashtag was trending, but there was no news. The original tweet had been retweeted sixty thousand times now. The Facebook page had hundreds of comments and shares. Some of the comments, directed at Mina's mum, had a nasty edge. 'Shame on you.' 'How could you leave her?' 'Unfit mother.' And worse. People had obviously worked out that she hadn't been home on Wednesday night, but it was starting to feel like the focus had shifted – they were spending more energy hating on her than looking for Mina.

She'd been missing for two nights now. Every flat had been leafleted. The bin stores and garages had been searched. He wondered if everyone else was thinking the same as him now. If she was just staying out, hiding or something, or if she'd had some sort of accident, she would have been found. Even if she'd run away, she was so little that someone would have noticed her. No, she'd been on her way home and something had happened. Somewhere between the café and her flat.

His bedroom window looked out onto the estate. He sat up, leaned over and pulled back a curtain. It wasn't raining anymore, but the sky was still heavy and grey. Together with the concrete of the blocks and terraces, it looked like an old photograph or a black and white TV or something.

There were so many windows, rows and ranks of them, in horizontal and vertical lines. Mina could be behind any one of them, taken by someone on this estate or any of the neighbouring ones or the ones beyond those. How do you find one little girl in a city of eight million people? Where do you start? What could he do to help?

The only thing was to open the café like normal, have the posters and flyers on display, spread the word. They opened at six-thirty to catch the early birds, so, after a shower and a bowl of cornflakes, he made his way downstairs. There was no sign of Dad so he started the morning routine without him, getting the chairs down from the tables, restocking the biscuits and crisps, checking the ketchup bottles and salt and vinegar pots. The café was bathed in the sulphurous streetlight coming in from the front – the shutters weren't down like they usually were. He'd moved into the kitchen to unload the dishwasher when Dad appeared, unshaven and with deep shadows under his eyes.

'You okay, Dad? Where'd you go last night?'

Dad shot him an aggressive look. 'Nowhere. I didn't go out.'

'I heard the door and the van—'

'I just moved it. Didn't want some idiot scraping the side or taking off a wing mirror.'

He grimaced and rubbed the top of his protruding belly with the flat of his hand. Den knew from experience not to argue any further.

'Dad, are you okay?'

'Yeah, I'm fine. Heartburn. Have you put the float in the till?'

'No, not yet.'

'Crack on, then, soft lad. It's nearly opening time. Hey, you do it today.'

He threw a bunch of keys towards Den who instinctively put out his hand and caught them. At the same moment someone starting banging on the door.

'Open up! Police!'

Den and his dad looked at each other.

'What the hell is this?' Dad said. 'Here, give me those!'

He took the keys back and walked to the front of the café. 'I'm coming!' he shouted. It seemed to take an age to undo the locks and bolts. All the time Den was feeling stabs of anxiety in his stomach. Was it really the police? Dad opened the door a fraction. Someone put a shiny boot in the doorway.

'Anthony Hammond?'

'Yes.'

'Open up.'

His boot was forcing the door inwards.

'Okay, okay.'

He opened the door. There were two officers, both in uniform, both looking deadly serious. One of them was the guy who took the CCTV footage away. Den didn't recognise the other one.

'What is it?' Dad said. 'Have you found her? Have you found the girl? Why are you—?'

'We're here for your son, sir,' looking past Dad towards Den. 'Dennis Hammond. We've got a few questions.'

Den started to panic. He was suddenly catapulted back a couple of years into a tiny windowless room, smelling his own sweat, seeing the distaste in the interviewers' eyes.

Dad was standing his ground, blocking their way in. 'Why are you picking on him?'

'Please, Mr Hammond, let's keep this calm. We just want to take him to the station for a few questions.'

'Ask your questions here! Are you arresting him?'

Nobody could outshout Dad when he got going. Hearing a

noise behind him, Den glanced round. Now Mum was in the café, her long plait curled round over the shoulder of her dressing gown.

'What's going on? Why are you shouting?'

Dad spun round. 'Go upstairs, Linda! I'm sorting this!'

'It might be easier if you just come now, sir,' the officer said, looking past Dad directly at Den. 'Let's get this over with, shall we?'

'He's not going anywhere!' Dad screamed and put his hands on Den's shoulders.

'Dad, it's all right,' he said, even though he felt the opposite. 'I've done nothing wrong. I'll help them as much as I can and then I'll come home. Please, go upstairs with Mum, have a cup of tea, then open the café. Carry on as normal. I'll see you soon, yeah?'

At least he had stopped shouting.

'I've done nothing wrong, Dad. It's going to be all right.'

Den stepped past him and walked to the waiting patrol car. Dad was still standing in the doorway as he got in. Behind him Den could see his mum's face crumple as she started to cry.

Day Two

Kath

I had my breakfast in front of the telly, watching the early news. I'd done my morning blood sugar test and despite all the excitement yesterday, and a large, iced bun, my number was okay today, so I took my usual pills and made a nice bowl of porridge.

They have segments of local news every now and again, but there wasn't really anything to report. They just showed the same footage as yesterday evening. As much as I wanted to be out there looking with everyone else, my legs needed a rest. There would be plenty of other people searching for her and I needed a quiet day after yesterday. The best-laid plans and all that, though – before I'd even finished my second cup of tea, there was a knock at the door.

I checked that my dressing-gown buttons were done up and went to the door, keeping the chain on as I opened it. I peered through the gap. It was Jodie, the female police officer.

'Morning, Kath!' she said, cheerfully, although her face was drawn and pasty. 'Can I have a word?'

'Oh, yes. Of course. Hang on a minute.'

I shut the door and unchained it, then I glanced in the mirror in the hallway and patted my hair down. When I opened the door again, Jodie smiled. 'Sorry to call so early.'

'Is there any news?'

'We haven't found her yet. Can I come in?'

I hesitated. It felt uncomfortable letting someone into the house in my nightie and dressing gown, even a nice policewoman.

'It won't take long. There's been a couple of developments.'

That was enough for me. I showed her into the lounge. My breakfast things were still on the coffee table, but apart from that it was tidy enough. I could see her taking in the room, just like Naz had done yesterday – I suppose when you're in the police you're trained to be observant. I sat on the sofa and Jodie took the chair. I muted the telly but didn't turn it off.

'I'm wondering if you might be able to help us,' Jodie said.

'Of course. Anything.'

'We'd like Sandy to do a press conference this morning. When people go missing, appeals for information are so much more powerful coming from the relatives than from the police.'

I'd seen plenty of appeals like that on the news – distraught parents, or partners, usually sitting behind a desk reading a few words out. Jodie was right. They were always emotional, tugged at your heartstrings. Mind you, with the partner or husband, you always wondered if they were putting on a show, that at the back of their minds they were thinking about the body they'd stuffed under the floorboards. A horrible thought entered my head. Was that what Sandy would be doing? Putting on a show?

'Sounds like a good idea to me.'

'Exactly, but she wasn't keen last night. You can understand it, can't you? It can be intimidating in front of a bank of cameras and she's got no one with her to support her.'

She looked at me meaningfully and the penny started to drop.

'Honestly, Jodie, I don't really know her. I'm ashamed to say it, but we didn't talk before all this.'

'I think it really helped having you there yesterday. She seems to trust you. Maybe you could just have a word with her? Offer to be at the press conference with her?'

Be at the press conference? This was all getting a bit out of hand. I hardly knew the woman. I'd feel like a fraud sitting by her side or whatever, being filmed for the telly. I could feel my heart fluttering – it does that sometimes – and I put my hand up to my chest.

'I don't know,' I said.

'I know it's a lot to ask, but I do really think you could make a difference. We need to search the flat properly too.' That was interesting. 'Easier when she's not there. It's all about Mina, Kath. Getting her back safe and sound. Will you do it?'

Well, how could I refuse when she put it like that?

''Course I will,' I said. 'I'll need to put some clothes on and make myself look presentable.'

'Sandy's still asleep. We're letting her lie in for a bit, but maybe you could come round at about ten, and then, if we can get her to talk to the press, we'll try to do it at eleven, so it'll get on the lunchtime news bulletins.'

'All right. I'll come next door at ten.'

Jodie stood up to leave. 'Oh, one other thing. The young man at the café – you spoke to him yesterday, didn't you?'

'I did. I called in there when I was on my way to the school. It was blowing a gale. Don't know what I thought I was going to find.'

'How did he seem when you spoke to him?'

'Den? He was lovely. He could see I was upset, and he got me a chair. He's a good listener, really nice young man. His dad's a bit of a tyrant, but I think it's all bluster.'

'So, he just seemed normal to you?'

'Yes. Well, some people might think he's a bit . . . over-friendly.'

She narrowed her eyes. 'In what way, Kath?'

'Well, when I was in the café yesterday, he—' I stopped. Maybe it was nothing.

'Yes? He what, Kath?'

'He put his hand on me, on my shoulder. Kept it there a bit too long. It probably wasn't anything but I felt a bit uncomfortable. I'm probably oversensitive. Like I said, he's a nice friendly lad. Why do you ask?'

Jodie smiled. 'We're just putting a picture together of Mina's last known movements.'

She moved quickly towards the hall. 'I'll be next door. See you in a little while, Kath. And thank you.'

As she closed the door, I was left musing. It had all been a bit Columbo, if you asked me. 'One last thing.' That's what he always said, didn't he, when he was onto something? A casual throwaway question that revealed a killer clue. Sounded like Den was a 'person of interest'. And what were the 'developments' she'd mentioned before? She'd never actually told me. Aching legs or not, perhaps I'd take a walk round the estate today, maybe call in at the café, see what I could sniff out.

Day Two

Den

It was only a ten-minute drive to the police station. Den stared out of the window, feeling almost as if he was saying goodbye to the outside world. For the first couple of minutes the route was studded with pops of yellow – ribbons for Mina tied around lampposts on either side of the road, some with posters underneath. Early as it was, there were plenty of people about; guys in work boots and high-vis jackets, pensioners with small dogs, grim-faced women walking purposefully towards the Tube station. Some of them were lost in their own worlds, earbuds in or just concentrating on putting one foot in front of the other. A few looked up as the police car swept by. One of them was Marlon, apparently holding court with a bunch of his workmates. He clearly clocked who it was in the car, stopped what he was doing and stared. Den felt the prickle of anxiety when he'd questioned him last night in the café surging again. He tried not to look away, telling himself, *I'm not a criminal. I've done nothing wrong.*

The car turned off the road, passed through some gates and down to an underground car park. It stopped right by a door and Den was escorted from the car, through the door and then straight to an interview room.

'I'll just be a couple of minutes,' one of the officers said, and he left, shutting the door behind him. Den sat and waited. There was a mirror on one wall and it occurred to him that if this was a cop show on the TV then it would actually be one-way glass and there would be people observing him on the other side. And then he felt himself going hot all over the surface of his skin, because of course that was what they were doing. Leaving him to stew for a bit and watching. And he was stewing. He could feel himself getting hotter and hotter, gently cooking in his own sweat.

'You're okay, you're okay,' he muttered to himself and then stopped, aware this might look and sound worse than just sitting quietly. But if he was too still, would that look odd too?

The door opened and the questions began. There were two officers, neither of whom he had met before. The smaller one, kind of stocky and in a nasty brown suit, introduced himself.

'Hi Den, I'm Detective Sergeant Fisher and this is Detective Constable Waite. We're investigating the disappearance of Mina Dimitriou. Thanks for coming in to help. We appreciate it. We're recording this conversation, for our records.'

'Of course, I'll help any way I can.' Den could feel himself smiling again. He couldn't stop himself.

'Can you tell us a bit about Mina? You told one of our officers that she came into the café.'

'Yes, but I wouldn't say I exactly knew her. She called in like a lot of the neighbourhood kids on their way home from school. I'd seen her for about a year, maybe less.'

'And what sort of girl was she?'

He shrugged. 'How can you tell from someone buying chips or sweets? I mean, she was quiet, small for her age, I would say. She didn't want to chat.'

'Big spender?'

He started to laugh at the absurdity of the question, then attempted to stifle it and started coughing. Sergeant Fisher pushed a plastic bottle of water across the table towards Den and he took a sip.

'She was, is, just a kid,' he said. 'So, no. Not a big spender. Sometimes she didn't have any money at all.'

'But she still came into the café?'

'She picked things up sometimes. I turned a blind eye. She was kind of sad. I think on some days she was hungry.'

'And you gave her things?' He looked down at some notes. 'Like a sachet of hot chocolate?'

'Yes. I let her pinch a few sweets, and I gave her little things. Not often.'

'More than once?'

'No. I don't know. I did give her the hot chocolate on Wednesday afternoon, the last time I saw her. She was absolutely soaked and shivering.'

'So you do remember that Wednesday.'

'Yes.'

'Because the first time our PC came into your café, on the Thursday, you denied that she'd been in there the day before.' He looked down at his file. 'You said, "No. I don't think so." Was that deliberate misdirection, Den?'

Den's palms were sweaty now, his throat dry. He took another sip of water. 'I can't remember what I said. I don't think I said, "No." I think I said, "Maybe." I wasn't sure, that's all.' *For God's sake, stop smiling, Den,* he thought. Why couldn't he stop smiling?

Constable Waite was making a big show of writing in a notebook. He underlined something, but Den couldn't read his writing upside down.

'So she came in on the Wednesday, soaking wet, and you felt sorry for her. You gave her some hot chocolate.'

'Yes.'

'Was it a bit more than that, Den? Did you invite her into the

87

back office? Upstairs to the flat? Did you boil the kettle and make that hot drink for her? Is that how it started?'

Den could feel his heart beating faster in his chest. 'No, sir,' he said. 'She bought a Kit Kat and I gave her a sachet of hot chocolate and she left. That was the last time I saw her. My dad was in the kitchen. My mum was in the flat. The CCTV will show this. I've got nothing to hide.'

'We've been looking at the CCTV, Den. Your father left the café soon after four. He was gone for an hour and a half. There's no coverage of the flat. So, what really happened? Come on, son, it's better if you just tell us. Tell us where she is now.'

'I've told you the truth. That's all I can do.'

Sergeant Fisher switched gear now, leaned forward and looked Den right in the eye.

'Okay, tell us about the scrunchie then. How did it come to be on the floor of the café? Did things get a little rough? Did she try to fight you off?'

In the heat of it all, Den had forgotten about the scrunchie.

'No, of course not,' he said. 'There was no fight, nothing at all.'

'She came quietly?'

'No, you're twisting things.' *Don't argue with them,* he thought. *Stick to the facts!* 'She bought the Kit Kat and she left. Maybe the scrunchie just fell off. We pick up all sorts of lost property at the end of a day in the café.'

The officers looked at each other, their expressions mirroring each other – neither of them believed him.

'You're an obsessive person, Den, aren't you? You get a thing for people, girls, and it gets a bit out of hand. You don't know when to stop. Tell us about Sarah.'

Day Two

Den

Den gasped. In his heart, he'd known that this was coming, but he still wasn't prepared for it. He buried his face in his hands, then took a deep breath and sat up again.

'Sarah was eighteen, like me. I wasn't obsessed. It was . . . I was in love with her. I thought she was in love with me, but it all went wrong. I thought I could win her back. It was my first relationship. I didn't know the rules.'

'She was a young woman, away from home for the first time. She complained about harassment, stalking.'

'I left her flowers. I . . .' Oh God, he knew how bad this would sound. 'I waited for her some days. I sang under her window one night. I thought I was being romantic. I didn't realise . . .'

'She'd told you to stop, to leave her alone, but you didn't, did you, Den?'

'I loved her so much. I still had hope that we'd get back together. I was foolish, I suppose. When I realised I'd got it wrong, it broke me. I never meant to frighten her. I never meant to be that person.'

'And when did you realise you'd got it wrong, Den?'

'When the police in Hull came to my room in the student halls. When they took me away and questioned me.'

His world had come crashing down that day; he'd seen his romantic hopes, his self-image, his academic career all in tatters. At some point, his mum and dad had come to fetch him home. There had been doctors and hospital rooms; there was medication and long days in bed behind closed curtains. It had been the worst time of his life. He started to cry.

Sergeant Fisher put a tissue on the table between them and Den grabbed it and tried to clean himself up.

'It's okay, Den, let it out,' he said. 'Everyone makes mistakes. We get that. We need to know what happened with Mina, though. We've promised her mum that we'd find her. Come on, Den, we're listening. Mina was another obsession, wasn't she? It's time to tell the truth.'

Day Two

Sandy

Just for a moment, when she woke up, she thought everything was normal. She felt rough, but just the usual morning sort of rough, when you know a coffee and a ciggie will make you feel instantly better. She could hear someone in the flat, moving around in the kitchen and wondered if Mina was going to bring her a cuppa. Then she remembered why it couldn't be her. Or could it? Was she back? Had she come back in the night?

Her heart started thumping, her stomach cramped and she could feel the jitters rushing through her arms and legs. She threw back the covers and stumbled out of her bedroom. She tried to shout Mina's name, but her throat was too dry and only a sort of squawk came out.

'Oh.'

The person in the kitchen was not Mina. Just for a moment she couldn't remember her name, but she knew she was a cop.

The woman – Jodie, that was it – turned round.

'Morning, Sandy.' Her tone was steady, calm. How could anyone stay calm in the middle of a shitshow like this?

'Have you found her?'

'No, sorry, love, but we did find something that might be hers. The lads are bringing it up now for you to look at.'

'Found something? What is it? Is it her cuggy?' The thought of it, that precious scrap of material, being found lying somewhere was almost too much to bear.

'Don't panic. It's an umbrella. You said you saw her take a brolly with her on Wednesday morning. Can you remember what colour it was?'

'It's blue,' she said, running her fingers through her hair, 'with pink spots on. I got it in the Poundshop. Mina loves it.'

Jodie's face seemed to change. The description matched, didn't it? She knew it was Mina's. Oh shit, oh shit, the day was going wrong before it had even started. Everything worse than yesterday, if that was even possible.

'Okay,' Jodie said. 'Let's wait and see. Now, the kettle's just boiled. Do you want tea or coffee? Toast or cereal? You'll need something – you didn't eat last night, did you?'

Sandy stared dully at this woman, bold as brass, taking over her kitchen.

'Just coffee,' Sandy said. 'Nothing to eat. What colour is the umbrella they've found?'

Jodie ignored her. 'You'll have to have something. You need to keep your strength up.'

'What am I? Five? Why aren't you answering me?'

Jodie didn't say anything, just made the coffee and put it on the worktop near to her.

'Sandy, drink this. They'll be up in a minute. In the meantime, we need to think about making that appeal. It won't take long. We'll get on the TV news and in the papers. It will keep everyone looking.'

She'd mentioned it last night, but Sandy couldn't even think about it then.

'I don't know,' she said, taking a sip of the hot coffee. Her stomach still hurt. Maybe it was just because it was empty. It *was* a long time since she'd eaten anything. It seemed disloyal to do normal things – eat, drink – with Mina missing, but she wouldn't be any good to her if she didn't keep herself together. 'Sorry I snapped before. I'll have some toast. Please.'

Jodie nodded and Sandy took her coffee into the lounge. She flicked the TV on, although she wasn't really watching. She was just facing that way while images danced in front of her eyes, as she sipped her coffee and lit another fag.

Jodie popped her head round the door. 'We need to do a proper search of this place today, too. We could crack on with that while you are out.'

Did Sandy really have any choice? She couldn't stand the thought of strangers, especially the police, poking around her things. She didn't have anything to hide these days, apart from a few private pics on her phone and she'd already got rid of those. They wouldn't find anything that would get her in trouble. 'I dunno,' she said. 'Let me think about it.'

The telly had moved on to a local news programme and suddenly Mina's face was right there on the screen, the photo that Sandy had given the police. A reporter was talking over it, about 'fears growing for missing Mina'. Sandy couldn't take her eyes off it. Jodie came in carrying a plate of toast.

At the same time there was a knock on the door. Jodie opened it and another officer came in, carrying a see-through bag. Sandy didn't need to examine it. She knew straight away. Bile or something, hot and sour, pressed at the back of her throat.

'It's hers,' she said. 'That's Mina's umbrella.'

Day Two

Den

They started the interview again, but somehow breaking down had given Den new strength. The tension had gone; he was calmer. Every time they fired another question at him, he took a deep breath before replying and then he gave his answer.

He didn't have his phone with him, so he had very little idea how long he'd been there. All part of their plan, he supposed: shut you in a windowless room, disorientate you. They kept going back over the same ground, and he sensed their growing frustration with him when there was a knock on the door and another plain-clothes officer stepped in.

'Can I have a word, Sarge?'

Sergeant Fisher got up and left the room. When he came back he was carrying something in a clear plastic bag.

'Would you mind taking a look at this?' he said, putting it on the table in front of Den with an air of triumph.

Den peered at the bag. It didn't take him long to realise that the object inside was an umbrella, some of the spokes at strange angles like the broken wing of a bird.

'It was found in the bin outside your café. Does that jog your memory?'

Den swallowed hard, trying to trick his face muscles into stopping smiling. It didn't work. 'Yes, of course. I found that on Thursday. It was on the pavement near the bin. I picked it up and put it in. That was all.'

'You didn't think it might be significant?'

'No. Not when I found it. I never gave it a second thought.'

'But it will have your fingerprints on it?'

Den shrugged. 'Yeah, I suppose. Unless they've washed off. Wait a minute, is it hers? Is it Mina's?'

'You tell us.'

'How would I know? An umbrella's an umbrella. *Is* it hers?'

'We're going to run some tests, but her mother has identified it, yes. So tell us again where you found it?' He emphasised the word 'found' so heavily that Den could hear the scepticism.

Den's calmness was dissolving. There was a tremor in his voice as he recounted the event.

'It was Thursday afternoon. Mina's neighbour, Mrs C, had been in, asking about her, and I held the door for her and spotted the umbrella on the ground. We keep our bit of pavement clean and tidy, so, of course, I picked it up. It looked broken, so I put it in the bin.'

'Mina was in your café on Wednesday. It was raining. She was soaked. And yet you say you found her umbrella on Thursday, a whole twenty-four hours later. That doesn't add up, does it? You had her umbrella somewhere in the shop or in the flat, didn't you? Did you have her bag too? Have you still got it? And the girl. Where's Mina, Den? Where is she?'

'I don't know!' His smile had finally gone, shocked away by the enormity of what was happening. 'I'm telling you the truth. I don't know where she is, I wish I did! I picked up her umbrella on Thursday afternoon. You've got to believe me.'

Day Two

Kath

I'm guessing Sandy didn't get much sleep because she looked rougher than yesterday and that's saying something. She was sitting in her lounge, smoking, with a mug of black coffee steaming on the crate in front of her.

'Hello, Sandy,' I said. 'Sorry there's been no news.' She squinted up at me.

'Oh Kath, they found her umbrella. Stuffed in the bin outside the café.'

My jaw dropped a little bit, my mouth falling open. The scrunchie and now the umbrella. Somehow that made it all seem more real.

I sat down next to her and looked at Jodie, who was standing in the doorway. She nodded her encouragement. I'd been rehearsing what I should say but none of it seemed right now I was here. To be honest, Sandy looked so frail, I wondered if it was fair to ask her to talk to the press. Her cigarette smoke was drifting my way, making my chest tight again. It caught in the back of my throat and I started coughing.

'Sorry,' Sandy said and stubbed the cigarette out in the saucer, which I thought was rather sensitive of her in the circumstances.

'Just her umbrella?' I said.

I looked towards Jodie, who nodded.

'Well, that's something, I suppose.'

'Her comforter – she calls is her cuggy – is missing too,' said Sandy. 'They haven't found that.'

That was new, too. Was it a 'development'? I'd have to ask Jodie or Naz when I could get one of them on their own.

'Maybe it's in her bag, love,' I said. 'They haven't found that yet, have they? Jodie here mentioned that you might do a public appeal – ask Mina to come home, ask people to keep an eye out. That right?' The little muscles underneath Sandy's ear were working as she clenched and unclenched her jaw. 'It sounds like a good idea, if you can face it. After all, if little Mina's just run away, she might be scared to come home. If she sees on the telly that it's okay to come back, that she's not in trouble, this might all be over in a few hours.'

Jodie gave me a secret thumbs-up.

'That's exactly it, Sandy,' she said. 'If you could say that no one's cross with her, that it's all right to come home, it might help.'

Sandy shoved the mug away from her sharply, so that coffee slopped over the rim onto the crate. 'Why are you both going on about that, about her being scared to come home? Her hair thing! Her umbrella! Someone's got her! That bloke from the café most likely. Why are you accusing me of something? We didn't have a row or anything! We didn't argue, okay? Someone's taken her! She's not run away!'

The force with which she spat out her words made me think that anyone who *did* row with her might have reason to be scared, very scared. I glanced at Jodie, who nodded again.

'No, 'course not,' I said, keeping my voice as light and soothing as I could. 'Kids are kids, though, aren't they? I know from my

Evie that they get things muddled up or out of proportion. If she has run away, it might be over something tiny, something you wouldn't give a second thought to.'

'Do you think so?'

'Maybe. It's got to be worth a try, hasn't it?'

She reached for the mug now, picked it up and cradled it. 'Yeah. I suppose so. The cameras, though. I feel really . . . grubby.'

I'd noticed that she was still in yesterday's clothes. To be honest, she stank a bit too.

'Have a shower, then. It'll make you feel better anyway.'

'I can't. My hot water's fucked.'

I shot another glance at Jodie, who shrugged.

'Your leccy's still on, isn't it?' I said, thinking about the kettle that had produced the boiling water for the coffee.

'Yeah, but the water doesn't get hot in the immersion. We haven't had hot water for a couple of weeks.'

'Weeks, Sandy? That's no good. Have you rung the landlord?' said Jodie.

'I rang but they didn't send anyone.'

'Could she use your bathroom, Kath?'

I hesitated. 'Um, yes, I suppose so. Would you like a shower at mine, Sandy?'

'Could I have a bath?' It was such a simple question, but it almost floored me. She seemed so childlike again and, in that moment, I started to feel sorry for her, however badly she'd treated Mina. People aren't all bad or all good, are they? Maybe it was just a case of not coping, dropping the ball. God knows, I knew about that.

''Course you can, love. Give me five minutes. I'll go and start it running for you. Shall I put some bubbles in?'

'Yes please.'

'Good girl.' I stood up with some difficulty – her sofa was low to start with and squashy with age. Then I had an idea. 'Would it help if you had something of Mina's with you at the press conference? A toy or a little jumper or something? Give you some courage?'

Sandy looked up at me. Her eyes were filling with tears. 'Her cuggy's her favourite thing.'

'Something else then. Do you want me to have a look?' She nodded. I walked past Jodie and went into Mina's room. It was as sparse as the lounge. Just a bed and a little table and chair next to it, and a wardrobe with a broken handle. I looked around, including turning down her duvet, picked up a pink cardigan and took it through to Sandy.

'You could hold this cardi, if it would help,' I said and handed it to her. She immediately put it up to her face, buried her nose in it, and started crying quietly. The tears seemed so much more genuine than the hysterics last night. Sometimes it's good to let the feelings out. I thought I'd better leave her to it, so I walked out into the hall, and Jodie followed me.

'Well done, Kath. You did that beautifully,' she said. 'Imagine not having hot water for two weeks when you've got a kid! I'd have played merry hell with the landlord.'

'Mm, me too. If only I'd known, they could both have come round mine.'

'You didn't know. It's not your fault. I'll bring her round in five minutes, and I'll let the press officer know we're good to go at eleven. The plan is to do it in the courtyard. No need to take her down to the station. Are you okay to come with her?'

I agreed. Although I wasn't used to all this fuss, I can't deny it was nice to feel useful after all these years. I've never been one to push myself forward, never craved the limelight, but it felt like sometime in my fifties, I started to become invisible. People just don't take any notice of older women. By the time you're in your eighties, if anyone pays you any attention at all, it's to pat you on your head for living that long. It never occurs to people that you might have something to contribute. Not until now, anyway.

I let myself back into the flat and headed straight for the

bathroom. When we moved in, avocado suites were quite the thing, although to be perfectly honest, it was all just a tiny bit shabby now. The grouting needed redoing and the lino was cracked and a bit mouldy in the corners. I just haven't got the puff for that sort of job anymore. Never mind, a hot bath would be more luxury than Sandy had had for a while. I turned on the taps and tipped more bubble bath than I intended into the flowing water. By the time Sandy appeared, there was a thick layer of froth brimming over the edge of the bath, like squirty cream on top of the best sort of hot chocolate.

'Oh, Kath, that's lovely,' she said, and burst into tears again. She was carrying a change of clothes with her and a towel, so it was too awkward to hug her, but I put a hand on the top of her back and gave her a little rub.

'Have a nice soak, Sandy. I'll put the kettle on for when you get out. Coffee, is it? Or tea?'

'Coffee please.'

'Black?'

'Yes, please.'

Funny how a little kindness had turned her all meek and polite. She was almost like a different person, someone you could almost start to be fond of.

Jodie was in the hall.

'Do you want a cuppa, love?' I said. 'I'm putting the kettle on.'

'Best not. I've had two already this morning. Do you mind if Naz and I do a little experiment? I want to see how much I can hear from your flat. That okay? Will you help me?'

''Course. I'll do whatever you need.'

I hovered in the hall while she went into the lounge. She beckoned me inside, then spoke on the walkie-talkie with Naz. 'Yeah. Okay. Just clap your hands or something. Yeah. Did you hear that, Kath?'

'Yes, but I've normally got the telly on. Sometimes I've got my aids in, sometimes not.'

'Have you got them in now?'

'Yes.'

'Okay. Let's put the TV on. Make it realistic.' She returned to the walkie-talkie. 'Now can you open and close the front door?'

She looked at me, watching for my reaction. I didn't hear anything. 'Has he done it yet?' I asked.

'Yes,' she said. Then, to Naz, 'Try slamming it.'

Now I heard it, the dull thud that I was used to. 'That's it,' I said. 'Heard it that time.'

'Interesting,' said Jodie. She seemed pleased, but I was bothered. I'd been so sure that I was aware of the comings and goings next door. Had I been missing half the picture?

'I'm sorry, Jodie,' I said. 'I reported everything in good faith. Now I'm thinking I might have missed things . . . I'm – what do you call it? – an unreliable witness.' I felt a bit wobbly, to be honest.

She registered my distress. 'Kath, it's fine. You've been a huge help. This would be so much more difficult without you. Why don't you put that kettle on now?'

I went into the hall and as I did, I heard someone singing. She had a lovely voice, I'll give her that much, but the song floating out of the bathroom made the hair on the back of my neck stand on end for a different reason. I'm not very up on Eighties pop, but I did recognise this one. Everybody knows it; it's one of those feelgood, upbeat songs which my Ray would call a 'standard'. And now Sandy was belting it out in my bathroom: *Walking on Sunshine*.

I turned back to ask if Jodie could hear it too, but the look of horror on her face told me everything I needed to know.

Day Two

Kath

Jodie didn't need to say anything. We looked at each other for a moment and then I shook my head and went into the kitchen to put the kettle on. Jodie followed me in.

'Can you believe it?' I said in a loud whisper. There was no way Sandy would be able to hear us, but I wasn't taking any chances.

'She's been under a lot of strain,' said Jodie, picking her words carefully. The set of her mouth made me think she wasn't as understanding as her words implied. 'People sometimes don't react to stress the way we expect them to.'

'Even so,' I said. 'Jodie, if Sandy knew where Mina was all the time, she wouldn't be worried, would she? I mean, most people would pretend, I suppose, but maybe they'd let it slip sometimes.'

Jodie sucked air in through pursed lips. 'We look at every possibility, Kath.'

The blood seemed to be running a bit colder in my veins. It was difficult to imagine anything more heartless. I stood in my little kitchen and listened to the woman with a missing child singing in my bathroom. The sound merged with the gurgling of pipes – she was letting the water out.

'It's important that we stick to Plan A,' said Jodie. 'Keep things as relaxed as possible, get her to do the public appeal. I can count on you to help, can't I?'

'Yes. If that's the plan,' I said, weakly, although I'd rather have done anything else than go to a press conference with that woman.

'You've been brilliant, Kath. You've got an important role to play. You're so calm. It really helps.'

'I don't feel calm,' I said, 'but I'm doing my best.'

Jodie looked past me to the fridge. 'Is that her drawing, Kath? Is it Mina's?' I turned round too, although I knew what she was referring to.

'Yes,' I said. Just looking at the picture was stirring up all sorts of emotions. 'I'd posted a little chocolate through the door to her. I never expected a thank you like that. Shows you what a nice girl she is. Difficult to believe with a mother like that.'

I could feel myself getting tearful again, but that was no use to anyone, was it? So I sniffed hard and took a couple of deep breaths.

It was ages before Sandy emerged from the bathroom. When she did, she looked quite different from before – smaller somehow, more wholesome. She was wearing clean clothes, no make-up and her hair was wrapped up in one of my handtowels.

'Have you got a hairdryer?'

No please or anything. The manners had gone then. They didn't last long.

'Yes. It's in my bedroom.' I couldn't help a measure of stiffness in my words. 'I'll fetch it.'

She dried her hair in the lounge, and I made her some coffee and a couple of pieces of toast and spread. It stuck in my craw to do all this, but Jodie was there and I'd given her my word. It might be old-fashioned but it still counts for something in my book. The clock ticked round towards eleven.

'We'll go straight out to the courtyard from here, Sandy,' Jodie said.

'I need to do my make-up,' Sandy said. 'There's no way I'm doing it without my face on.'

'Better not, to be honest, love. The message will have more impact if you don't look "perfect", if you know what I mean. I'm not going to lie; it can be quite an emotional thing. We don't want mascara running down your face, do we?'

'I've got waterproof. I'm telling you, I'm not doing it like this. I've got the basics in my handbag. I've left it next door.'

'The black one? I'll go and fetch it. I'll drop your old clothes back in too,' said Jodie, quickly, and disappeared before Sandy could protest, leaving us alone together. Talk about awkward silence. I didn't know what to say to her. She didn't seem nervous at all now, roaming round the lounge, running her hands over my ornaments and photographs on the mantelpiece.

'This your family?' She'd picked up the framed one of Ray and Evie at the seaside, when Evie was about four. I couldn't keep my eyes off her hands holding the frame. I didn't want her touching it, wanted to snatch it away.

'Yes,' I said. 'Just one daughter, like you.'

'And a husband, unlike me.' She put it down and trailed her fingers over the urn next to it.

'He's in there now. Well, his ashes are,' I said, deliberately trying to startle her. I know it was mean but having her here was making me edgy. She looked at me, glanced back at the urn and then took her hand away.

'Oh. Sorry. What's your daughter doing now?' she said.

'She's in Australia. She's been there for ages. Got two boys, both grown up now.'

'Wow, Australia. Do you go out there?'

'Not anymore. The flight's too much – too expensive and too long.'

Jodie came back in with Sandy's bag.

'Great. Is the best mirror the bathroom one?' I nodded. 'I could do your make-up if you like, Kath, in a minute. There'll be lots of cameras down there today.'

'Not for me, thank you. I'm not bothered by all that,' I said.

'Suit yourself.' She retreated into the bathroom again. When she re-emerged, she looked older, harder. She'd drawn in her eyebrows, put eyeliner and thick mascara on and bright red lipstick.

'That's better,' she said. 'Shall we go and do it? Is it time?'

Day Two

Sandy

She was feeling much better after her bath. It was amazing how being really clean and warm pepped you up. With her face back on, she almost felt on top of her nerves. That confidence only lasted until they stepped out of Kath's front door.

She could hear voices drifting up from the yard below, where the press was assembling, like a wolf pack, and then as they walked past her flat the door was ajar and she got a glimpse of someone wearing a crinkly white boiler suit, the sort you see on the telly at crime scenes, where there's a body. It suddenly made her skin crawl.

There was quite a gang of people trooping down the stairs with her: two detectives, Jodie and Naz, a press officer and Kath. When they came out of the door at the bottom of the staircase, a volley of shutters went off and people crowded round. The cops made them stand back and she walked through, clutching Mina's cardi a bit tighter. She was shivering, from the cold or the nerves or both. Beside her, Kath took her arm and gave it a squeeze. She wasn't a bad old stick, was she?

The press officer greeted people and introduced the detective in charge, Detective Inspector Andy Haynes. He started talking, but Sandy didn't really hear what he was saying. She was scared now, trying to remember what she needed to do. Her mouth had gone dry and her legs were wobbly.

She suddenly realised that he had stopped talking and everyone was waiting. It was her turn. She took a step forward. Just that movement made all the cameras go off again, startling her. She'd written some notes on a piece of paper, but when she looked at it, the words swam in front of her eyes. Still clutching the paper, she looked up at the bank of cameras. She focused on one guy and spoke to him.

'The last forty-eight hours have been the worst of my life,' she said, her voice breaking up. 'My little girl is missing and all I want is for her to come home.' It was too much. She started crying and covered her face with her hands, but pressing the soft cardi into her skin, getting the faintest scent of Mina, made it all worse somehow. Kath passed her a hanky and she dabbed her eyes, leaving big black smudges on the cloth. She tried to carry on. 'Mina, if you can see this, please come home, darling. You're not in trouble. I just need you home, angel.' She couldn't do it. She held her hand up, bowed her head and waited for someone else to take over.

Kath put her arms round her, as the detective stepped in. 'Thank you, Sandy. As you can see, this is a painful time. We need to get Mina home. If you have any information at all, please contact the police. You can do it anonymously; we just need to find Mina now. Thank you!'

There was a sudden hubbub as journalists shouted questions.

One voice rose above the others. 'Sandy, is it true that you didn't come home on Wednesday night? That Mina was missing for twenty-four hours before anyone noticed?'

There was silence for a moment, then someone booed. A woman's voice called out, 'Shame!'

Sandy burrowed her head into Kath's shoulder.

Another voice shouted out, 'Have you arrested someone, Inspector? Can you tell us more? Is this now a murder inquiry?'

Sandy gasped and started sobbing. DI Haynes said, 'Mina is missing. This is a missing persons inquiry, but we're keeping an open mind.'

'But you've arrested someone?'

'We haven't made any arrests. We're pursuing a number of lines of inquiry, and people are helping us with that, but that's all I can say for now. Thank you.'

He turned towards Sandy and Kath and, holding both arms out, ushered them towards the stairwell again. He looked rattled, like things hadn't gone according to plan.

'Well done,' he said. 'Let's get you back.'

'You did it,' said Kath. 'It's over now. You were very brave.'

Kath was walking slowly, using a stick, so Jodie took over from her, putting her arm round Sandy and walking her to the stairs.

'They hate me, don't they?' Sandy said to her as they climbed to the second floor.

'They're just stirring, Sandy,' she said. 'Try not to let it get to you. You did very well.'

'Why would they ask if it was murder, or whether you've arrested someone? Do they know something? Is there something you're not telling me?'

'No, love. We'll tell you of any development as soon as we can. That's my job. You can trust me. We're interviewing all sorts of people, but we haven't arrested anyone. We'll get there.'

They were still searching the flat when they got upstairs. Sandy wasn't ready to go back in anyway. It was starting to feel really claustrophobic in there. She waited on the walkway, lighting a cigarette to calm herself down. She didn't know whether it was the nicotine or the cold air, or maybe the adrenaline rush of the press conference, but she was starting to feel better. She'd done her bit – the appeal would go out on the telly at lunchtime and millions of people would see it.

Kath came puffing along the walkway. She was in a bit of state, limping and leaning heavily on her stick. Sandy could hear her breath wheezing in and out as she came closer. *It can't be nice being that old and knackered,* she thought.

'I just wanted to say thanks, Kath, for being there today. I couldn't have done it without you.'

'You're welcome, love. Let's hope it does some good, eh?'

They both looked out over the courtyard. Below them, the press pack were going their separate ways.

'People can't just disappear, can they?' said Sandy.

'No, love. So we'll find her.'

Kath leaned her stick against the wall, turned towards her, grabbed both her arms and looked her square in the face. There was something in her eyes, a kindness and decency that seemed to warm Sandy, there and then, standing in that cold wind.

'We'll find her. There's always hope, Sandy. You must never give up hope.'

'It would help if there was a reward. The papers do that, don't they, when kids go missing? The *Sun* or the *Mirror*? Should I talk to them about it?'

Kath shrugged. 'I haven't the foggiest, love.'

'They offered five thousand pounds for that girl a couple of years ago. Do you think they'll do that for Mina?'

Kath looked at her. 'Not my department, Sandy. Maybe Jodie could help.'

'Lot of money, Kath.'

'Yes, love, that's a lot of money.' She winced as she moved towards her front door. 'I've got to go in now. My legs are killing me. I'll see you later, Sandy. Try to keep your chin up, love.'

Sandy watched as Kath let herself in and closed the door behind her.

Jodie emerged from her flat. 'They've finished searching,' she said. 'You can go back in in a minute.'

'Nice,' said Sandy, dropping her cigarette onto the walkway and grinding it under her foot. 'Jodie, who do I see about getting a reward put in the papers?'

Day Two

Kath

I don't have a smartphone-whatchamacallit but I do have a laptop. I went to a thing at the community centre, Get Connected they called it, where they taught oldies like me how to search the internet, send an email and join a neighbourhood forum to keep up with local information. It was all very good and I came away from those Thursday afternoons quite pleased with myself, but as soon as I got home, I couldn't remember what we'd done or how to do it. The printouts didn't help much. No good telling me to select an icon from the toolbar, if you don't know what an icon is or where to find the toolbar.

Anyway, I can just about search for things if I have to, so after I'd talked to Jodie and Sandy on the walkway, I headed back inside and tried to find out who it was the police had taken in for questioning. It seemed like the sort of thing the internet might tell you. Well, it wasn't on Google, or at least not on my computer. There was a lot of nasty stuff about Sandy on the neighbourhood chat, though. Lots of people calling her out for neglecting Mina. To be honest, they were only saying what any sensible person would be thinking. I wondered what those same people would say if they knew how keen she was on someone putting up a reward? I mean, it might just be she wanted to see an incentive out there to encourage someone to come forward, or there might be more to it.

I didn't know how to post without it being obvious it was me – my username isn't exactly subtle: KathinNelson1933 – so I reckoned I should go back to the old ways, the 'bush telegraph' my Ray used to call it, and take a walk down to the corner shop. They'd know what was what. Might even call in at the café on the way. After all, with the scrunchie and the umbrella being found near there, it seemed like that was at the centre of things. Den seemed like a nice young chap, but you never really know, do you?

I knocked on number seven as I passed. Jodie came to the door.

'I'm going to the shops,' I said. 'Do you need anything?'

'I don't think so, Kath. Thanks for asking. Do you want a hand with that trolley?' she asked, looking at my tartan terror on wheels.

'No, ta, there's nothing in it,' I said, 'apart from a bit of recycling for the bins downstairs and that doesn't weigh anything. I'll be glad when the lift's fixed, though.'

There weren't any photographers or press in the courtyard, but there were police officers in uniform, who looked about twelve, patrolling the estate. I trundled my trolley to the bin store, which was more like an open-sided concrete shed, and dumped my tins, cardboard and plastic. I peered into the recess behind the bins. Obviously, it had been searched, like everywhere else on the estate, but I just couldn't stop looking, hoping to find something that everyone else had missed.

The gang of teenagers I'd seen watching the press conference were near the garages next to the bin store. I kept my eye on them as I was emptying my trolley. I know some people are scared of them, but not me. I'm too old to be intimidated by some scrawny kids. They're only hanging around outside because there's nothing better to do, although, of course, at that age they should have been in school.

I started walking towards the shops, then turned back. The kids were always around, weren't they? Watching, taking things in? I wondered how likely they were to tell the police anything they'd seen. Not very, I'd have thought, but they might talk to a harmless old bat who reminds them of their nan.

They looked surprised when I walked right up to them; five lads, none of them over sixteen, I would have said, and an ugly little dog, one of those ones with bandy legs and an attitude. It was wearing a collar with studs on to make it look even tougher and it kept sniffing round my bag.

'All right, boys?'

They glanced at each other, confused. One of them, astride a bike, smiled in a sort of cocky way. 'We're all right. Don't know about you, though, Grandma.'

The others laughed.

'To be honest, love, I'm not all right.' I kept studying his face for signs of human empathy, but there wasn't a flicker. I ploughed on regardless. 'I'm worried about that girl who's missing. She's my neighbour, see. You probably know her too, don't you?'

The boy shrugged. 'We've seen her. Don't know her.'

'I reckon you see everything round here. Did you see little Mina the day before yesterday? Did you see her around here at about half past three?'

He stopped meeting my eyes then, looked down at his hands gripping the handlebars of his bike.

'Who do you think you are? Luther or something?'

Another snigger from his audience. *Luther* wasn't one of my favourites on the telly. Bit too violent for me – I'm more of a *Midsomer Murders* kind of person.

'I'm just someone who's worried about a little girl. She's only eleven.' My chin started to wobble and I blinked hard. That got them. They might try to appear hard as nails on the outside, but they couldn't cope with a crying nan.

'Okay, okay. We didn't see nothing on Wednesday. It was pissing down, wannit? We were in Vince's place.' He looked towards one of the other boys, who nodded.

'True dat.'

'Fair enough. Just thought I'd ask. You know, as you're out and about so much, if you do see anything, please tell someone. Tell the police or any grown-up. Tell me, if you like. We do need to find her.'

There was a glimmer of warmth and a mumbled, 'Yeah. Sure. But they've nicked someone for it, haven't they? Taken the nonce from the café in. Reckon it's all over.'

My heart was off again, thudding away in my chest. 'They've taken who in?'

'The young guy, Dennis. They took him in this morning. He was seen.'

'Oh,' I said. 'I didn't know.'

He smirked. 'Your friendly neighbourhood pedo, innit?'

'Sorry?' I said, not sure I'd heard what he said. I do miss things when people mumble and youngsters are the worst.

He laughed. 'Don't worry about it, Grandma. He's off the streets now. Won't be following girls in his van or lurking by the school gates anymore.'

'Den did that? You saw him?'

'Nah, but Vince's little sister did. A big guy, she said, asking which class she was in. Trying to find out how old she was, I reckon. Pervert.'

'Oh, right.' My mind was reeling. This was all new information. I wondered why Jodie hadn't told me they'd arrested someone. Maybe the boys had got it wrong.

There was only one way to find out. I left them to it, whatever 'it' was, and headed towards the café, dragging my trolley behind me.

114

Day Two

Kath

There were yellow ribbons tied to all the lampposts. I found it strangely moving, a sign that the community was holding Mina in its thoughts. Yellow's usually a cheerful colour, isn't it? I crocheted a yellow and purple baby blanket when I was expecting my Evie. I've still got it and it always makes me smile.

As I rounded the corner, I saw a couple of people outside the café taking photographs and someone up a stepladder. I did a double-take when I realised it was Mrs Hammond, scrubbing at the shutters with a sponge and a bucket of soapy water. I screwed my eyes up, trying to make sense of the painted words she was trying to get rid of, then got a sick feeling in my stomach as I realised they said, 'PEDO SCUM'.

It was true, then, I thought. A man being questioned or even arrested. It was Den.

I walked right up to the photographers. 'Haven't you got anything better to do?'

They brought their cameras away from their faces.

'Just doing our job, love. If we don't take pictures, someone else will.'

'Well, you've got them now, so why don't you clear off?'

They looked at each other and shrugged, then, to my surprise, slung their bags over their shoulders and walked away. Got their shots already, I supposed, or perhaps they still had a shred of decency. I went and stood at the bottom of the stepladder and called up, 'Mrs Hammond? Mrs Hammond!'

She paused and dashed a stray strand of hair out of her eyes. 'We're closed today,' she said, flatly.

The sponge in her hand was stained bright red, but the 'P' from 'PEDO' was still there, just smudged a bit.

'Have you got another sponge?' I said. 'I'm no good on ladders, but I can have a go at the bottom bit.'

Her expression softened. 'It's okay. You don't need to do that.'

'I know, but I'm offering. I've been cleaning up mess all my life. I'm not frightened of a bit of elbow grease.'

She smiled sadly and picked her way down the ladder. 'I'll fetch another bucket,' she said, 'and a hard brush. Maybe that'll be better.'

She wasn't gone for long. She came back with some strong cleaning spray, a second bucket of water and a small stiff brush. 'I wanted to get rid of this before Den gets back. I don't want him to see it.'

'Understandable. Is he the one they're questioning?'

'Yes.'

'I'm so sorry.'

'Do you have children, Mrs Cartright?'

'A girl,' I said, hardly missing a beat. 'And do call me Kath.'

She smiled. 'Linda,' she said.

I picked up the spray and started tackling the 'M', while Linda climbed back up the ladder. We had a go at the whole thing, but after twenty minutes we ended up with a blurry mess which was still legible, and I was jiggered.

'Come on, love,' I shouted up at her. 'Let's have a cuppa.'

She nodded to me and we packed up. She tipped the paint-stained water down the nearest drain and carried the stepladder into the café. 'It's only on one side of the shutter,' I said. 'It won't show when the café's open.'

'If it opens,' she said, gloomily. 'Who'll want to eat here now? Mud sticks.'

She locked the front door and led me through the empty café to some stairs at the back.

The flat itself was more spacious than you might imagine. I sat at the table in a nice kitchen diner, while she made tea for us and put some little cakes on a plate.

'I shouldn't really,' I said. 'I'm not meant to have sugar.'

And then she did a lovely thing. She reached into the fruit basket on the kitchen worktop, picked up a mango, peeled it and cut slices onto a plate.

'I've never had mango,' I said.

'Ah, you're missing a treat! Try it.'

The fruit was shiny with juice. She handed me a fork. I speared the smallest bit I could find and nibbled the end. It was delicious, earthy and sweet. She raised her eyebrows in enquiry.

'Gorgeous,' I said, and I helped myself to some more, although I suspected it had as much sugar in it as a Mr Kipling's Country Slice.

She set a pot of tea down, along with two china cups and saucers. It was all rather fancy.

'This is nice,' I said, then immediately regretted it, because I was only here due to things being so awful for her. She took my words at face value, though.

'Yes,' she said. 'It is. I don't get many visitors.'

'You and me both. Surely this place is busy, though?'

'I'm mostly up here. I do book-keeping for people, including us. I leave running the café to Den and Tony and that isn't as busy as it used to be. People would rather go to a Costa or a

Starbucks these days.'

'I'm sorry about that.' I took another sliver of mango. 'Maybe this Mina business will bring people together.' I suddenly thought of the graffiti on the shutters and regretted opening my big mouth. Too late now, so I tried to dig myself out of the hole. 'Sad if it takes something like this to help us talk to each other. I don't mean just you and me, but all of us, the community round here.'

'Oh, I agree. Sad if it pulls us further apart, though.' She poured tea into the two cups. It was a beautifully rich, red-golden colour.

'Do you have some milk?' I asked.

'Try it without first. See what you think.'

I did as she said. It was delicious, fragrant and refreshing. 'Do you still want milk? I don't mind if you do, honestly. I'm not a dictator.'

'Maybe a drop. And a little bit of sugar. What tea is it?'

'Assam. I get it from the Asian shop. We live on stuff from the cash-and-carry, have to nowadays with things being so tight, but I buy myself little treats now and again, with my own money. I keep a little back every week. Tony doesn't know. Is that very bad of me? Nice to have something in the cupboard for special occasions.'

I felt rather honoured that I was considered special.

'No harm in having little secrets,' I said. 'Or doing your own thing. I think it's healthy.'

'Definitely. I think I'd go mad if I didn't have my knitting club and yoga class, Kath. Gets me out of the house, and we have a good chat and a laugh. Do you get out much?'

I think you'd describe the sound that came out of me as a hollow laugh. 'No. Not anymore. I can go days without seeing anyone, Linda.'

'You could come with me to the community centre.'

'Maybe. I don't know. I'm sorry you've had an awful day. There are some little shits around here, pardon my language. You wonder where the parents are, don't you?' I could have bitten my tongue off as soon as I said it, what with her son being questioned by the police as we spoke.

'Probably at work, like Mina's mother. Everyone's just trying to hold things together round here, us included.'

'Oh, I know all about that. I always worked round my Evie, though. After I lost my Ray, I did bits of cleaning when she was at school and took in sewing jobs and ironing for the evenings, so I could be there for her. I'm not saying it's easy, but I never left her alone.'

She smiled. 'Sewing? Do you knit as well? You could come and "stitch and bitch" with me on a Sunday. You'd fit right in. You're like me. I took up book-keeping because I could work at home. I was always here for Den. It's not the ideal place to bring up a family, but we did our best.'

I noticed the desk now, tucked into a corner of the room with shelves above it lined with lever arch files, all neat and tidy, everything in its place. I rather liked the cut of Linda's jib.

'Mind you,' I said, 'it was different times then. The estate was new and full of young families. We all left our doors open and had babies out on the walkways in their prams getting some fresh air. You don't do that now, do you? Kids were in and out of each other's houses and playing on the yard.'

'There are still kids on that yard, but not little ones.'

'Those teenagers? I think they're mostly harmless. I had a nice chat with them on my way over. We're not quite on "hug a hoodie" terms but they were polite enough. A lot of this tough stuff is all for show, isn't it?'

Linda shook her head. 'I don't know, Kath. I don't like walking around here after dark. I always keep my keys in my hand, not that I go out very much. And I worry if Den's out. Young men are more likely to be victims of crime than us.'

'Linda,' I said, 'are you worried that your Den had something to do with this?'

She was pouring another cup of tea and her hand didn't waver, not even a little bit.

'You know what it's like, Kath. Den has been a constant worry to me. He wouldn't hurt a child, though. I know him, Kath. He wouldn't do this. I don't know what happened to that little girl, but I do know Den's got nothing to do with it.'

'It's been two days, Linda, and no sightings. I can't understand why no one's spotted her somewhere, the poor little scrap. People don't just disappear, do they? You know, the more this goes on, the more I think someone's taken her, but I wouldn't be a hundred per cent surprised if Sandy knew who.'

Linda arched her eyebrows and put her cup down. 'Really?'

'She's not as upset as you'd expect, Linda. Not behind closed doors. All that for the cameras, that was just crocodile tears, I reckon. She was asking about a reward this morning.'

'Are you saying it's all fake? She cooked something up with someone to keep Mina hidden away until they can claim a reward?'

I took another sip of tea. 'I'm not saying anything, Linda. I'm not one to gossip, but I wouldn't be surprised, that's all.'

Day Two

Sandy

'I want to tell you this before you hear it from someone else, Sandy. The person we took in for questioning – we're letting him go.'

The adrenaline surge from the press conference had worn off and Sandy was feeling tired and disorientated. She just wanted this all to be over.

'What does that even mean? Are they still a suspect or what? Do you know where Mina is?'

Jodie held her hands up. 'Whoa, whoa, slow down, Sandy. All it is, right, is that someone was questioned at the station, but they haven't been arrested or charged. We haven't found Mina. It's just another step in the investigation.'

Her head was spinning now. 'Who was it? Who were you bloody questioning?'

'We're not releasing any details, Sandy, so it's better not to tell you right now. All I can say is that it's a twenty-one-year-old man.'

'Twenty-one? Okay. So, do you still think he might be the one? Do you think she's still alive?'

'I'm sorry, love, that's all I know at the moment.'

'Twenty-one. Twenty-one.' She didn't really know anyone locally. There were groups of kids and gangs of older ones who hung out on the estate, but this was just one person.

'Sandy, don't try to second-guess this. I'll tell you more as soon as I know, okay? Let me make you a coffee.'

'Coffee. Yeah, ta.'

She needed some caffeine, but she needed nicotine too, and some fresh air. She grabbed her packet of cigarettes and went straight to the front door. Then she leaned on the balustrade and lit up. There was a couple of photographers in the courtyard below, and as she looked down, someone shouted and they swung round and pointed their lenses at her. She resisted the urge to flick them the Vs but only just.

Two blokes in high-vis jackets were walking past, one a really tall guy with a big dog on a lead. They saw the photographers and looked up at Sandy too. One of them pointed and shouted, 'Slag!' Then they both laughed. What the hell? They must have known who she was, that her daughter was missing. How could they be so cruel? That was it. She stuck her middle finger up at them, but they'd looked away and were carrying on walking towards the shops. The photographers saw, though, but Sandy was past caring. She turned her back on them, took a long drag and blew smoke up into the air.

She got out her phone to check the FindMina Facebook page. There were hundreds of notifications and messages. God, it was vile stuff. People saying it was all her fault, that she was an unfit mother. Death threats. Rape threats. Her hands started shaking. She didn't want to look any more but couldn't stop scrolling. She took another drag from her cigarette and her phone slipped from her fingers and landed with a crack on the concrete by her feet.

Jodie came through the doorway, carrying a mug of coffee.

'Whoops,' she said, seeing the phone on the ground.

'Have you seen what they're saying about me?' Sandy said, bending down to retrieve the phone.

Jodie held the mug out towards her. 'I'm sorry, love,' she said. 'It's a pile-on. It's best not to read those things.'

'I've got death threats and all.'

She frowned. 'We can do something about that.'

'They're not going to do anything, though, are they? They're just little boys probably still living at home and wetting themselves every time they troll someone.'

'It's not on, though. I'll report it to our team. See what we can do. I know this is tricky, Sandy, but try not to worry.'

Try not to worry? Her daughter was gone, and she was public enemy number one. She opened Facebook again and tried to look through the comments for clues about the guy who had been questioned. It didn't take long to find the name.

Den Hammond. The son of the café owner. That café. She knew it.

And now they'd let the bastard go.

'I'm going out,' she said to Jodie.

She looked alarmed. 'We need to know where you are, Sandy. It's important . . .'

'I'll have my phone with me. You can't keep me here. This won't take long.'

Day Two

Den

They emerged from the lift and Fisher peeled off into an office, while Waite conducted Den along a corridor and through some doors, which he unlocked with a swipe of his ID card. As soon as they were through Den heard someone shout his name, and there, on a chair in a rather forlorn row underneath some Crimestoppers posters, was Dad. He leaped to his feet and Den started running towards him. There was a moment's hesitation and then they hugged each other, Den resting his head on Dad's shoulder and trying very hard not to cry. Dad's hand squeezed his neck.

'Hey, son. It's all right,' he said into Den's ear.

They pulled apart. 'I didn't know you were here, Dad.'

'I was just about to ring a solicitor. You've been here nearly five hours. They've told me nothing. Nothing,' he repeated, turning up the volume and addressing the woman behind the desk. She looked up and gave him the sort of fixed smile she clearly reserved for her more trying customers. 'Let's get you home. The van's out front. There are some reporters outside. Keep calm. Don't say a word, head down, into the van.'

'Reporters? Why? For me?'

'Yeah. Sorry, son. The police haven't released your name, but it's out there anyway now. Common knowledge.'

Den felt like the ground was moving beneath his feet, but really it was his legs threatening to give way. 'I don't know if I can do this, Dad.'

Dad put his hand on Den's shoulder and gripped hard.

'Come on, son. Grow some balls. It's a storm in a teacup. It'll die down. It'll be okay.' He fished in his pocket for the keys to the van. 'Ready?'

Before Den could protest, Dad was heading rapidly for the door. Den trotted behind him, trying to keep up. As soon as the door opened, the shouting began. People were shoving cameras in their faces and firing questions at them.

'Do you know where Mina is, Den?'

'Are you going to make a statement?'

'Were you the last person to see her?'

People were pushing and shoving, trying to block their path. 'Dad!' Den shouted. He was some way ahead now, almost at the van. He turned around.

'Hey, get out of his way, you fucking animals!' He started back towards Den, like a rodeo bull charging out of the gates, and making a similar sort of noise. The crowd parted miraculously, and Den darted forward. Dad grabbed his hand and pulled him towards the van, bundled him into the passenger seat and ran round to the other side. He started the engine and they were off, slowly at first as he tried to negotiate their exit without running anyone over. He kept up a running commentary, gesticulating wildly, until they were clear of the scrum and out on the open road.

'Get out of the fucking way! Clear the road! Move yourselves!'

Thankfully, traffic was light and, as Den looked in the wing mirror, he could soon see the remnants of the press pack on the pavement, receding into the background.

'"Keep calm. Don't say a word, head down." Good job, Dad!'

'Ha! That was for you! I never said I'd keep calm. How can I, with those fucking vultures pecking at you? They were round the café too, asking questions, phone ringing all the time. We didn't open up today.'

That, more than anything, brought Den up short. 'You didn't open up?'

'Not today, son.'

'But we never close. That's our thing, our USP. We can't afford to lose a day's takings.'

'It's only one day, Den. This'll all blow over. Hey, it means we get to watch the cricket.'

Dad's expression was stoic, but Den could see a little muscle at the corner of his eye twitching rapidly.

'I'm so sorry, Dad.'

'It's not your fault. You've done nothing wrong. People will have forgotten it by tomorrow. You'll see. Text your mum – tell her we're on our way.'

Day Two

Kath

There was a noise from the back of the building – a man shouting, the sound of an engine. We both looked up as two vehicle doors slammed and then the door downstairs opened and shut. Linda got up from the table and started towards the top of the stairs.

'Tony, is that you?' she called.

Footsteps clattered on the stairs and then Mr Hammond and Den came into the kitchen. The older man was flustered. Den looked decidedly rough. His mother flung her arms round him. It felt wrong to be witnessing this private, family moment, and yet I couldn't tear my eyes away. I made a show of standing up and starting to put my coat on. Den shrugged off his mum.

'I feel dirty, Mum. I need a shower.'

'Yes, of course. Are you hungry?'

'Yeah, kind of. Oh—' Den had spotted me now. He and Mr Hammond turned to me.

'I was just going,' I said. 'I only popped out to buy some milk.'

'Well, we don't sell milk here and besides, we're not bloody open,' Mr Hammond said. 'Anyone can see that!'

'Tony, shh! Mrs Cartright – Kath – kindly helped me clean something up.'

'What are you talking about?'

'There's some graffiti, some nasty stuff. I wanted it gone before you came back, and she helped me.'

His expression softened. He suddenly looked exhausted. 'Oh, I see. That's very good of you. Thank you, Kath. Was it milk you needed? You can have some from our kitchen downstairs.'

'There's no need, I can walk to the Co-op.'

'No, no. I'll fetch the milk. Anything else?'

'No, honestly, you've got enough on your plate.'

'Kath, sit there. Please.' He was so on edge, you got the feeling of a massive amount of pent-up energy with nowhere to go. So I didn't argue. I sat down and he went back to the café. Den was still standing near the door. He was a big lad, but soft around the edges, if you know what I mean. Vulnerable. I could understand what Linda had said about him not being capable of hurting a child. And yet a mother doesn't always know best, and certainly doesn't know everything about their kid. Everyone has their own life, inner thoughts they don't tell anyone, and I didn't suppose Den was any different. Who knows what went on behind that rather gormless face?

'I suppose you know where I've been,' he said, directing his words to me, but not quite able to meet my eye. 'I didn't have anything to do with it, you know.'

'No, love. I never thought you did,' I said, doing up the buttons on my coat. 'Must have been nasty. I'll leave you to it. Keep your chin up. I'll find your father in the café on my way out. Thank you, Linda.'

She smiled and nodded. I was almost at the top of the stairs when I heard shouting outside, then a furious banging. Someone was bashing the front door of the café. I felt bad for Linda and Tony. Graffiti was bad enough, physical violence was something else.

'What's that?' Linda said.

'Stay here, Mum. I'll go.' Den moved past me and hurtled down the stairs. Linda and I looked at each other wide-eyed as we heard Tony shouting.

'We're closed! Can't you bloody see?! Not open today! Hey! Hey!'

Linda started walking towards the stairs. I let her go in front of me and followed as fast as I could. I wasn't going to miss out on this, not on your nelly. By the time I'd got to the bottom of the stairs, along a little corridor and into the shop, all hell was breaking loose.

It didn't take long for me to realise that the person outside screaming and banging on the front door was Sandy. Even through Tony's shouting and Den's attempts to calm him down, I could hear her: 'Where's my daughter? Give me back my daughter, you fucking pedo!'

Behind her, camera flashes were going off like a firework display. Linda and I had stopped by the counter. She turned back to me.

'Kath,' she said, 'you know her, don't you? Can you calm her down?'

The way she was going at that window it seemed unlikely, but it was worth a try. I shuffled forwards. 'Mr Hammond,' I said, tapping him on the shoulder, 'do you mind, just for a minute?'

Mr Hammond swivelled his head round, like a furious owl. His mouth was open; his forehead was all sweaty. For a moment I thought he might take a swing at me, then he seemed to come to his senses. 'Kath?'

'Step away for a minute. Let me talk to her.'

Sandy hadn't stopped hitting the glass and screaming. I couldn't see her very clearly through the shutter. I needed to get her attention. I tapped on the glass door with the handle of my walking stick. She didn't take any notice, screaming her head off. So I knocked harder. There was a tiny lull and I shouted as best I could, 'Sandy, it's me. It's me, Kath!'

'Kath? What are you doing there?'

'They're friends, Sandy. Let's talk, shall we, love?' The effort of shouting was making me feel wheezy – my lungs aren't the best these days.

'I dunno.'

'If you calm down, I reckon Mr Hammond will let you in to talk.' I was making it up as I went along. I glanced round at Den and his dad. Den was looking startled, like he'd rather be anywhere else, while his dad was frowning at me, but I ploughed on. 'No point shouting in front of the press. Do you want to come in?'

A long, agonising pause, then: 'Okay.'

I turned to Tony. 'Is that all right? Will you let her in? She's been going through hell, love. And so have all of you. Let's take a bit of heat out of it.'

Tony was still puffing and panting like a marathon runner. Finally, he snorted in disgust, and nodded his head.

'Will you open the door, then, or should she come round the back?'

'We'll talk in here but send her round the back. I'd have to go out and do the shutters otherwise.'

I indicated to Sandy that she should walk to the rear. She got the message and Linda went to let her in. She brought her back into the café. She was in a shocking state and, once again, I was reminded how young she really was. Not much more than a child herself. When she saw me, I held my arm out, remembering all those times I used to open my arms for my Evie when she was a little tot learning to walk.

Sandy stumbled towards me – her only ally – and I took hold of her arm. And there we were, all standing there, looking at each other.

A deathly silence hung over us. I had two hands locked round one of Sandy's arms, partly for support, partly because I didn't trust her not to throw herself at Den and start a fight. I doubt I could have restrained her, but perhaps I'd have slowed her down.

Linda was staring at her, like she expected some sort of outburst. Den and Tony were standing together. Den looked petrified, blinking rapidly and wiping his clammy hands on his trousers. Tony was breathing hard, nostrils flaring, like a prize bull.

I could feel my heart fluttering again – I'm really not good under stress. I was just about to suggest that we all sat down when Sandy, looking solidly at Den and with an unmistakeable edge of contempt in her voice said, 'Well then, you little shit, are you going to tell me what you've done with my daughter?'

Day Two

Sandy

'I didn't do anything with her! I don't know what happened to her!'

He was spluttering. Sandy could see saliva literally spraying out of his disgusting mouth. She had been in the café a few times but never taken much notice of him before. A bit pasty, a bit doughy-looking, a bland sort of face – nothing much going for him. Certainly not fanciable. Now the thought of him touching Mina, hurting her, was too much.

'I don't believe you. The police couldn't get it out of you but I will!'

She broke free of Kath's grip and lunged towards him.

Everyone started shouting at once. Den's dad got in between them and blocked Sandy, who was reaching round, trying to grab or scratch Den.

'Oi, oi, oi!' Den's dad was yelling. 'Calm down! Behave yourself!'

He put his hands on her shoulders and pushed her backwards, away from Den. Now she turned her attention to him.

'Get your hands off me! You can't touch me! That's assault, that is! Do you know what your son's done? Do you?'

She was trying to shrug Tony's hands away, but he gripped harder.

'Listen to me. He hasn't done nothing! I'm telling you, you need to calm down. Look at me. Look at me!'

Sandy stopped craning over his shoulder and looked at Tony. They were much the same height, so their eyes met easily. He'd served them himself when they'd come in for Mina's birthday – the day she'd taken the photo that was now everywhere. She'd thought then that he was a bit of a grumpy old sod, but she saw now that he wasn't that old. The grip on her shoulders was strong and rather disturbing. She hated being touched like that.

'We want to find Mina as much as anyone. I swear on my mum's grave that Den didn't have anything to do with this. He's a good boy.' She looked from Tony to Den and back again. 'Please, this is a terrible time for you. We want to help. Sit down. Let's talk.'

There was something about the tone of his voice that she responded to. She nodded, a signal to him that she was calmer now. He let go of her shoulders and pulled out a chair for her. It felt like the whole room breathed a sigh of relief as she sat down. Tony indicated to a wary Den that he should sit at the same table, opposite Sandy, while he pulled out the chair next to her and helped Kath to sit down.

'Let me get you all a drink. Tea? Coffee?'

'Whatever – I don't care,' Sandy said, suddenly feeling defeated.

'Tea for me, love,' said Kath. Sandy was glad she was there, like she had someone on her side.

Den was sitting bolt upright, looking like he was ready to make a run for it if things got nasty again. Sandy could hardly look at him. She fiddled with the black shoulder bag which she'd put on her lap. She was craving a cigarette but knew she couldn't light up in here.

'Den,' said Kath, 'why don't you tell Sandy about the last time you saw Mina. I'm sure she'd like to hear it from you.'

Den was biting his lip, looking down at the table. 'Would you?'

Sandy nodded and he told her about Mina coming into the café, how cold and wet she'd been, how she bought a Kit Kat and he'd given her the hot chocolate sachet to take home.

Tony brought a tray with a large teapot, milk, sugar, four mugs and a plate of cakes. Kath and Den leaned back as he squeezed between them to put it on the table.

'And that was it?'

'Yeah. She was only here for a couple of minutes. You could watch it on the CCTV if you wanted to, couldn't she, Dad?'

Den looked up at Tony who was standing slightly behind him now, with his hands on his hips. 'Sure, it's what they've already shown on the telly, but you can look here if you want to.'

Linda reached into the middle of the table and started pouring tea.

'I don't need to see it again if it's what's been shown. How was she, though, Den? How did she seem?'

'Like I said, she was cold and wet. Apart from that, I don't know. I wish I could tell you more, I really do.'

She looked at him properly now, searched his face. He met her gaze this time, although it was obviously an effort. He seemed genuinely distraught, but was this the face of a liar?

'So why were the police questioning you? What about the scrunchie and the umbrella? Is it just a coincidence that they were found here?'

'She said the umbrella was broken. I guess she left it outside the café. I don't know about the scrunchie. It could have been here for days, tucked under a table leg or something. I know it looks bad, but I'm telling you the truth.'

'Why did you give her stuff? The hot chocolate.'

'I felt sorry for her.'

A silence descended on the room. Those five words seemed to have sucked the oxygen out of the air. Everyone was studiously avoiding looking at her now, but she felt the weight of their disapproval all the same. They all agreed with Den. They were

134

sorry for Mina. Suddenly it was too much. She scraped her chair back and stood up, nudging the table so that tea slopped out of all the mugs at once.

'You're all quick to judge, aren't you? Just like everyone else. Did any of you ever stop to think how hard it is trying to bring up a kid on your own? Did you?'

She didn't wait for an answer, but rushed out of the room, blundering into the hallway and towards the back. As soon as the door opened the others heard a volley of shouts from the photographers. The press pack had sighted their quarry.

Day Two

Kath

'I'd better go after her,' I said.

'What about your tea?' said Linda.

'I'm awash anyway.'

'At least take a cake. Take one for Sandy too.'

Tony put two iced fancies in a paper bag and gave them to me on the way out. I made my way back across the courtyard. I couldn't see Sandy, and she hadn't said she was going home, but I was tired anyway and ready for a sit-down. The group of lads I'd spoken to was splitting up. A couple of them set off on bikes, tipping them up on their back wheels and generally showing off. Part of me really wanted one to tip over backwards and land on his backside. The ugly little dog sniffed round my trolley again. After my cakes, I should think. It looked pretty hungry and was quite persistent. I fended it off with my stick and it gave up eventually and set off after them.

Another pair of lads walked along the front of Nelson House and round the corner. The last one hung back. I hadn't really noticed him when I was talking to them earlier, but now he left the bench he'd been sitting on and headed for the entrance to my stairwell. I didn't think much of it until I trundled my trolley in through the door and there he was, lurking at the bottom of the stairs, hood up, hands in pockets.

He peered out from under his hood and stepped forward. Like I said, I'm not scared of the local kids, but I did gasp when I saw him. It was obvious he'd been waiting for me.

'Hello,' I said, trying to brazen it out. I think generally people are less likely to do bad things if you talk to them, if they see you as a real person.

'Can I talk to you?' He wouldn't make eye contact, seemed to be talking to his feet.

'Yes. Of course. If you'll carry this trolley upstairs for me.'

'Um, okay. Can we talk here first, though?' Here was a badly lit space that smelled of cigarette smoke and urine. Not my first choice for a chat. I didn't want to put him off though, so I agreed.

'What is it, love? What's bothering you?' He was silent for a while, like he was summoning up the courage to speak. I let the silence run, encouraging him to break it.

'It's the girl. Mina.'

'Well, I thought it might be. What about her?'

'What Danno said, it wasn't quite right. He – we – knew, *know*, Mina. It was a sort of game. We didn't mean anything bad.'

I felt a shiver run up and down my spine. Whatever their 'game' had been, he knew damn well they shouldn't have been doing it.

'I'm sorry, love, I don't know what you're talking about. What was a game? You'll have to spell it out.'

'We used to, I dunno, follow her a bit, tease her.'

Follow her a bit. I didn't like that.

'Five of you and one of her. Following her in the dark and calling her names.'

'Yeah.'

'Any way you think about it, that's not very nice, is it?'

'No. I'm sorry. It felt wrong, but if you don't join in, the others pick on you.'

He had the grace to look ashamed, shuffling his feet in the damp concrete. I didn't want him to clam up on me.

'Perhaps they're not really friends then. Not good friends.'

'No.'

'So was that it? Was that what you wanted to tell me?'

'Sort of. The thing was, you were asking about Wednesday.'

'Yes, love, and your friend – Danno? – said you were all indoors, in someone's flat.'

'Yeah. We were. But we didn't all get there at the same time. And I was walking across the estate about half-three and that's when I saw her.'

'You saw her? Where?'

He nodded towards the door. 'Here. Well, just outside. She was coming in here.'

'Are you sure it was Wednesday, love?'

'Yeah. It was pissing down – sorry, raining – wasn't it? She was wet through, running across the yard and jumping over the puddles.'

'Have you told anyone about it?'

'No.'

'You should do.'

He shuffled his feet again. 'The thing is, a few seconds later, I saw Danno come in here. He came into the stairs. It's not even the same block as Vince's.'

'He was following her, you mean. Have you asked him about it?'

'You're shitting me. Sorry—' He glanced at me, checking for disapproval over his language but I just shook my head a fraction to show him it didn't matter to me. 'I can't say anything. He can't know I saw him. He'd fucking kill me.'

Like he killed her. He didn't say the words out loud, because he didn't have to. We were both thinking it.

Day Two

Kath

'You mustn't tell anyone about this. You've got to promise.'

He tipped his face up to the light a little and I could see that it was screwed up in agony. Poor kid, I caught myself thinking, he spends his whole life between a rock and a hard place. Now more than ever.

'I can't promise that, I'm afraid. We're talking about a young girl here. We need to find her.'

'Yeah. All right, but keep me out of it, yeah?'

'Well,' I said, truthfully, 'I can't give them your name because I don't know it, do I?' He looked at me. We both knew that he'd told me Danno's name. 'Now, help me with this trolley, will you? The lift's still out. I wish they'd fix the blessed thing. Up to the third floor, please. There's a good lad.'

Probably not a good idea to give away exactly where my flat was, but, like I said, I'm not scared of these boys. Not this one, anyway. He grabbed hold of the trolley and started hauling it up the stairs.

'Jeez, it weighs a ton!'

He didn't wait for an answer. Despite his protest, he raced ahead of me up the stairs like a mountain goat. When I caught up, he was just outside the stairwell on the third floor, looking out over the estate.

I got a better look at him in the light. Bit younger than I thought before – maybe as young as thirteen or fourteen. His hood was still up but there was a lick of ginger hair curling out onto his forehead and when he turned to face me, I noticed a spattering of freckles across the bridge of his nose. Nice-looking lad. My Evie had a touch of ginger to her hair when she was a baby. You only really saw it when the light caught it at a certain angle. Ray was adamant it didn't, wouldn't even let me say the word. The closest he would get to it was 'strawberry blonde', bless him. Funny the bees people keep in their bonnets, isn't it?

'What have you got in here?' he said, looking down at my trolley.

'There's just some milk and other bits I got from the café.' I watched to see if there was any reaction from him but his face didn't register anything. 'Don't suppose you know anything about the graffiti on the front of it, do you?'

I looked him up and down, checking for spots of red paint.

'Nah. I seen it, took a snap of it, but it wasn't me. Don't know anything about that.'

'You sure? He's a good kid, Den. I was there just now. The whole family's so upset.'

'Yeah, well. P'rhaps he's not so nice, after all. If you know what I mean.'

My senses were tingling again. My new friend was proving an excellent source of information.

'Not really, love, no,' I said, mildly. 'He's always been nice to me, really kind and thoughtful, and I've often seen him giving lollipops to kids in there.'

''Zactly.' He wagged a finger at me. 'A grown man giving kids sweeties. If that isn't suss, what is?'

It made me sad to admit it, but he had a point. I suppose I've got a sunny view of human nature – even after everything I've been through – but one man's kind gesture could be another pervert's grooming. You have to be so careful in this day and age. Maybe I was wrong about Den after all. Maybe I'd been wrong to give Mina that Freddo frog. What a sad old world it is.

I suddenly felt tired. I needed my sofa and the telly and Warwick and Richard and Bradley, but my afternoon's work wasn't over yet.

'Thank you for helping me,' I said, taking hold of the trolley's handle. 'I'll be all right from here.'

'Okay. No problem. You take care, all right?'

Our eyes met for a moment and there was a connection, an understanding. He was asking me to take care of both myself and him. By waiting for me, telling me about Danno, he knew that he'd made himself vulnerable. He was trying to do the right thing, bless him. But he was scared.

'Don't worry,' I said. 'I'll take care of things. You're a good lad.'

There was a glimmer of a smile and then he turned and disappeared into the stairwell. I started walking towards my flat. I stopped to knock on the door of number seven. Jodie answered.

'All right, Kath?'

'Yes, love. Is Sandy here?'

'She got back a while ago. Went straight into her room. Do you want her?'

I thought of the two cakes in my trolley. Was it very bad of me to keep quiet? Everyone's allowed a little wickedness now and again, aren't they?

'No, that's fine,' I said. 'I was just worried about her. As long as she's safe and sound. It was you I really wanted to talk to. I've got something for you.'

Jodie looked at me expectantly. I beckoned to her and she stepped onto the walkway, pulling the door to behind her.

'I just had a very interesting chat. There was a sighting, Jodie. Mina was seen coming into this block and there's more . . .'

Day Two

Den

After Sandy and Kath left, Den dived into the shower. It felt like the stench of the police station was sticking to his skin along with a crust of stale sweat. The trauma of being questioned, then seeing the paint daubed across the front of the café like blood in a slaughterhouse and coming face to face with Sandy – his nerve endings were too raw to cope with it all. He stood under the stream of water and let it rain down onto his skin.

Later he lay on his bed and scrolled through his phone. His name was everywhere, along with the vilest insults and threats. He could feel the sweat seeping out of his pores again. He'd already been judged and found guilty. Every message made him feel sicker and more panicky, yet he couldn't stop looking.

A vigil was due to take place in the courtyard at seven. People were invited to gather quietly and light candles for Mina. Was it mad to want to join them? To show that he had nothing to hide? That he, too, was hoping and praying for Mina's safe return?

When Mum tapped on the bedroom door, offering him some soup, he got up and joined her and Dad in the kitchen. Dad was subdued and conciliatory, treating Den like he was ill or had to be humoured. That changed when he raised the subject of the vigil.

'No way, son. Are you out of your tiny mind?' Dad was off on one again. 'They'll hang, draw and quarter you!'

'It's a vigil, Dad. A peaceful gathering. I haven't done anything wrong. I want to show them that.'

'You being there isn't going to help. We've got to keep a low profile now. Hope that people move on to the next thing soon.'

There was no point arguing. But Dad wasn't the only one with a stubborn streak. So when the time came, Den didn't say anything but simply put his jacket on and slipped his phone into his pocket. Mum appeared at his side, with her coat on and a thick scarf over her head.

'Linda, where are you going?' Dad said.

'I'm going to stand with the other mothers in this community. I'm going to stand with our son.'

It wasn't often that Mum stood up to him like that. Den could see him processing the situation.

'It's like that, is it? Well, if you're both going, I'm coming too! We'll do it together.'

She put a hand on his arm. 'Please, Tony. I love you, but we can't have shouting or ranting this evening.'

He looked pained. 'Linda, what do you think I am? Some sort of monster? I'm just going so we can be seen as a family sticking together. To show we've got nothing to hide. Come on. Let's go. Stay together, though. Don't split up.'

It was cold and clear outside. Den looked up and fancied he could even see a few stars in the darker pockets of sky between the streetlights. People were streaming past the café towards the flats, but there was hardly any noise – no chatter or banter. It was the same in the courtyard, a sombre gathering. He could see that flowers and yellow ribbons had been tied to a piece of railing. Tealights and other candles were being placed on the ground in front, creating a sort of garden of light.

'We should have brought something, Mum,' he said, feeling guilty at being empty-handed.

'I've got these.' She reached into her bag and brought out three tealights and a box of matches. 'One each.'

'You think of everything.'

He wondered if they should stay at the back. It felt like nobody had really noticed them and that suited him just fine. Despite saying he wanted to be seen there, he realised it was more about just being there. It wasn't about him, or his family, or their business. This was about Mina.

Maybe Mum felt the same. She had stopped walking and had linked her arm through his, but now Dad tipped his head towards the front and started to make his way through the crowd.

'Come on.'

Den and his mum exchanged long-suffering looks and followed in his wake.

A little to the side of the candles, Den could see Kath standing next to Sandy, with a female police officer nearby. If he didn't know better, he'd have said that Sandy was looking bored. She was rolling her eyes, not looking at the candles or the flowers, like she'd rather be anywhere else. Beside her, Kath looked tired. Den managed to catch her eye as they got closer and she smiled. They were almost at the front, tealights in hand, when someone stepped brusquely in front of them.

Marlon was in Dad's face, glowering past him at Den.

'What do you think you're doing here?' he said. 'For God's sake, show some respect.'

'That's why we're here, sir,' said Dad. 'To show respect like everyone else. To light a candle.'

'No way, man. You're not welcome.'

He was a big guy. His physical presence, this close, oozed threat. Den was painfully aware of his mum next to him, his need to keep her safe. He put his hand on Dad's shoulder and leaned forward. 'Dad, let's go,' he said, into his ear.

Marlon was still eyeballing him. Den tried to hold his gaze but he couldn't. Instead, he looked down past his high-vis jacket his paint-spattered trousers and heavy work boots.

'Please stand aside, sir,' Dad said, as if he hadn't heard Den. 'Let us light our candles and then we'll go.'

Marlon didn't move. In fact, he raised his hand up and pushed Dad in the centre of his chest, making him stagger back into Den, who himself was forced to step backwards. There were shouts of protest in the crowd behind him and someone jabbed at his back.

'I said you're not welcome.' Marlon was walking forwards, shoving them, barging them back. People all around were looking – a ripple of awareness spreading out – and Den could tell they knew who they were now. Somebody jeered.

Mum tightened her grip on his sleeve. 'Let's go, Den. Tony! We need to go.'

Den looked down at her. Her face was creased with worry.

'Okay, okay. We're leaving.'

But Dad wasn't going anywhere. Den could see him quivering like a testosterone-fuelled bulldog. This was going to end badly.

Then, out of nowhere, Den heard a female voice ring out. 'That's enough of that. Pack it in!'

Both Marlon and Dad looked in the direction the voice was coming from. The crowd parted to reveal Kath standing there in her padded coat and her mittens and with the streetlight reflecting off the lenses of her glasses. She lifted her walking stick from the ground and waved the rubber end at them.

'We don't want any of that here. We're here to send our prayers for a little girl. Everyone's welcome, as long as you're quiet and respectful.'

'Kath,' Tony said, 'that's what we're here for, to show some respect.'

'And you're not welcome,' Marlon chipped in. Tension fizzed between them, like electricity in the air.

'Stop that right now. This isn't about you. Move away.' Kath

145

tapped at Marlon's leg with her stick. Astonished, he stepped back a couple of paces, holding his hands up.

'Okay, Grandma. Take it easy.'

Dad looked from him to Kath and back again. Den moved to his side. 'Dad,' he said, 'we're not helping things. Let's just go.'

Kath nodded to him and they exchanged the briefest of smiles. Den put his arm round Dad's shoulders and they turned round, gathered up Mum on the way, and walked to the back of the crowd. As they left, Den looked back over his shoulder. Marlon had disappeared, but Kath was making her way to the front. People were gently patting her shoulders and he noticed a cluster of cameramen training their lenses on her. He felt a surge of gratitude to her for defusing the situation so quickly.

'I'm so sorry,' he said, as they arrived back at the café. 'That was all my fault.'

'I did try to tell you,' Tony sighed. 'It was a bad idea from the start.'

'People's ignorance is not your fault, Den,' said Mum.

'No, but my foolishness is. How I behaved two years ago. I wouldn't have been taken in if I hadn't been on their list as someone to watch.'

She put her hands on the top of his arms, making him face her.

'Everyone makes mistakes, Den. The foolish thing is not to learn from them. You're young. You're learning. I'm proud of you.'

He heard Dad snort, a noise that somehow meant more to him than a thousand of Mum's kind words. Mum meant well, but no one would ever be truly proud of him while the stench of suspicion still clung to him. You couldn't wash that sort of thing off. He would only be rid of it when the spotlight had switched to someone else.

Day Two

Kath

I watched people gathering for the vigil from the walkway, bundled up in my coat and mittens. I heard the door to number seven open behind me and Sandy appeared. She was wearing only a thin T-shirt and some leggings and her bare feet were in slip-on plastic mules, the sort of thing you might wear round the pool on holiday.

'Sandy,' I said, 'you need a jumper on and a coat. It's chilly out.'

Her arms were stick-thin and covered in old scars, which made me feel a bit funny looking at them. There was an awful lot I didn't know about her.

'Jodie said they were going to have a vigil for Mina down there. She said I should think about going.' She joined me, looking over the edge, leaning on the concrete parapet.

'There's already quite a crowd.'

She sniffed. 'Nobody will want me there, Kath. I'm public enemy number one. The world's worst mother.'

'It might feel like that, Sandy, but it's just the press whipping things up. Most people, normal people, will feel for you. It's any parent's worst nightmare.' She folded her skinny arms across her chest, which didn't stop her shivering. I'd judged her as much as the next person, but what I said was true, too – I couldn't help feeling sorry for her. Losing a child is just so unimaginably awful. 'You can light a little candle, add your prayers to everyone else's.'

'It's not going to bring her back, though, is it? Nothing's going to bring her back.'

My blood ran a little colder in my veins. 'Why do you say that? Everyone's looking, Sandy. You mustn't give up hope.'

'It's been two days now. She's not coming back. There's no reward or anything.'

Again, the reward thing. She seemed strangely calm and clear-sighted. If I hadn't heard her with my own ears, I wouldn't have believed it.

I had no idea what to say. Was I in the presence of evil or just an inadequate young woman who became a mum too soon? I guess I was gaping like a goldfish because she looked at me and said, 'I've shocked you, haven't I? Well, sorry about that, but I'm just being realistic. All this hope and prayer. I can't do it. It would be like pretending and I can't.'

'Sandy—' I said, but at that moment I heard movement behind us and Jodie came out of number seven. She was holding Sandy's parka.

'Thought you might need this,' she said.

'Oh, ta.' Jodie put the coat on. 'I was thinking I might go out somewhere. It's doing my head in stuck in that flat.'

Jodie glanced at me. 'Sure, where are you thinking?'

Sandy shook her head. 'Dunno. Just out. Go for a walk or something.'

My lips pursed. I couldn't help it.

'You can go anywhere you like, Sandy, as long as we can contact you in case there's news. Don't you think it might be a good idea to go to the vigil, though? You don't have to make a speech, just spend a few minutes there quietly.'

Sandy sighed. 'I can't face it.' She sounded like a sulky teenager. The internet had told me she was twenty-seven, but honestly, she seemed an awful lot younger. Immature.

She sent me a look of appeal, wanted me to back her up.

'Sandy was just saying that she would find it difficult to be at the vigil.' I was choosing my words carefully. 'It's a lot of pressure.'

That got a rare, grateful smile. 'I'd go with you, though, Sandy, and Kath, too – wouldn't you, Kath?'

Why can't I say 'no' to people? It's always been a problem. 'Yes, of course,' I said, automatically, even though I'd just about had enough of things for one day. I'd got a lot to think about and I needed to put my poor old legs up.

Sandy caved, and so I locked up the flat and off we went, down the stairs again and out into the yard. Although there were more people there than for the press conference, it was quieter, almost eerie. People looked at Sandy as we made our way to the front past a little field of candles and flowers, but nobody shouted out, thank God, although there were cameras trained on us, clicking away.

We stood near the low wall and watched as people came forward and lit candles. All those people there and I hardly recognised anyone. I was scanning around for a friendly face when I spotted Den, from the shop. He was heading our way, with his mum and dad next to him and that's when it all started kicking off.

A great tall slab of a man – one of the organisers of yesterday's search party – stepped in front of them and seemed to barge Tony. Voices were raised and there was a ripple effect in the crowd, people being pushed backwards and forwards.

Everyone was looking now. Jodie jumped onto the wall, so she could see what was going on, but she didn't dive in. I got a glimpse of Linda's face through a gap and didn't hesitate. I left Sandy by the wall and plunged into the crowd.

It didn't take me long to get close. I'd never have done this when I was younger, but when you get into your eighties, I think you stop caring so much about what people think of you. I took as deep a breath as I can manage these days and bellowed as loud as I could, 'That's enough of that. Pack it in!'

Guess what? It worked. Tony and the big guy with the high-vis jacket on both stopped and looked at me. I told them to have some respect. The big guy told Tony that he wasn't welcome but he backed off when I gave him a little tap with my walking stick. Tony, Den and Linda wisely decided not to push things and left and that was that. A nasty little incident which could have exploded was over and I felt – what do they say these days? – epic!

I took myself back to Sandy and there were people smiling at me and there was a little ripple of applause. I tried to shush people, because that's not what we were there for, after all. We stood together, looking at the candles and flowers and messages from people and then Sandy said, 'I've had enough. I'm going back up.'

'Not for a walk?' I said, unable to keep a touch of sarcasm in my voice. She didn't appear to notice.

'Nah, Jodie's convinced me it wouldn't be a good look. Are you coming? We could, I dunno, watch some telly or something.'

'I'll stay for a little while, then I think it's an early night for me.'

'Suit yourself,' she said and walked towards the stairs.

I stayed at the vigil for longer than I expected. They started singing – hymns and pop songs – and I found myself joining in. It felt good to be part of something communal, gentle and positive. When things started to break up, I was approached by that lovely reporter from the local news, the one with fifty smart coats in primary colours. Today's was bright red with rather nice military-style buttons.

'Can we talk to you for a minute?'

'Of course.'

She told me to say my name and age into the camera, like a sort of screen test. Then she started talking. I wasn't sure if I was being interviewed or if this was just a chat.

'We saw you step in just now to defuse a sticky situation. Why did you do that?'

Daft question, if you ask me, but I didn't want to make her look stupid so I did my best to answer. 'We're here for Mina. It's all about her. I just wanted people to calm things down and focus on that.'

'I think a lot of people will admire you for that.'

I couldn't help feeling a little proud. I mean, you would, wouldn't you? 'I'm just doing what I can.'

'You live here, in this block?'

'That's right, love. Next door to Mina and her mum.'

'This must be very upsetting. What are they like?'

She might be a bit dim, but she had such a nice way about her. So easy to talk to.

'Well, you know how it is with most kids. They're noisy, charge about. Mina's not like that. She's very quiet. She's a good girl. Her mum's working a lot and I know how hard that is, so I sort of look out for Mina. Keep an eye on her.'

'But you didn't notice when she didn't come home on Wednesday?'

'I didn't hear her on Wednesday and I was worried. I thought she might be with friends or something. But I got really worried when she didn't come home on Thursday. That when I went looking for her.'

'You went out looking? How old are you, Kath?'

I didn't know what that had to do with things. 'I'm eighty-five.'

'That's marvellous. Did you see anything at all?'

'I found a scrunchie, you know, a hair thing.' I stopped, not sure if I should mention where I found it. Things were already pretty inflamed.

'Where was that?'

Like I said, she was so easy to talk to. It just seemed natural to tell her. I didn't mean to make anything worse for Den and his family. 'In the café.'

'So you're quite the Miss Marple, aren't you?'

'I wouldn't say that. Like everyone round here, I just want that little girl back safe and sound, and I'm not going to stop until she is.'

We chatted for a little longer, then she wrapped things up with a 'Thank you, Kath. God bless.' What a lovely woman. You can't always judge a book by its cover, or a TV presenter by their coat. I could tell that this wasn't just a job to her – she really cared.

The yard was almost empty now. The rest of the press people had gone and there were just one or two folks still looking at the candles. The group of lads was hanging around by one of the benches. I could see them out of the corner of my eye.

I headed into Nelson House and climbed the stairs slowly. Would they never fix that lift? I took a breather at the top and looked out over the yard, just as a police van and two cars pulled into the entrance. A dozen or so officers piled out of the van and surrounded the lads. They targeted two of them, pulling them away from their mates and quickly bundling them into separate cars. And just like that, they were gone. The whole thing had taken a couple of minutes.

Officers stayed talking to the ones who were left for a minute, then they, too, left. I watched as the yard emptied and felt a little surge of satisfaction – a word here, a word there, it was surprising how much good you could do.

Day Three

Den

They all watched the late news. Den and Mum sat on the sofa together, but Dad wouldn't stop pacing. In the end, he perched on the arm of an armchair, looking like he might take off again at any minute. There was coverage from the vigil including footage of their confrontation with Marlon and Kath remonstrating with him.

'I know him from somewhere,' Mum said. 'That big bully. I can't quite place him.'

'He comes into the café,' Den said.

'Mm, it's not that, though. I've seen him somewhere else.'

After they had shown Sandy and others gathered round the candles, and there was a long interview with Kath.

'She's coming across well, isn't she?' Mum said. 'Good on her.'

Kath and the interviewer seemed to be getting along famously. Den could see that she was a gift for a roving reporter – happy to talk, likeable, a bit of a character. He shuddered to think of his own appearance the night before, his face shiny with sweat, looking shifty and ill at ease. Why on earth had he spoken to them at all? For a moment he was back there again, a rabbit trapped in the headlights, then Dad brought him back into the room.

'Why did she have to mention the café?' he exploded. 'That's all we need! We might as well close the doors for good – we're finished as a business.'

'Shush, I can't hear,' said Mum.

'Miss Marple, though?' Dad snorted. 'Where do they get this shit from?'

'Tony! It's harmless, isn't it? It's the only good side to this story. Neighbours getting involved. People seeing that this estate isn't all bad.'

Dad huffed and puffed a bit more but didn't say anything as they continued to watch.

'You must have seen some changes around here, Kath,' said the interviewer.

'Here we go,' said Dad. 'This is when we find out that the nice little old lady with her shopping trolley is ever so slightly BNP.'

Den wished he'd shut up, but he knew his posturing and cynicism were his reaction to the evening's events. He himself could still feel the adrenaline pulsing through his veins. Fight or flight. They'd chosen flight, but that left all those feelings still in your system with nowhere to go.

'There are comings and goings. That's London, isn't it? That's part of what makes this city what it is. You want me to say it's gone down the toilet; well, I'm not going to. There is crime round here, but that doesn't mean we like it or accept it. We're a community here. Being a neighbour means something. Always has done.'

Mum looked at Dad and raised her eyebrows. 'Just a nice little old lady after all. Good on her.'

'Hah. And maybe our very own Miss Marple will find little Mina and we'll all live happily ever after.'

She rounded on him now. 'Tony, what's wrong with you?'

'I just don't like being in the middle of this. This is our business. This is our home.'

154

'I know, but like you said earlier, it will all blow over.'

'Will it, though?'

Den couldn't stand any more. He stood up. 'I'm sorry,' he shouted. 'I get it! It's all my fault and I'm sorry, okay?'

'Den—'

He stormed off into his bedroom and slammed the door firmly shut, but it didn't help. It was more like a prison cell than a sanctuary, and now he'd shut himself in. Four walls confining him, the sound of the TV and his parents bickering coming under the door. He went over to the window. The curtains were still open and he gazed out at the array of light-studded tower blocks. Surrounded by people – so many people – and yet he felt so lonely. What was it about him that marked him out? Why couldn't he connect? What was wrong with him?

He closed the curtains and lay down on the bed, but his head was full of an uncomfortable kaleidoscope of images, noises, memories and feelings. The interview room, his interrogators' faces, the blood-red graffiti, Marlon's hostility and endless cameras clicking, flashing, recording every move. Hot bile was moving up his oesophagus. He had a phobia of being sick, could feel panic gripping him as the pressure increased inside. He sat upright and swallowed hard, switched the bedside light on and tried to slow his breathing.

He sat there for a long time, until the TV was turned off and his parents went about their bedtime routine – switching off lights, visiting the bathroom in turn. The water pipes gurgled in the wall behind him. Sirens wailed in the distance, while overhead another plane started its rumbling approach to Heathrow.

For a moment he saw himself, like he was in a film – a young guy, already balding, sitting on the edge of a single bed in his parents' flat. The camera panned out, taking in the café downstairs, the graffiti on the shutters: 'Pedo scum'. Twenty-two years here and this was what people thought of him.

His family's business was wrecked. He didn't want to spend

his life serving in the café, certainly didn't want to take the business on from Dad when the time came, but this was home, too. He wanted, *needed*, to feel safe here. That couldn't happen while Mina was still missing.

He padded through the darkened flat and down into the café. Soft yellow light filtered through the shutters. In the office, he didn't bother flicking on the light, just sat down in the office chair and fired up the computer. No wonder everyone suspected him – he'd been the last person to see Mina, plus there was the scrunchie and the umbrella. He needed to fight back, find some proof that it wasn't him. He had to move the spotlight somewhere else.

Day Three

Den

He called up the CCTV footage and played the section from Wednesday afternoon. He felt his stomach lurch again when Mina made her appearance. He couldn't imagine a time when this moment – the image of it caught forever – would not make him feel like this. There she was. He couldn't get a good view of her face due to the camera angle, but it was clearly her. She was drenched, hood up to start with, but then she took it down and there were her plaits, both still done up.

She checked over her shoulder, then picked up a Kit Kat and put her money on the counter. He could see himself talking to her and slipping a sachet of hot chocolate across the counter. Mina checked behind her again. That was odd. He stopped the video, went back and played it again. Yes, she'd checked behind her twice. Was she scared of something? Someone? Had she been followed before she came into the café?

Her hair was drenched, the plait on the side nearest the camera draped on her shoulder like a rat's tail. He bent closer to the screen. There was definitely a scrunchie holding the bottom of the plait together. Was there one on the other side? He let the footage play, then froze it as she turned round to leave. Wait a minute. The plait was done up on the other side too, held in place with a scrunchie. He pressed play again and watched as she walked out of the camera's field of view. Nothing fell to the floor. He was pretty sure she had both scrunchies in her hair all the way through – entering the café, standing at the counter and leaving. That must mean that she'd dropped the scrunchie beforehand, on another day, or that it was a spare, that had fallen out of her pocket or bag.

If she was checking behind her, who was she worried about? Perhaps they'd been in the café. He rewound the footage to ten minutes before Mina came in and watched carefully, pausing it and noting down descriptions of customers for the whole period until half an hour after Mina had left the café.

Of the sixteen people on his list, he had names for a few, but it was mostly descriptions. More than half of them were women, young mums with toddlers mostly. They wouldn't take a girl off the street, would they? He put a line through them, which left five men. He scanned the list again and then rewatched some of the footage. The first guy into the café, who came in just seconds after she had gone, was horribly familiar. The high-vis jacket, the alpha-male strut, the shaved head – it was Marlon. Ever-bloody-present Marlon. He'd only bought a drink from the chilled cabinet – it had taken all of a minute and a half and then he'd left.

He let the video play on until the timer was nearly at four o'clock, then he paused it. He knew that if he played the footage for another minute or two, he'd have a sixth name to add to his list. He sighed and pressed play, then watched as Dad clearly left the kitchen with his coat over his arm. He'd gone to the cash-and-carry in the van. It was a perfectly normal thing to do, but why go at four in the afternoon, when the traffic was building up? He usually went mid-morning – after breakfast and before the lunch rush.

He stopped the film, shut the file and leaned back. The screen was sending blue light across the desk, which was even more of a mess than usual. Heaps of paper were spilling over the keyboard. Den started to gather them up, shuffle them into a tidier stack. The top one was an electricity bill. Didn't they do all this online now? This was a warning. Urgent. Pay within seven days or court proceedings would be instigated. Den leafed through some more. Unpaid bills for water, for the contractor who'd fixed the leak in the customer sink, for the council tax. Jeez, Dad, what was going on?

Above him he could hear someone walking around, making the boards creak, the toilet flushing, the tap running in the kitchen. Then the pacing. Footsteps moving backwards and forwards, over and over. He wasn't the only one having a sleepless night.

Day Three

Den

After Hull, Den had sworn off social media for the most part. He'd kept a Facebook profile but he never posted on it, the same with Twitter. When he did dip back into these places, he wasn't a participant. He was a watcher. He kept an eye on the timelines of the people he'd known in Hull. Not 'friends' because they'd all dropped him. Some of them had blocked him, too, but it was surprising how much stuff was public.

They'd all graduated this year. Some had gone travelling. Others were starting new jobs, new lives. The one who was hardest to track was Sarah. Obviously, she'd blocked him on every platform and so had her friends. She wasn't invisible, though. He'd tried not to look, to 'stay away', but he just couldn't. The last time he'd checked was only a few days ago, in fact. One of her friends had tagged her in a photo – a group of people round a pub table. Sarah was in the middle of it all, sitting right next to a guy he didn't recognise, a guy with his arm round her shoulder. It shouldn't matter. It was years ago now, so why did he feel hurt? Betrayed. Angry.

He vowed to stop. It wasn't doing him any good. He should

take Facebook and Twitter and Snapchat off his phone for good. He should have done it. But he didn't. And so, when it became public knowledge that he'd been taken in for questioning, the onslaught of abuse started. People posting on his wall, message requests coming in. Hundreds of notifications, more coming in all the time. He'd thought perhaps that the feeding frenzy would calm down after he'd been released, but it seemed to be accelerating. Why? With a feeling of dread, he opened up Google on the office PC and typed in his name.

The first page of links were all national news sites. The list of images, spread horizontally across the page, were all the same one, repeated. A still from the awful vox pop interview he had given on Thursday evening.

He clicked on one of the articles, from *The Express*. He was front-page news. Alongside his photo, there was one of Sandy, making her appeal for Mina to come home, the anguish on her face clear. Next to her was a photograph of a girl Den hadn't seen for two years, a girl who still made his stomach flip. Underneath the pictures, the headline read, 'Stalked by Mina Suspect – My Year of Hell'.

Den made himself read the whole article. It painted a damning picture of a complete obsessive, a young man who had pestered Sarah relentlessly, turning up at her home uninvited, following her to lectures and when she was out with friends. Because of him, Sarah had messed up her exams, had to undergo therapy and take antidepressants, which she was still on. Her life had been ruined. Apparently. But it was lies, wasn't it? She was going out, socialising, laughing while he was stuck in his childhood bedroom, with a single bed, posters on the wall and the smell of chip fat hanging in the air. Who was the real victim here?

He didn't hear Dad come downstairs and clearly Dad didn't expect to find him in the office. 'Bloody hell, son. What are you doing here? You going through my stuff, were you? Poking your nose in?'

He lunged towards Den and grabbed his shoulder, wrenching him out of the chair. Den was taken by surprise. He staggered to his feet.

'No, Dad! I was just looking at the CCTV.'

'What are you doing that for? I thought you of all people would know that spying on people, stalking them, is wrong.'

It wasn't just Dad pulling him around that shocked Den, it was his cruelty. How could he strike so low?

'I was looking for clues, to see who was around at the same time as Mina.'

'That's for the police to do, son, isn't it?'

'I know, Dad, but I'm all over the morning's papers. They're crucifying me. I just thought, the only way to stop all this is to find out who's really got her.'

'How the hell are you going to find out? The whole country's looking for that girl.'

He'd relaxed his grip on Den's shirt now. His hand was resting on his shoulder, less threatening, almost comforting.

'I dunno, Dad. I've just got to try.' He paused.

'I don't think we'll be able to open again until they've found her. People won't come in here, and if they do we'll get a load of abuse. I'm sorry, Dad. I know things are tough right now. We need the money.'

Now Dad brought his face closer, peering at him sharply. 'What do you know? You *were* poking around, weren't you?'

'No, I wasn't. I moved some papers. I was tidying up. That's all. There are a few red ones there. Are we in trouble, Dad?'

Dad stepped back and ran his hands over the top of his head. 'It's nothing for you to worry about. It's just business. I'll get it sorted.'

'Dad, I'm twenty-two. You can tell me.'

'It's nothing, okay. I'm going out.'

Den checked the time on the computer screen. 'It's half past three in the morning.'

'I can't sleep, okay. I need to clear my head. Go to bed, son. You're not doing any good here. All of this—' he gestured at the desk and the PC '—it's not doing you any good.'

Den stood in the doorway of the office, listening as Dad let himself out through the sticky back door. Then the van door slammed and the engine started up.

Day Three

Kath

I wasn't expecting anyone to call, so when someone rapped on the door at just after nine, my heart fluttered. I put the chain on and peered out. There were two male police officers, not ones I'd seen before.

'Morning, madam, can we have a word, please?' the older of the two said.

I pushed closed the door and took off the chain, my fingers stiff and clumsy, then opened up again. Mornings are such a bother when you get old: it takes so long to get going.

'What is it?' I said. 'Have you found her?'

'No, we're searching all the flats in the block, including yours. It won't take long and we won't make a mess. Can we come in?'

'Your colleagues have already been in,' I said.

They looked at each other and then down at their phones. 'Today? You're still on our list.'

'No, not today. They were round here yesterday. I let Mina's mum use my bathroom.'

Their faces relaxed a little. 'Ah, this is different. It won't take long.'

I must say I don't like unannounced visitors but they sort of squared up to me, their body language indicating that I didn't have a choice. If I'd known they were coming, I would have cleaned round, made sure everything was spick and span, although I didn't suppose they'd be judging the standard of my housework.

'Okay,' I said. 'Come in.'

I opened the door wide and went in, leading them into the lounge. I noted with approval that they both wiped their feet on the mat, then the older one followed me to the lounge, while the other, who honestly looked about eighteen and was sporting a smear of facial hair under his nose in an effort to prove something, walked further down the hall. It felt odd having strangers in, unsettling. I wanted to be in two places at once, keeping an eye on them both.

'You were on the telly last night, weren't you?' my guy said. 'I hear they're calling you the Fincham Estate Miss Marple.'

I'd thought I was too old to blush, but I was wrong. I could feel my cheeks going pink with pleasure. 'I don't know about that,' I said. 'Are they?'

'We could do with more people like you round here.'

'Is there any news about those boys? I saw them being taken away last night.'

He moved a little closer. 'You know I can't divulge that sort of information, Mrs Cartright.'

'I was the one who tipped you off about them. I'm your – what is it? – mole.'

His eyebrows went up a little and he smiled. 'Ah, in that case, I'll just say that we didn't keep them in, but we're keeping an eye on them.' He tapped the side of his nose. 'A close eye.'

I nodded, satisfied, then stepped into the hall to see where Junior had got to. He was coming out of my bedroom and going into the second bedroom.

'Wait a minute!' I called out, my voice louder than I meant it to be. He stopped, his hand on the door handle.

'Is there someone sleeping in here?'

'No. No, love, it's not that.'

He looked at me and I knew he was registering my alarm. 'Don't worry if it's a mess,' he said. 'Believe me, we see all sorts in this job.'

'It's not a mess,' I said, 'it's just that I don't often let people in there. But it's okay. Go ahead.'

He pressed the handle down and opened the door. He went in and I hovered in the doorway. The room was just as it had been for the past forty years: orange paint on Anaglypta wallpaper, pink and orange floral curtains with matching duvet cover and pillowcase, posters of Blondie Blu-tacked all over the walls.

The officer looked around the room and smiled. 'Wow, Blondie. Still going, aren't they?'

'I don't know,' I said, truthfully.

'This your daughter's room?'

'Yes. She left home a long time ago, but I can't bear to change it somehow.'

He didn't react, just opened the wardrobe, had a quick scan under the bed and made to leave. Just before he went, he noticed the recessed rectangle in the ceiling above the bed.

'Loft?' he said.

'Roof space. It's to give access to the maintenance guys. We've never used it in over forty years. My husband, Ray, painted over it 'cos there was a draught sometimes. I think we all have them on the top floor. I expect that's the first place you looked next door, isn't it? Sort of place a little girl might hide, if she was scared.'

He studied it, then nodded and smiled at me. 'Okay, I think we're done. Thank you.'

I stepped in and smoothed the duvet down, while he walked past me and went to find his colleague who was coming out of the kitchen. I was just closing the bedroom door when I heard him ask, in a low voice, 'Do you know if they've checked the roof space next door?'

'We need to check,' the other one said, then called out to me. 'Thank you, Mrs Cartright.'

I saw them out but kept the front door slightly ajar and stood by the opening. I was letting the cold air in, but I wanted to hear what they were saying. They knocked at number seven and Jodie answered. 'Don't want to teach anyone to suck eggs,' one of them said, 'but did the search team go into the roof? There's a hatch in number eight and she says they're in all of the flats on this floor.'

'I'll check,' Jodie said. 'Thanks, guys.'

The door shut again and I quietly closed mine. I stood there for a while, leaning against it, feeling rather pleased at developments. The Fincham Estate Miss Marple, eh? Who'd have thought it?

Day Three

Sandy

They were searching the estate today. Jodie had told Sandy that they thought Mina had come back there on Wednesday after school but hadn't said who had seen her. What did that even mean, thought Sandy? That she'd come to the flat? That she was there overnight? If she'd been there, Sandy would know, wouldn't she? Maybe she had been here and left again, taking her cuggy. But where would she have gone?

Brett hadn't texted since last night. Sandy could feel him slipping away from her since he'd been interviewed by the police. They'd done it in his flat, hadn't taken him in or anything, but she could tell it had pissed him off. *So there goes another one,* she thought. He was all right, too. Would she even be able to work there now? The thought of going back to work seemed so odd, so unlikely. If they didn't find Mina, things could never go back to normal, could they? The world might move on, forget about her, but Sandy never could. What the hell would she do with her life? How could she even have a life after this?

She'd turned her phone's sound off because the notifications had been driving her round the bend when she was trying to sleep. Now she looked at the screen. Twenty plus notifications on Facebook. Twenty plus on Twitter. She didn't need to read them. *Unfit mother. Scum. Waste of space.*

There were new texts, though. Maybe it was Brett. She opened them up.

Oh no.

It was *them*.

Alex, can we call you? M & D

Is there any news? We're here for you. M & D

We'll see you later. M & D xx

What the fuck? Alex. Just seeing the name made her hear her mum's voice, that trademark tone which could indicate judgement, disapproval and disappointment so effortlessly. She hadn't seen her parents for about seven years. It had been a relief to finally cut the apron strings – a massive weight off her shoulders. They'd called and texted for six months or so and always messaged at Christmas and on her and Mina's birthdays, but she'd hadn't replied and she hadn't sent them her address here.

We'll see you later? She guessed the whole world knew where she lived now.

Day Three

Kath

Sandy's parents weren't what I would have expected at all. They were very Marks and Spencer, if you know what I mean. Nicely turned out, quiet sort of people. Too posh for Fincham, well, our bit of it anyway.

I heard them knocking next door and then a bit of a kerfuffle. Sandy was shouting. The door slammed. They knocked on it again and then I heard another voice, Jodie's I think. All this took about a quarter of an hour.

I couldn't help myself; I opened my door a little and peeked out. They were standing on the walkway, looking lost. I knew who they were straight away, though. Sandy's got her mum's eyes and her dad's colouring – Mediterranean, you'd call it, I suppose.

I opened the door a little wider.

'Your daughter?' I said. I gave her mum a sympathetic smile, and she nodded. 'She's been very up and down. You can't really blame her, can you? Where've you come from?'

Sandy's Mum said, 'Epsom.'

'Very nice.'

'Suppose we'll just head back. We're not wanted here.'

She looked quite forlorn. Her husband, in a nice camel coat and black leather gloves, was tight-lipped and tense. It didn't feel right to leave things like that. And I had so many questions . . .

'Would you like to come in for a cuppa before you go?'

They looked at each other enquiringly until the husband – clearly the senior partner – gave the nod.

'That's very kind,' Sandy's mum said. 'I'm Rebecca, by the way, and this is Richard.'

'Kath,' I said. 'Nice to meet you. Come and have a warm-up – this walkway's always draughty.'

I opened the door a bit wider and ushered them into the lounge. God bless them, you might expect people like that to look down on all my bits and pieces, but Rebecca was so nice. She stood in the middle of the carpet, taking it all in, then said, without a hint of snottiness, 'What a lovely room.'

'Thank you.' I couldn't help glowing a little. 'Do sit down. Tea or coffee?'

I took their 'order' and hurried to put the kettle on. When I came back with the drinks and a plate of biscuits on a tray, they were sitting next to each other on the sofa, both perched on the edge like they weren't planning on stopping for long.

'Help yourselves to sugar,' I said.

Neither of them did. More self-discipline than me. I put two spoons in mine. I needed a little boost.

'It's a shame she didn't want to talk,' I said, testing the water gently, 'but it's a terrible time for her.'

'I'm so glad she's got you next door, Kath. We saw you on the news and the police officer told us how helpful you've been.'

'I wish I could have done more. Can't help feeling guilty.'

She leaned forward, nearly spilling her tea. 'But you mustn't. Everyone says you've been marvellous. Have you been here long? This estate, it's not very . . . I mean it's probably perfectly nice but it's not . . . ideal for a child.' She was digging a bit of a hole for herself here but had the grace to recognise it. 'I'm sorry. That must sound rude. You see, we didn't even know where Alex and Mina were – she didn't send us her address last time they moved. She'd cut us off. We've been missing Mina terribly. And now—' She wasn't able to continue and fished in her pocket for a cotton hanky, which she pressed firmly into her nose.

'Oh, I'm so sorry, love.'

There was an awkward silence while Rebecca tried to get her composure back.

'Do you have children, Kath?' Richard said, making a brave attempt to fill in the gap.

'A daughter. Evie. She's in Australia, with her kiddies,' I said, 'so I do know a bit about missing your family. Not that it's the same, of course.'

Rebecca lowered her tissue. 'Was she happy here, Kath? Was Mina happy?'

What could I say to that? I felt really put on the spot. 'I honestly don't know, Rebecca. She was a quiet girl. Is that what her mum was like when she was little?'

Rebecca sighed. She clutched the tissue in both hands on her lap. 'She was a lovely girl, Kath,' she said quietly. 'Only child. I had pre-eclampsia and they advised me not to have any more. But it didn't matter because she was everything we ever wanted.' Richard was looking round the room. Either he'd heard all this too many times before or he was embarrassed. Perhaps a bit of both.

'It was all fine until she was fifteen. She was such a sunny girl, but then it all went wrong. She started staying out, being very defiant, lying to us.' I gave a little grunt of recognition at that. 'By the time she was sixteen we were at our wits' end. It was obvious she was on drugs. We stopped her allowance but she just . . .'

'We don't need to go into all that,' Richard cut in. Rebecca nodded, looked almost grateful to be given permission to stop.

'We tried grounding her but she ignored us. I used to go out looking for her, to bring her home, but honestly, I didn't even know if I wanted her in the house anymore. And it got so bad—' she looked at him for reassurance '—that we had to ask her to leave.'

'Is that the last time you saw her?'

'Oh no, she's been in and out of our lives. She reappears when she hasn't got anywhere else to go or needs money. She came home when she was pregnant. She said she was clean and wanted to stay clean and we helped her as much as we could. To be honest, I did believe her, but we haven't seen her for years. Do you think she's clean, Kath? From what you've seen?'

'I couldn't say, Rebecca. I don't know her that well.'

'Was there anything that you noticed, though?'

'Well, she did keep funny hours, and then there was the . . . well . . . shouting.'

The tissue was clamped back under her nose. You could see the effect of all this on her.

'There's another thing,' I said. 'I hope you don't mind me mentioning it. I think she owes people money. There's a man who comes round collecting. I've seen him at her door.'

Richard looked at Rebecca sharply. 'I don't like the sound of that.'

'She was asking about a reward,' I said. I didn't like to mention it but I felt I owed it to them to tell them the whole truth.

'Do you think she's involved, Kath?' said Rebecca. 'Arranged Mina's disappearance to claim a reward?'

I shrugged. 'I don't think she'd do that. I really don't.'

I did, though, and so did they, and they were the ones who knew her best. Knew what she was capable of.

Day Three

Den

Den didn't go back to bed after Dad drove off in the van. He sat in the office, going over the CCTV again and again, freezing frames, wishing he could freeze time, rewind it, do things differently. He would make Mina the hot chocolate and invite her to sit at the table nearest the counter. Encourage her to chat as she drank it, ask about her day, ask if there was anything worrying her. He was well aware that if he had done that and it was all on film, things would look even worse for him, but perhaps no one would ever have seen that tape. There would have been no need. Mina could have told him if something was wrong. She wouldn't have gone missing.

No point dwelling on it, but what else could he do? He knew so little about Mina, but maybe he could find out a bit more. Maybe he had some information right here. He started sifting through the CCTV videos, starting with Tuesday and working backwards, watching each one for ten minutes either side of half past three. She wasn't there every day, but she popped in once or twice a week, always on her own. Den became completely absorbed in his task. He copied the sections of film as he came upon them and put them all together in one file. He was pasting one snippet in when the final frame caught his eye. Someone was coming into the picture, a hand and leg, frozen as they walked towards the counter. He went back to the original footage and pressed play. Mina was turning towards the door. The man coming in stopped her. They were talking for just over a minute.

Den replayed the footage. It was a difficult angle, but the man was tall, with a clean-shaven head, and he was wearing work clothes and a high-vis jacket.

The clock in the right-hand corner of the screen ticked on. It was after four now. Where had Dad gone? He was used to Dad's insomnia, the pacing, the dark shadows under his eyes in the mornings, and, yes, he came and went at odd times of the night. But to do it when the whole estate was in agony over a missing girl. What was going on?

The more he thought about it, the worse it seemed.

At ten past five, Den heard a noise at the side door. He was determined to confront Dad, have it out with him, not to let him slink upstairs this time and pretend nothing was happening. He pushed the chair back, jumped up and went through to the hallway.

There was a small plastic bag on the floor. It was open and Den knew what was in it before he even got close – the smell was unmistakeable. He nudged it to one side with the tip of his slipper and yanked open the door, adrenaline surging through him. He stepped out in the street and looked around. He saw a figure running round the corner of the alleyway. It was too dark to distinguish much about them – if he was pushed he'd say male, tall, but that wouldn't narrow things down much, would it?

He stepped back inside, quickly fetched some rubber gloves from the kitchen and picked up the bag. Wincing, he tied the handles into a knot and, holding it at arm's length, went out again to put it in the dustbin. As he was closing the lid, he heard the familiar sound of their van's engine and, sure enough, it came round the corner and pulled into their parking space.

Dad got out. He walked over to Den slowly, shoulders hunched.

'What are you doing up? We're not opening today.'

'I was waiting for you, Dad, and then I was dealing with the present that someone posted through the door.'

'The what?'

'Someone posted a bag of shit through the door just now. I've put it in the bin. You can see it there if you don't believe me.'

'No, no, I believe you. Just now? Come on, let's get in the van, see if we can find them. They can't be far away.'

He was already halfway back to the driver's door.

'And then what? Beat the crap out of him? Have a nice man-to-man chat and sort it all out with a bit of banter?'

Dad stopped. 'Somewhere in between. Just make this stop. Make all this stop.' There was something different about Dad. He'd lost his normal bullishness. He looked smaller, emptier, almost defeated. Den found him difficult to deal with in normal times, but this version was worse. This Dad made the knot in his stomach twist and tighten.

'Dad—' He was on the edge of asking him. Where did you go at four o'clock on Wednesday? Where do you go in the middle of the night?

'What?'

He couldn't do it. 'I think we should open today.'

'I don't know, son. I don't want to invite abuse.'

'What happened to "When they go low, we go high", Dad? Rise above it and all that.'

Dad stepped towards him, put his hand on his shoulder and squeezed. 'Ha! Maybe you're right. Perhaps you're growing a spine at last,' he said.

He always knew how to hurt him. Was it deliberate or just a pattern they'd fallen into? Den wished that just once he could make Dad proud of him. This close, Den could smell the sourness of Dad's stale sweat.

'Do you want to go and get showered while I get ready to open up?' he said.

Dad looked at him. 'Yeah. Okay, son.'

He walked to the bottom of the stairs.

'Dad!'

Dad stopped and looked back. 'Yeah?'

'You've never asked me if I had anything to do with this.'

'I don't need to ask, Den. I know you would never harm anyone.'

'Because I haven't got the balls,' Den said, getting in there before his dad could.

'No, mate. Because you are a decent man. I reckon you've got your mum to thank for that. It didn't come from me.'

Day Three

Sandy

Sandy had texted them, told them not to come, but they'd come anyway, appearing on her doorstep, with faux concern on their I-told-you-so faces. Dad in his bloody camel coat, like the bank manager he was. He was such a cliché. Manager of a small branch, Rotary Club in the evenings, golf at the weekends.

And Mum.

Actually, Mum looked different.

She'd stopped dyeing her hair. Obviously she looked older. It was nice, though, grey mixed in with mousy blonde making it ashy. It suited her. Her face was different too. Had she always had those lines at the corners of her eyes and round her mouth? Her jawline was softer, saggier. She'd put on a bit of weight.

Sandy hadn't let them in. It would have been giving in to them, wouldn't it, letting them win? She couldn't go back to being their little girl, accepting their way even when she disagreed. She needed them to see her as she was now – independent, a mother herself. They should respect that. Respect her.

The conversation, if you could call it that, hadn't lasted long.

Now, with her front door shut, she was back to sitting on the sofa with Jodie for company. Waiting.

She pictured Mum's face again, the softening, the sagging, and it made something soften inside her. What had it taken for them both to come here? Mum had looked genuinely upset. She hadn't seen Mina for years – had she actually been missing her all this time, the way Sandy missed her now? Perhaps they, of all people, could understand how she was feeling, what she was going through.

She slipped her feet into her flip-flops. Jodie looked up from her phone. 'I'm just going outside.'

The air was cold and sharp, a stiff breeze blowing along the walkway. She leaned against the concrete balustrade and looked across the courtyard. It had been half an hour or so. They'd be long gone, wouldn't they? Where would they have parked? On the street somewhere? In the multi-storey?

Below her, a photographer angled his lens upwards and snapped, snapped, snapped. She flicked him the Vs. Honestly, people had no respect.

She heard a door opening behind her. It was Kath's and she could hear her voice.

'You're welcome, love. You take care now.'

Dad stepped out first, doing up the buttons of that bloody camel coat. He looked up at Sandy and froze. Mum emerged behind him. 'What've you stopped for, Richard? Come on, it's cold. Let's get home. Oh—'

Caught unawares, Mum's face was unguarded. It was the face Sandy had seen from her cot, the face she'd seen when she'd run out of her classroom at the end of the day in infant school, the face that had soothed her and sung to her when she had a temperature. There was no judgement there, just love. Uncritical love.

'Mum? Dad? Please don't go.'

Day Three

Den

Den had left it all day but couldn't put it off any longer. He had too many questions. It was torturing him.

'Dad, I want you to look at something. I've made a list. People who were in the café just before and just after Mina. I went through the CCTV.'

'Oh yeah? What are you doing that for? The cops have all the footage. I told you to leave it to them.'

'I know, but I need to do something. Innocent until proved guilty doesn't seem to mean much round here. I need evidence that I'm innocent – that means I need to find out who did it.'

'I get that, but it's not your job, mate.'

'The thing is, I want you to look at it. See if you've got any information on any of them.'

Den was tense, scared of what he was about to do. He'd added Dad's name to the bottom of the list. He knew it was likely to provoke a reaction, but he needed to put his mind at rest, one way or another. Sometimes things had to get worse before they got better.

It was closing time at the café. As they'd suspected they'd had hardly any customers in. Mud sticks. Dad had been tired and tetchy all day, his mood getting worse as the day went on.

'Not now, son, okay? I've got to clean down the kitchen. Just let me get on with it unless you want to do it.'

Den wavered. It would be so much easier to avoid the issue, but he'd made up his mind. He needed to do this.

'Please, Dad. Just look at it.'

Den held the piece of paper out towards him. Dad sighed, put his soapy cloth down, and took the sheet. He frowned as he scanned down the names. Den could feel a pulse in his throat as he watched. His stupid nervous smile was twitching on and off like a Belisha beacon.

Dad's gaze reached the bottom of the page. He stared at the paper for a long time without saying a word. Den could see the muscles in Dad's jaw working. The skin on his neck was growing mottled. Den took a step back. Dad's volcanic eruptions were famous – it was nearly always bluster, almost pantomime. Nearly always. Den could remember the few times when Dad was angry, really angry, with hideous clarity. He was tempted to back off, but he knew he needed to stand his ground this time.

'Are you serious?' Dad said, his voice low and uneven. 'Is this some sort of joke?'

Den swallowed, hard. 'It's not a joke, Dad. I'm worried. I'm worried how the things you do might look to other people. I'm worried about what's actually going on.'

There. He'd said it. Now he held his breath, waiting for the reaction.

Dad put his hand up to his face, which had gone dark red, like he'd just done a weights session at the gym. He squeezed the bridge of his nose, hard. Then, much to Den's horror, he started to cry. His shoulders shook and he kept gasping, like he couldn't get hold of enough oxygen. Tears seeped out of the corners of his eyes.

Den couldn't remember ever seeing his Dad cry before. It was like standing on the edge of an abyss. This was bad – mortifying – but he felt like it was going to get a whole lot worse.

'Dad! What is it?'

Dad's legs had buckled as he gave in to his grief. Now he sat on the tiled floor, leaning against a cupboard door. When he spoke, his voice was an octave higher than usual as he fought the tears. 'It's all in the lockup.'

Den's heart was in his mouth. 'What is?'

Dad shook his head. 'You never know what you're capable of until you're pushed into a corner.'

Day Three

Sandy

Her parents weren't emotional people. They were 'doers', always busy mowing the lawn, cleaning out cupboards, watering houseplants, making lists. Growing up, Sandy had sometimes wondered what would happen if they just stopped. Would they collapse, implode, explode, spontaneously combust? That was a thing, wasn't it? People sitting in armchairs just bursting into flame and smouldering like human candles, leaving their charred remains in an otherwise untouched room? Was the answer to this enduring mystery simply that this is what happens when middle-class people stop pottering?

Now, they were on her sofa, doing nothing, just sitting. Neither of them took their coats off.

'Why did you—?'

'Don't, Mum. Just don't.'

'No, I'm sorry. You must have asked yourself the same thing.'

'Don't apologise, Bex,' Dad said. He was the only one who called her that. 'We've all been wondering. I mean, what were you thinking?'

Sandy could feel her teenage self, elbowing its way stroppily to the front of her brain. She thought she'd left that person behind but, of course, she hadn't. 'I was thinking that I need to earn money to pay the bills, Dad. I was thinking that Mina was sensible, probably wouldn't even notice I wasn't there. Or maybe I wasn't thinking at all. What do you reckon, Dad?'

He shifted uncomfortably in his seat. 'You could have come to us.'

'I wasn't that desperate.'

'We would never have wanted Mina to go without, Alex.'

'It's Sandy, Dad. My name's Sandy. I didn't want her to go without either. Do you think I wanted this?' She gestured at the bleak room and the tide of defiance started receding alarmingly quickly. *This.* This flat. This life. It didn't add up to much, did it? And now she'd lost the only good, pure thing in it.

Mum looked like she wanted to cry again. Her hands were clasping the tissue so tightly, it was mangled into stringy bits.

'I was proud of doing things on my own,' Sandy said. 'I've been clean all this time. I thought I was doing all right. Well, not all right, but not terrible.'

They lapsed into silence again.

'I – we – are very proud of you for staying clean. Aren't we, Richard?' Mum's words were so quiet Sandy wasn't sure if she'd heard them. 'I know it can't have been easy.'

'It wasn't. Isn't. And I'm not using again, I promise you. I'm skint because it's too hard to live on your own in this city and earn a living and look after a kid and pay the rent and . . . and . . . you don't understand.'

Dad brushed some imaginary dust off the side of his coat. 'Actually, you'd be surprised,' he said. 'I see people struggling every day. Mortgages, bills, debts. It's brutal out there.'

Sandy frowned. She'd never heard him talk like that before. 'It is brutal.'

'People are pushed into corners; the banks play their part in this. I understand more than you know.'

Mum looked sideways at Dad like she was seeing a new side of him. Sandy guessed it wasn't what they talked about as they ate dinner off a tray in front of *Top Gear* or *Antiques Roadshow*.

'Alex – Sandy,' Mum said. 'We all do things we regret. You can go over and over it and it doesn't help.'

'Mum—'

'No, listen. Whatever you've done, we – Dad and I – will always love you. We always have. We'll stand by you.'

Sandy wondered if she was just talking about her night away, or whether she was getting at something else. Whatever. It wasn't easy to say any of this. It wasn't easy to hear it without saying something sarky back, but she understood, finally, that it was sincerely meant.

'Thanks, Mum,' she said. 'And Dad.'

She looked at him cagily. He was brushing that imaginary dirt again.

'Right. Well,' he said. 'Are we done here? I mean, do you want us to stay?'

In a sudden rush of blood to the head, Sandy almost begged them to take her with them. Anything to get out of this place, away from here. But instead, she shook her head. 'No, I've got Jodie and Kath next door. I'm all right.'

'But you'll keep in touch now, won't you? Let us know how things are going? We can come back any time. Day or night,' Mum said.

'Yeah,' said Sandy. 'I'll keep in touch.'

Day Three

Den

Dad undid the padlock and started heaving the door upwards.

Den watched with trepidation as the gap at the bottom of the door inched wider and wider, anticipating – *dreading* – what was inside. A body? Or a live, frightened girl? Oh, Dad, what have you done?

He peered into the dark space. To start with he couldn't see anything out of the ordinary. There were the normal heaps of toilet rolls and paper towels, some catering-size containers of cooking oil and the big chest freezer at the back wall. Shit, the freezer. Dear God, no.

'Dad?' he said.

'It's here.' Dad walked into the lockup and took hold of the bottom of a green tarpaulin draped over something near the left-hand wall.

It. *It?*

Dad drew the cloth up to reveal three petrol cans and a heap of rags.

'What's this?' This was so different to what Den was expecting that for a while at least he didn't understand what he was seeing. Even when his blindsided brain figured it out, he still couldn't grasp the significance.

Dad looked at him squarely. 'We're in so much trouble. It's the only way to save the family now. We've got to torch the lot.'

Den felt like he was having an out-of-body experience or a bad dream or something. This couldn't possibly be real.

'Torch it? The café? As in set fire to it?'

Dad nodded. 'It's the only thing that makes sense.'

'Can you hear yourself? It makes no sense. When were you going to do this? What about Mum? What about the Singhs next door?'

Dad let the tarpaulin fall back down. 'Obviously, we'll wait until your mother is out. We'll make sure it's caught in our place, then raise the alarm. I've thought it all through. No one will get hurt.'

'Hang on a minute, there's no "we" here and you're not going ahead with this. It's completely fucking nuts.'

'We don't have a choice. The business is finished. It was dead anyway. You being nicked by the police was the nail in the coffin.'

Here we go, thought Den, *I was the nail.*

'I wasn't nicked, Dad. I was questioned and then let go. I haven't done anything wrong. I'm so sorry the café's being targeted, but it'll blow over. When Mina is found, it will all be over. People will come back and we'll be fine.'

'You don't understand.'

Dad sank down onto a bale of kitchen rolls, leaning his head in his hands. He was right. Den didn't understand. Trade was down but the café was still popular enough. Takings were reasonably steady, certainly enough to meet their overheads and pay the wages. He felt a cold surge of dread. This wasn't about the business, was it? There was something else.

'So tell me.'

He sat down next to him and listened as Dad told him of the loans he'd taken out and failed to pay back, the corners he'd cut, the tax he hadn't paid.

'But the café's doing all right, isn't it? I mean, people are still coming in. We don't exactly take massive wages out, do we? We're not flashy. Why do we need loans? Where's all the money gone?'

There was a pause. 'I play cards sometimes.'

It sounded so innocuous. Nothing wrong with getting together with a few mates for a games night. Den almost felt relieved that was all it was.

'Is that where you go?'

'Sometimes.'

'You play for money and lose?'

'I owe people.'

'Okay, but it can't be too bad, surely. Like how much? Hundreds?' Even as he said it, Den knew it wasn't enough. Not to bring Dad this low, to rack up so many unpaid bills, to even contemplate destroying his business and home. 'Thousands?'

Dad grunted.

'Dad? Thousands?'

'Thirty thousand.'

Den let his words sink in. It was difficult not to just stand up and walk away. It was difficult not to take Dad by the shoulders and shake him until his teeth rattled. Instead, he took some deep breaths and tried to think. 'Does Mum know?'

'She does the books. She knows the business is in trouble. She doesn't know why.'

'We've got to go home and we've got to tell her. We can sort it out. It's just money, innit?'

'Easy for you to say. It's never "just money". It's threats and violence. It's security. It's lies. It's indigestion so bad I keep thinking I'm having a heart attack. It's insomnia. It's our whole world.'

'But we can sort it. We'll start by getting Mum onside.'

'I can't tell her, Den. She'll kick me out. It happened before, years ago. I got in a muddle. We did sort it out that time, but she warned me – never again. I've thought about this, believe me

– you'll have to trust me on this. I've got insurance. If the café goes up, I can pay off my debts, start again. If you take Mum out for a while – evening would be best – I'll just do it. Or I could take her and you—'

'Stop it! We're not doing it! We'll think of something else, but not that. For fuck's sake, Dad.'

Den stood up and started pacing around between the piles of supplies. He didn't know what to do with himself. He started punching a tower of toilet rolls, his fists slamming into their plastic wrapping.

'Hey, hey!' Dad was on his feet too now. He put his hand on Den's arm. 'It's all right, Den. It's all right. I messed up. I'll sort it.'

Den stopped throwing punches and turned to face Dad. 'By talking to someone? Getting help?'

'Yes, yes. You've got to promise me you won't tell your mother. Promise me, Den. I can't lose her. I just can't.' Dad's eyes were feverish, overbright in the garage's harsh light. His voice was thick with emotion. He tightened his grip on Den's arm. 'Promise me, yeah?'

'Okay. I promise,' said Den. 'But if you can't talk to her, talk to me. Let me help.'

Dad moved his hand up from Den's arm to his shoulder. 'You're a good boy. Let's go home.'

'We've got to get rid of that stuff, though. The petrol cans. Give me the keys to the van – I'll take them to the tip or dump them somewhere.'

'Not now, mate. The tip'll be closed. Leave it today.'

Day Three

Kath

Sandy's mum and dad didn't stay all day, but they had a good hour next door and I knew they'd parted on better terms. I kept the telly on mute and opened the front door a crack when I heard them making a move. Obviously, I couldn't take all the credit for their little reunion but, if I'd never invited them in, they'd have gone back to Epsom well before Sandy had second thoughts. So, I marked it down as another little triumph.

There were no updates on Mina. I watched the local news, then logged onto my laptop and checked the local sites. There was quite a flurry about Nelson House being searched flat by flat. Apparently one man had been arrested for growing cannabis and the RSPCA had been brought in to advise a woman who had been found keeping eighteen cats. You never know what goes on behind closed doors, although neither of those things was a real surprise if I'm honest.

I couldn't find much gossip about the lads I'd seen taken in, although that had to be the reason the police were focusing on the flats, hadn't it? Mina had been seen going into the stairwell.

Did she make it home? Did Danno get to her before she got to the third floor? If the police had let him go after questioning him, that must mean either he had a convincing story or they didn't have a strong enough case to charge him. Could a toerag like him kill someone and dispose of the body without leaving any evidence? Just thinking the word 'body' made me feel a bit sick. I mustn't go down that road – much better to keep hoping. My Ray used to say that if you expected the worst you'd be pleasantly surprised if things actually turned out okay, but I always like to look on the bright side.

By the end of the afternoon I was getting a bit twitchy. Another day without any progress – no arrests, no sightings. I couldn't just sit there. It was too frustrating. Besides, the weekend quizzes aren't my favourites, although I do like Alexander (I like to think we'd be on Xander and Kath terms if we ever met) and Richard. Such nice men! I'm not bothered by the so-called celebrity editions of any of the quizzes, though. I mean, I've never heard of half the people.

I'd go and pick up a pint of milk and something nice for tea, see if I could pick up any gossip on the way. I trundled my trolley along the walkway, hoping that perhaps the focus on Nelson House would have prompted the housing people to send someone out to fix the lift. No such luck. The stairs seemed to get steeper every day. The way my knees were going, I'd soon be stuck in the flat and then what would I do? Seemed a bit of a stretch to imagine Sandy fetching my shopping for me. I could ask the council about meals on wheels but I really don't like eating other people's cooking. It's never as good as mine and I can't take anything spicy.

Going downstairs was almost as bad as going up. The strain on my poor old joints was unbearable. It felt like my knees could give way at any time, just buckle and then I'd be headlong down to the next landing. I was breathless too. Who gets breathless going downstairs? I really am an old croc. I kept a tight grip

191

on the railing, trying not to think too hard about all the other hands that had touched it – the sweat, the grime, the snot, the God-knows-what-else – except that maybe there was a trace of Mina left here too. Had her little hands gripped this metal rail as she ran up the stairs, trying to get away from that thug? It made me shudder to think of it.

However many times I've trudged up and down here, I've never got used to the smell. Even when it's been cleaned with disinfectant, which happens once in a blue moon, there's still a back note of disappointment, fag smoke and urine. Now as I neared the ground floor, puffing hard as I paused on every second step and lifted my trolley down, I noticed a different edge to the air. It was almost metallic. There was something familiar about it, but I couldn't put a name to it. Another sign of ageing – words just out of reach, difficult to pin things down, label them.

There was a skittering noise, the sound of feet on concrete, and looking down I saw a little shadow run out of the open door. We get rats in here sometimes, but this was much bigger. A blessed dog on the loose. They're a menace on this estate.

I was only a couple of steps from the bottom when I noticed the dark mass on the concrete floor, under the stairwell to my right. A coat or maybe a heap of bedding left there by last night's occupant. The smell was stronger here, that metallic twang.

I heaved myself down the last two steps and put my foot in something wet. A pool of dark liquid coming out from under the coat. That was when I remembered what the metallic smell was. Blood. It was blood.

'Oh no,' I murmured. 'Please God, no.'

Day Three

Den

A cluster of cars and vans and two ambulances were gathered in the far corner of the courtyard by the entrance to Nelson House. Den could see blue and white tape marking the area off. A crowd was gathering at a distance, people huddling together. Den looked up and people were dotted along the walkways of Nelson House, looking down, filming on their phones.

He and Dad threaded their way through the crowd. The back of the ambulance was open, bright lights inside making it look like a theatre set or TV screen. Kath, in her familiar padded coat, was sitting in a wheelchair, on the lowered tail lift while a paramedic tended to her.

'It's Mrs C!' Den said to Dad. She seemed to be getting agitated, remonstrating with the woman trying to help her.

Den ran over to the van. 'Mrs C! It's me. Are you okay?'

A second ambulance worker stood in his path. 'We need to keep this area clear, sir.'

'I'm her friend. She hasn't got any family, not here. Is she okay?'

Kath saw him now. 'Den!' she said. She was gasping for air, struggling to get any words out. 'Let him through.'

The guy stood aside and Den went forward. He kneeled down so that he was at Kath's eye level.

'Mrs C, are you okay? What's happened?'

'Oh, Den, it's awful.' She paused to try to catch her breath. 'In there . . . by the stairs.'

'What is it?'

'So much blood, Den. I found it. I found a—'

A body?

Another team of paramedics emerged from the stairwell, carrying a stretcher. People were craning to see who it was.

Suddenly, he heard screaming from overhead. He looked up. They were so close to the block that the lip of the balconies obscured the watchers above, apart from those who were leaning over, peering down, filming it on their phones. One of the faces peering down from the top floor was Sandy.

'Nooo! My baby!'

Even from a distance, Den could see that her face was contorted with pain. She was leaning over dangerously far. Now hands gripped her shoulders and pulled her back out of sight. The screaming continued, though.

He looked at Kath's face, which was hideously pale, almost grey. Her breathing was fast and shallow, her mouth gaping like a fish out of water, little flecks of white spit at either corner.

'It's not her,' Kath said. 'It's not Mina. It was a lad who was attacked. I don't know if he's alive or not.'

Den looked across as the stretcher was loaded into the second ambulance. The person being carried had a blanket over them but the face wasn't covered up. He had an oxygen mask on and was clearly still breathing.

'He's alive, Mrs C.'

'Thank God for that. I'd never forgive myself if he . . . if my interfering had meant that . . .'

'Mrs C, please calm down.'

'It's my fault, though, Den. This is all my fault.'

194

Day Three

Den

Den and Dad stayed nearby as Kath was tended to by the paramedic. The police were waiting to talk to her, but before she'd let them in, she beckoned to Den.

'Den, Den!' She was agitated. 'My trolley's over there.' She pointed to the wall near the entrance to Nelson House. 'Bring it here before someone nicks it.'

Den did as he was told. A constable questioned him as he reached for the handle but let him take it when he explained.

As he trundled it back towards the ambulance he passed a group of men, talking. Marlon, in his high-vis jacket, was among them, standing with his back to Den. What was he doing here on a Sunday? Surely he hadn't been working on site? He had a big dog on a leather leash with him – a Rottweiler or a Doberman, Den could never tell the difference. As he walked near, the dog lunged towards him, jerking Marlon's arm and making him spin round.

'Hey, Tyler, no! Oh—' Their eyes met. There was no mistaking the animosity there. The dog was straining to reach Den and Marlon fought to get it under control. Den moved on quickly.

As he walked away, the hair on the back of his neck was standing up, and he half-expected the dog to be let free to jump at his back or sink its teeth into his arm.

Back at the ambulance, he overheard the paramedic talking to Kath. 'Your heart's running a little bit fast, Kath. We're going to take you in, just for observation. You've had a nasty shock.'

Den was surprised at the vehemence of Kath's response.

'I'm not going to no hospital. Once you go in there, you don't come out again. No way.'

'Kath, you've had a nasty shock. This is just a precaution.'

'I know my heart jumps about a bit – it's done it for years. I've got pills for it. I'm not going to feel better in that place. I need my own place, that's all. I'm going home.'

The paramedics exchanged glances.

'We're not going to force you, but I understand you live alone.'

She flapped her hand towards Den. 'That's all right. My friend here will take me up and make sure I'm okay. You will, won't you?'

Den stepped forwards. 'Of course. I'll look after Mrs C.'

'I'll go back home,' said Dad, 'let Mum know what's happening. We'll bring some soup over or whatever – let me know how you're getting on, yeah?'

'Okay, Dad.'

'The police want to talk to me, Den. Can you wait, love?' Kath said. She looked so vulnerable in the wheelchair, her hair – ruffled by the wind – was sparse and wispy. He could see her mottled scalp underneath.

''Course I can, Mrs C. I'll just be here, guarding your trolley.'

Now Den wondered who the boy was. He tried listening in to the low-level chatter all around him, but he couldn't make out anything concrete.

'Gangs round here . . . knives . . . someone should do something . . . parents . . . no respect.'

Knives. It was another stabbing then. They seemed to happen almost every week. Turf wars, teenage squabbles that had got out of hand or muggings. Someone had been killed for their trainers a month ago or so. Growing up around here, there had always been trouble now and again, but it seemed to be getting worse. Den, never part of a gang himself, avoided eye contact and crossed the road if he saw a group of lads coming the other way when he was out at night. It was happening even during the day now, though.

Maybe Dad was right – the place was going down the toilet. Maybe it was time to get out – he should talk to Dad about selling the café, rather than burning it down. Pay off the debts and move on somewhere. Start again.

'Den? Den!'

Kath was calling to him.

'They've finished with me. Can you take me home, if they'll let us into the stairs?'

Kath clutched her tissue to her mouth and tears glittered in the corners of her eyes.

'It's all right, Mrs C,' Den said, kneeling beside her and putting a hand gently on her arm. 'We'll get you home soon.'

'You don't understand, Den,' she said. She lowered her tissue a little. Her bottom lip was wobbling like a blancmange. 'I know who it is. I recognised him. It's a lad called Sam and—' she gave a gulping gasp '—he'd be perfectly okay now if I hadn't opened my big mouth.'

Day Three

Sandy

Jodie got a call even before the ambulances and cop cars started arriving. Her face was so serious as she listened that Sandy knew that it wasn't good news from the very start.

Jodie clicked the 'call end' button and clipped her phone to her belt.

'Sandy, it's going to get noisy in a minute – they've found someone in the stairwell.'

Sandy didn't wait to hear the rest. Sirens and lights were filling the courtyard as she yanked open the front door. Emergency vehicles were converging on the entrance to the block. She peered over the edge of the balcony. A crowd was gathering too, mostly silent, looking towards the door to the stairwell, just watching. She leaned further to try to get a better view. She didn't want to see Mina's body there, lying on the concrete, but if this was happening she *needed* to see it.

Her screams were heard above the sirens, making people look up, a blur of faces.

Jodie came up behind her and grabbed her shoulders.

'It's not her, Sandy. Come away. Come inside.'

Sandy tried to shrug Jodie's hands away, but that cow wasn't letting go. She manhandled her away from the edge.

'We're going inside. I need to talk to you.'

'No! Let me see her! I'm her mum!'

'It's not her. It's a teenage boy. Looks like a stabbing.'

It took her a while to be calm enough for Jodie's words to sink in.

'I need to be sure. I need to see it with my own eyes.'

'Trust me, you don't. I've dealt with too many cases like this. It's ugly. He's still alive, just. My colleagues are dealing with it. It's not Mina.'

She led Sandy inside. As the news sank in, numb despair replaced the panic.

'What's going on round here? It's like everything's out of control . . .'

'Could be anything, Sandy. Knife crime is pretty prevalent around here. We did interview two lads yesterday as part of the investigation, though.'

'Two lads? Why?'

'We had reports that one of them had seen Mina on the Thursday. We're still checking everything out.'

'Why didn't you tell me?'

'It's a fast-moving investigation, Sandy. We're following every lead we find, but we haven't made any arrests yet. I'm not told about every last thing.'

Sandy slumped forwards in her chair. 'I never even thought about kids with knives . . .'

'Chances are this is completely unconnected – a gang thing. Try not to think the worst.'

What else was there to think about, though?

Day Three

Den

'Park it just inside the door, love. Ta,' Kath said as she led Den into her flat. He wheeled the trolley into the hall and put its brake on with his foot. The contrast between the breezy cold evening outside and the cloyingly warm air inside hit him. He took off his coat and wondered if it would seem odd if he peeled off his jumper too.

Kath had disappeared into a room on the left. Den followed and found her in an armchair, leaning her head back, eyes closed, apparently gasping for air. The climb up the stairs, as well as everything else, had taken it out of her. Perhaps the paramedics had been right – she should be in hospital.

'Can I get you some water?'

Her eyes fluttered open. 'Oh, yes please, love, and can you bring my bag of pills in? It's on the top, next to the microwave – a sponge bag with flowers on.'

Den did as he was asked, then watched her scrabbling through the bag, pressing two pills out of a blister pack. 'A cup of tea now, yeah?' he said.

'Mm.' She didn't speak as she was struggling to get the pills down, taking gulps of water and tipping her head back as she swallowed. Den left her to it and pottered about her kitchen. It reminded him of his nan's – all the cupboards full, orderly and clean. A place for everything and everything in its place. He made tea for both of them and found a packet of Jammie Dodgers in the cupboard, put everything on a tray and carried it through.

Kath had put her glass on the coffee table. She looked a little less grey in her face now but she was still in some distress, breathing noisily through her open mouth like a fish out of water. He handed her a china mug.

'See if this helps,' he said. 'I've put some sugar in.'

'I shouldn't with my diabetes,' she said but then, seeing him reach for the mug to take it back, chipped in quickly, 'but I reckon I need it for the shock. Thank you, Den. You're a good boy.'

He sat on the sofa opposite her. They both sipped their tea. Den looked round the room, which was cluttered, almost floor to ceiling, with ornaments and keepsakes. Little china animals – kittens, elephants and hedgehogs, tiny cottages and figurines – jostled with vases and boxes, dried flower arrangements and bowls of ancient potpourri. There were framed prints on the wall – the type you'd find in any charity shop – and a few framed photographs, family snaps, some in black and white.

'Some people would say it's a lot of old rubbish.' Kath was looking at him, examining her décor. He felt caught out.

'Not at all, Mrs C. I can tell it's all precious to you.'

She smiled. 'It's all I've got now. This is it. My whole life in a few rooms.'

'Mum said your daughter's in Australia.'

'That's right, love,' she said, mildly. 'Other side of the world. Almost like she's out of the picture. Awfully sad to start with, but you get used to it.'

'That must be hard.'

'Mm. You have to let them go, don't you? If they want to fly away. I bet your mum's glad to have you still at home. Don't you fancy spreading your wings a bit? Oh, you did, though, didn't you?'

From anyone else, that would have sounded pointed, a sly little dig, but Kath was so guileless. The sort of woman with no filter – she just said what was in her head. He wondered if that was an age thing or if she'd always been like that. He realised she was staring at him then and he felt himself growing hot with embarrassment, reminded again that everyone knew all about him. His story, what he'd done, was public property.

'I'm sorry, love. I didn't mean to upset you,' said Kath. 'What I say is, there's two sides to every story. The papers aren't interested in balance, are they?'

She went quiet again, but the invitation was clear. He could speak to her, tell her all about it. And after a few moments' hesitation, he did. He found himself spilling out the whole sorry tale from arriving in Hull to being sent home in disgrace.

'I think I sort of lost my mind, Mrs C. I thought I was being romantic, but it was something else. I frightened her. I didn't mean to.'

She put her cup down and heaved herself forwards in the chair, reaching out to him, taking his hand.

'Everyone makes mistakes, love. Sometimes, if we're lucky, we get a second chance. We get to make things right. You're so young. Your turn will come. You'll find someone who loves you just the way you are.'

Her words were so comforting. He was moved that a relative stranger could have such absolute faith in him. Dad always undermined him, whether he intended to or not. Mum was his cheerleader, but she had to be, didn't she? That was her job. Kath was different. In the middle of all this mess, he'd met someone who could really inspire him. It was unexpected and somehow rather wonderful.

'Thank you,' he said. 'I hope so.'

'I know so.'

'Like you and your husband.'

'My Ray? Yes, he was a diamond. One of a kind.'

She let go of his hand and sat back in her chair. He could see that her chest wasn't working as hard, her breathing was easier. He wouldn't leave her, though, until he was sure she didn't need him to call a doctor.

'Heck of an evening,' he said. He was naturally curious about what she'd said earlier about the boy she'd found, but he didn't want to upset her again. 'Do you want to talk about it?'

She looked down at her tea and then up at him, eyes blinking hard behind the thick lenses of her glasses.

'You know the gang of kids that hangs around the yard?' He nodded. 'I spoke with them yesterday. I wondered if they'd seen anything on Wednesday, cos they always seem to be there, don't they? Anyway, later one of them—' she swallowed hard '—the one who . . . he waited for me. Wanted to tell me something. You see, he did see Mina on Wednesday. She was being followed into Nelson House by another lad – Danno, his name is.'

'Okay.' Den's mind was racing now, anticipating where this was going.

'So I, of course, said I'd have to tell the police. He asked me, begged me, to keep him out of it. I didn't. I didn't know his name but I gave them a description – he's quite distinctive with that ginger hair – and the police took them both in for questioning.'

The bottom half of her face was wobbling now as she battled against tears.

Den leaned forward in his seat and put his mug down on the table. 'You think Danno stabbed him?'

'Almost certainly. This was punishment, Den.'

'I'm so sorry.'

'He's a nice lad, decent, I think, just got in with the wrong lot. People just get caught up in things, make mistakes and can't undo them.'

'Do you think they might come after you? Maybe you should ask for police protection or go somewhere else for a while?'

'A safe house? You've been watching too much telly, Den. I'll be all right. I'm not part of his gang, haven't broken their rules. He won't bother with me.'

'It's not nice walking round here at night, though, Mrs C. If you need to go out, you can always ring me. I'll be your, what's the word . . . chaperone. I'll look after you.'

'That's very kind, Den. I've lived here all this time. I'm not going to start letting people intimidate me now.'

Her words were admirably defiant, but somehow her expression didn't match. Behind a brave façade, she was scared. Den tried to think of something to distract her. From his experience in the café a little encouragement to reminisce could go a long way and took a lot of older people back to a happy place. It was worth a try.

'How long have you lived here, Mrs C?' he said.

Kath seemed to visibly relax.

'We were some of the first to move in when the flats were built. Nineteen sixty-seven. My Evie was two. It doesn't look like it now, but we all thought this place would be paradise for families and it wasn't bad to start with . . .'

They sat together for another half-hour or so, Kath talking about the old days and Den listening. Kath was much pinker in the face and more relaxed, half asleep in fact, speaking for a while and then drifting off a little.

'I'll leave you to it, Mrs C. But remember, you can call me whenever you need to. I'll come and see you tomorrow, yeah?'

'All right, love. I'll see you out.' She gripped the arms of the chair, starting to get up, but Den leapt up.

'No, no, you stay there. I'm fine.' He paused in the doorway of the lounge. 'What were you going out for earlier? Do you need me to fetch you anything?'

Kath looked distracted for a moment, then seemed to collect

her thoughts. Den imagined that everything before she found the boy in the stairwell must seem like a long time ago now. That was a hell of a thing for anyone to experience, let alone someone in their eighties. 'Oh, it was nothing. Sometimes it's just nice to get out. I don't need anything. Thanks, love.'

Day Four

Kath

I was too old for all this. It was bad enough Mina going missing. To be honest, and I know this sounds bad, but I was enjoying getting involved in trying to find her. I loved doing my bit and people actually listening to me. Calling me 'Miss Marple of Fincham' was going a bit far but I can't pretend I didn't like it.

But yesterday it all got too much for me.

Sam was in intensive care, apparently. He'd had an operation to patch him up but he was still very poorly. I couldn't stop thinking about him. If he hadn't spoken to me. If I hadn't told the police. If I'd never got involved . . . he'd be perfectly okay. I was going to have to live with that for the rest of my life. Something else to carry with me, and I'm not sure I've got the strength these days.

The internet was still covering the story, but it was all nasty stuff, tainted with prejudice about estates like this, people like us.

'*Broken Britain – how one estate sums up the state we're in*'

'*Hope Fades for Missing Mina – another casualty of sink estate London*'

'Stabbed on the Streets – just another day on the Fincham Estate'

I scanned the headlines but then shut my laptop down. I wouldn't do any more investigating. I'd done quite enough damage as it was. In fact, I wouldn't go outside today. I liked to think I wasn't worried walking around the estate on my own, but that was a lie, a white lie I tell myself to get me out of my front door. The truth was, I was nervous. Now, with what had happened to Sam, I was scared more than ever.

So, I would leave the hunt for Mina to the experts and go back to my routine before all this happened. Breakfast in front of the telly, a bit of cleaning, then settling down for *This Morning* and then *Loose Women* – they get on my nerves but I like the company. Then an afternoon watching the quizzes. Somehow, though, it seemed so empty and pointless (no pun intended). I'd never be able to fully settle until Mina was found. It seemed wrong to even try and I couldn't do it anyway. Thoughts of her, of what had happened on Wednesday, of where she was now, kept going round and round my head.

True to his word, Den checked in with me. He'd been through a lot over the past few days, too, but he was turning out to be a little diamond. He sent me a text first thing, and then rang later. We chatted about this and that.

'Have they found Danno yet?'

'Don't think so, Mrs C. They will, though.'

'You opening up the café today?'

'Yeah. Need to keep Dad on the straight and narrow.'

'What, love?' I wasn't sure I'd heard him correctly.

'Doesn't matter. Private joke. Shall I bring you some lunch up? Fish and chips? Special delivery?'

My legs were killing me, so this was music to my ears. 'All right, love. That'd be very nice. I'll give you the money.'

'Shall I bring some for Sandy?'

'That's a nice thought. I don't suppose she's eating much at the moment. I'll tell her it's on the way.'

I could really have done with a day off from her next door, but that was just me being selfish. She couldn't have a day off from it all, could she? She was still stuck in this nightmare. I needed to show a bit more charity, even if she was hard to like. I gave myself a bit of a talking-to, then pottered around and knocked next door at around eleven. Jodie opened up. She looked worse than ever. This business was taking its toll on everyone.

'Oh, Kath, I was going to call round. How are you? Nasty shock yesterday, eh?'

'I'm okay. I keep thinking about him. That poor lad. You know it was Danno that did it, don't you?'

'We don't know anything for sure, Kath. There are no witnesses yet or at least no one is willing to talk.'

'People won't. Too scared. I am too, to be honest, love, but I'll stand up in court and tell him to his face if it comes to that.'

Jodie smiled. 'I know you will, but let's hope it doesn't come to that. We'll be looking at DNA and forensic evidence. If there's enough of that, we'll wrap things up, maybe get a guilty plea.'

'It's on my conscience, though. How me talking to you caused it.'

'You can't think like that. You were doing the right thing. Violence like this is the perpetrator's fault. No one else's. We all have choices.'

That was one way to think about it. I wasn't sure I completely went along with it, though.

'Anyway, I just wanted to let Sandy know that the café are sending a hot lunch up.'

'Oh, that's nice.'

I realised my faux pas at once. 'I should've asked them to send one for you, shouldn't I? I can ring.'

Jodie laughed. 'Don't worry about it. I'm off shift in half an hour. Naz will be here soon. Are you having some food too?' I nodded. 'Nice idea to eat together. I'm sure Sandy will appreciate it.'

That wasn't quite what I'd suggested, but now Jodie had it would look mean to back out.

'Yes, that's what I thought,' I said. 'We could both use the company.'

Day Four

Sandy

Sandy knew she hadn't been an easy teenager. How had it spiralled out of control so quickly, though? They were all about control – Richard and Rebecca – that was their thing, and yet they'd lost it spectacularly with her. The worse she behaved, the more uptight they became and the wilder she got. It had been like equal and opposite forces, straining against each other until one side broke. Looking back now, she wasn't sure who it was who had broken – maybe all of them – but she remembered what caused the rupture, the day they'd asked her to leave, and felt a hot flush of shame.

She'd known it was wrong, but somehow it didn't count. She'd asked them for money. They'd cut off her allowance, so what did they expect? In her eyes at the time, they were equally to blame for her rifling through their things, selling what she could. Some opal earrings Mum had inherited from Grandma. An enamelled box she had been given for her eighteenth birthday. Her engagement ring.

All gone for a couple of hundred quid, handed over in a pub car park, so she could get that day's fix.

They'd waited for her to come home – they didn't always stay up – and she got the coldest of receptions. Both of them were shut down, drained of emotion.

'We'd like you to leave. You can stay tonight, but you'll have to go in the morning.'

But she didn't stay. She'd packed a few clothes into a bag there and then, and left. Out of there at sixteen and didn't look back. Not strictly true – she visited occasionally when she had completely run out of options, but she'd never lived there again. It wasn't home. She wasn't welcome.

Thinking about it now, who could blame them? She'd been a nightmare. If Mina started acting up like that, Sandy didn't know what she'd do, but it wouldn't happen because Mina was a good kid. And Sandy could help her not to make the mistakes she'd made. She'd promised herself she'd be the opposite of her parents – she'd be Mina's friend; they'd talk, be open and honest with each other.

Sandy sat on the side of her bed. Who was she kidding? She and Mina didn't have that sort of relationship. It wasn't 'friends sharing a flat', two girls together. It was her working all hours and still falling short. It was Mina fending for herself half the time, never complaining. It was knowing that you never had enough money at the end of the week to buy a takeaway as a treat and didn't have the energy to cook anything other than oven chips. It was borrowing money to pay for basics from people who charged interest that spiralled up and up, completely out of reach. People who wouldn't hesitate to hurt you.

Things would have to change when Mina came back. This wasn't how she wanted them both to live. It all came down to money. If they had enough money, a bit of breathing space, they could press the reset button and start again. No one had put up a reward. Didn't a kid on a council estate count? Even without a reward, though, maybe there were ways to cash in on this, to make

211

something good come out of this awful situation. When Mina was back, she was sure someone would pay for an interview and a photo. Maybe they could even have a holiday. She just needed her back now. She needed this to end.

Day Four

Den

He felt chills walking into the stairwell. It had been scrubbed and disinfected, but a few inches of blue and white tape remained, hanging mournfully from the end of a handrail. The concrete floor was darker than it should be – still damp, he guessed. It was impossible to be there without thinking of the lad who had fought for his life here, of the heartless soul who had thought nothing of sticking a knife in and running away.

The other side of that spot, near the lifts, a couple of workmen were just packing up their tools. They noticed Den coming in and one of them said, 'All done, mate. Want to test it out?'

Den shrugged. He didn't mind the stairs, but then again, why not?

The stood back as he entered the lift and there was a moment of awkwardness as he stood inside and the guys watched him as they all waited for the door to close. Just as it moved across, he saw the glint of recognition in one of men's eyes and felt a twinge of panic. If they, like the rest of the world, thought he was public enemy number one, they could trap him in here. Leave him. He wasn't normally claustrophobic but he started to feel the four walls closing in.

The lift lurched off the ground. Den looked up to the ceiling. There was a small opening, like a trapdoor. Maybe he could get out that way if he needed to. Who was he kidding? He had the upper body strength of a kitten. *Come on, come on, don't stop.* He willed the lift to make it to the third floor. The digital display changed to '3' and the lift slowed and stopped with a slight judder. The door opened and he breathed a sigh of relief.

Unsure of his reception at number seven, he rang the doorbell and stood back. Like lighting the touchpaper on a firework.

Day Four

Sandy

'I don't want anything from him.' It was a struggle to keep things that civil. Really Kath was too nice, too forgiving. Why the hell was she sucking up to one of the main suspects? Who could still be holding Mina somewhere, for all they knew?

'It's fish and chips, love. When's the last time you had a decent meal?' Kath blinked at her kindly through her thick lenses and Sandy could feel herself softening.

'I dunno. I haven't been hungry. I'm not really hungry now.' She wasn't sure that was true, though. The achy, sicky feeling in her stomach could just be because it was empty.

'You don't need to see him or talk to him. He's just bringing the food and going.'

'Okay. Whatever. He's not coming in, though. The thought of that creep in here . . .' She shuddered.

The doorbell rang a few minutes later. The smell of hot fat wafted through to the lounge when Naz opened the door. It smelled so good that saliva rushed into Sandy's mouth, confirming that she was actually famished. She jumped to her feet and went into the hallway where she caught sight of Den outside on the walkway. He was handing over a white plastic bag bulging with paper parcels.

He looked at her briefly, then quickly turned his eyes away, as if trying to deflect any hostility. It was a submissive thing. She realised he was a bit scared of her. Good! He should be. If she was allowed five minutes alone with him, she'd get the truth out of him. Honestly, she'd beat the shit out of him if she had to.

'Fish and chips for three,' he said, and gave a nervous laugh. 'I've put some extras in. Peas. Curry sauce. Ketchup.'

'Cheers, mate,' Naz said, taking the bag gleefully.

The smell was almost making Sandy feel faint.

'Is that Den?' Kath called from the lounge.

'Yes, Mrs C. Dinner's ready!' he shouted back.

'Come here, love.'

He glanced at Sandy, seeking her approval. She didn't exactly welcome him in, but she did take the bag from Naz and disappear back into the lounge. Den stepped inside tentatively and hovered in the hall.

'Shall I fetch some plates from the kitchen?' Naz said.

'No need. We can eat it like this, can't we?' Kath said, quickly. 'You could fetch some forks.'

'I put some in,' Den said. 'Wooden ones. And serviettes.'

'Bless you. Do you wanna sit down, love?'

Den looked warily at Sandy, who was busy unwrapping a parcel on her knees.

'I'd better get back,' he said. 'I've left Mum serving in the café and she doesn't really like it.'

Kath rooted in her bag and brought out her purse. She unclipped it and started bringing out notes.

'No, no, no!' Den held his hands up. 'This is on us. Honestly.'

'Thank you, love,' said Kath, who was putting her purse away. Sandy had a flashback to the last time she was in the café with Mina. Did she buy her a burger to go with her chips? She couldn't

216

remember. Mina liked it, anyway. A little treat. She rested her chip fork on the side of the polystyrene tray, suddenly disgusted with herself for digging into the food like this when Mina was still missing.

'It's okay. At least the lift is fixed now. Saved my legs!'

'Is it? Well, that's something.'

Den left and they all tucked in. Despite her self-disgust, Sandy couldn't resist the hot food.

'That was nice of him, wasn't it?' said Kath, when she'd come to an end with hers. She'd managed all the fish but had a few chips left over.

'Yeah. Still doesn't mean he's off the hook, though, does it?' said Sandy, looking over at Naz, who was maintaining a poker face. 'I mean, I still think it could be him. They say criminals return to the scene of their crime, don't they? I've never seen him in this block before, and now he's bringing fish and chips.'

'You might have a point there,' said Kath. 'On *Vera* and *Unforgotten* and whatnot, the detectives are always studying who turns up at the victim's funeral or is lurking behind the tape where the murder happened. Not that we're talking about murder here,' she added quickly, 'but you know what I mean. I've got nothing to say against Den, but he's been twice in twelve hours now.'

'Twice?' said Sandy.

Kath nodded. 'Mm. He brought me back home last night. I was feeling a bit funny after . . . you know. I had a very interesting chat with him, actually. He's a very troubled young man . . .'

Naz's ears had pricked up. 'Is there anything you think we should know, Kath?'

'Not specifically. We had a bit of a heart-to-heart. I don't think he's got anyone to really talk to. Bottles things up, if you know what I mean.'

'I do know what you mean, Kath. I do.'

Naz put his polystyrene tray down, moved into the hallway and took out his radio.

Sandy caught Kath eyeing the remains of her chips, even though she hadn't finished her own. 'Do you want these?' she said.

Kath reached out for them. 'If you don't mind, love. I'll take them home, warm them up later. Shame to waste them.'

Day Four

Den

He took the stairs on the way down. He'd been shocked at the state of Sandy's flat. Now he felt a sharp pang of regret. He'd known, deep down, that Mina was neglected. She'd stolen sweets, for goodness' sake, not because she was a bad kid, but because she was hungry, because she had so little joy in her life. Why hadn't he said anything? Why hadn't he rung someone? Because he saw it all the time. There were so many kids like Mina. Was that an excuse?

The smell of disinfectant caught the back of his throat. He walked swiftly out of the stairwell and emerged into the daylight. It was a dull sort of day, the muted light seeming to emphasise the flat tones of the blocks, the paving, the tarmac. Den caught a flash of colour – Day-Glo yellow, the opposite side of the yard. It was Marlon, in his high-vis jacket, carrying a plastic Co-op bag bulging with shopping, and walking purposefully away from the estate. No dog with him this time.

It was Sunday, wasn't it? Den glanced towards the corner, around which was the café. He hesitated and then set off at an angle, across the yard, away from home. Even if he lived round here, who wears their work clothes seven days a week? He followed Marlon out of the yard and through the streets of terraced houses. Nearer the estate the housing was more modern, little rows of two up, two downs with handkerchief-square gardens in front. Beyond them, the terraces were older – red brick stained darker by years of pollution.

Den kept Marlon in sight but maintained his distance. It already felt like he wouldn't need much of an excuse to give Den a good beating. Den knew these streets. They weren't far from the café's lockup garage with its do-it-yourself arsonist's kit. Jesus, he had to get rid of that stuff.

Marlon was heading to the end of the road where a hoarding surrounded a patch of land. An old cinema had been demolished and housing was coming in its place. He'd stopped now. Den waited behind a bus shelter and watched. Marlon put the bag on the ground, undid a padlock on a door in the hoarding, and – with a quick look over his shoulder – opened the door, picked up the bag and stepped inside.

Day Four

Den

'Not on a Sunday, mate,' a man walking past called out to him. Den was snapped out of the trance he'd been in, staring at the opening in the hoarding, wondering whether he should follow Marlon inside. What if Mina was there, still alive, being kept in a shed or a Portakabin or something?

'Sorry?'

'No buses here on a Sunday. If that's what you're waiting for. Oh—' In that moment, Den knew he'd been recognised. 'You're that nonce. The one they arrested.' He walked towards Den.

'I wasn't actually arrested. I was questioned.' Den winced as he heard the word 'actually' come out of his mouth. Why had he said that? It had been as involuntary as his smile, which was back, twitching on and off.

'Oh, pardon me.' The guy's faux politeness was as menacing as his direct aggression. 'My mistake.'

Den tried smiling at him for real. 'That's okay. No problem.'

'What you doing here then?' The guy was advancing and Den started backing away.

'I was . . .' following someone. Yeah, that would help. 'Just going for a walk.'

'Looking for your next victim? People like you make me sick. Where is she? Where's that little girl? What have you done with her?'

He was close now. He wasn't a big guy but he was hard, you could tell and, looking down, Den could see that his right hand was balled into a fist.

'Honestly, I haven't done anything. I don't know where she is.'

Den had backed into a wall now, his heels scraping against the brick. There was nowhere to go. The guy was so close Den could smell his breath – fag smoke and booze, fresh out of the pub for his Sunday pint.

He held his hands up in surrender.

'Please, mate, just let me go. I haven't done anything.'

The guy looked at him for what seemed like a long time, disgust etched into his face.

'If it is you, you'd better hope you do get arrested. People round here will fucking end you.' He turned to go. Just as Den was starting to relax, the guy twisted his head round and spat at Den. The glob of phlegm hit his cheek. He wiped his sleeve across his face, fighting the urge to gag, then stood there, taking in what had happened as the man carried on walking away. Den's legs felt wobbly, like he'd just run a marathon. His breath was coming in fits and starts. He leaned forward and put his hands on his thighs, trying to calm down. At the end of the street, the door in the hoarding was open. Marlon was standing on the pavement, with the dog next to him, looking his way. Den had no idea how long he'd been there, but clearly his cover was blown.

Day Four

Den

He just wanted to get home, hide away. Marlon and the dog were running now, running towards him. Shit. Even with a head start of twenty metres or so, Den had no chance of outpacing him. He'd look stupid even trying, so he took a few deep breaths and stood his ground.

'Hey,' he said, unconvincingly, when Marlon was close. 'All right?'

Marlon's face was a picture of contempt. 'Are you following me? Are you snooping?'

Den swallowed hard. There was only one way to go now – he'd have to brazen it out. 'Yes,' he said.

'You what?'

'Yes. I was following you. I wondered what you were doing in your work clothes on a Sunday.'

'What the hell's it got to do with you?' He stepped closer to Den, invading his space.

'Everyone thinks I had something to do with Mina disappearing, because I was the last one to see her, but you came into the café just after she left, so I reckon maybe you saw her too.'

Doubt flickered in Marlon's eyes. 'No, mate. I never saw her. Don't think I was even in the café on Wednesday.'

An alarm bell rang in Den's head, triggering a pulse of excitement. Marlon was lying and Den could prove it.

'You were there. It's all on CCTV. Did you see her outside? Was she leaving when you were going out?'

'I never saw her at all that day.'

Marlon put his hand up to his face and rubbed the back of his neck and Den realised he was nervous.

'You knew who she was, though.'

'What?'

'I've seen you in the café talking to her.'

'Yeah, like I said, she's in my daughter's class at school.'

'Are they friends? Has Mina been round to yours?'

'Just fuck off, man. I don't answer to you.'

He was sweating now, though, little beads of moisture glistening on his top lip.

'I don't know if they're friends. I don't live at home at the moment. Oh, just fuck off. It's nothing to do with you. I haven't seen her. She's not on my site, so you can stop following me like a little creep.'

Somehow Marlon was back on the front foot, his swagger restored.

'Yes. I mean, no.' Den just wanted to extricate himself without getting a pasting now. 'It was only . . . I'm desperate to find her.'

'Aren't we all? Now fuck off before I set the dog on you.'

Den forced himself to look into Marlon's eyes. They held each other's gaze for moment, then Den turned and started walking away, praying that Marlon would just let him go. He made himself maintain a normal pace, even though his instinct was to break into a run and keep going until he got home.

At the end of the street, he glanced over his shoulder. Marlon was still by the bus stop, watching him. His dog was squatting in the gutter. Den realised that he still didn't know why Marlon had gone to work on a day when the site was closed. Was he just looking after the guard dog or was it more than that? Was this more than a workplace? He'd left a bag of groceries there. Perhaps it was home. Perhaps, despite his outright denial, he had company.

Day Four

Sandy

'It has now been four days since Mina was last seen in person and we remain as committed as ever to locating her and bringing her home to her family.

'Our officers have now got a very good picture of Mina's movements on the afternoon of Wednesday 14th November. We know that she came back to the estate and we're very confident of finding out what happened next. The whole community is working together on this but we need you to come forward if you know anything at all.'

The perpetual breeze blew around the yard as the press conference began. Sandy stood between her parents, feeling numb, not knowing where to look as DI Haynes addressed the cameras.

'Are you linking the attack on Sam Stirling with Mina's disappearance?'

'We are not ruling anything out in our investigation. In that connection we are urgently trying to find Daniel McVey, known as Danno. He's sixteen, five foot eleven, white with a distinctive

226

shaved eyebrow. We ask the public not to approach him, but to ring 999 immediately.'

The officer took more questions and fielded any directed at Sandy. All the way through, although he was in the spotlight, Sandy felt that all eyes were on her, looking for a reaction. She didn't know how to act. What was the 'right' way to look?

When it was over they trooped back to the flat. As they started to move, Sandy allowed herself a glance up at the journalists and onlookers gathered around. At the back of the crowd she saw the unmistakeable bulk of Frank's collector. He was standing perfectly still, arms folded across his chest. She hadn't got anything to give him apart from the extra £50 she'd got on Wednesday night. He might as well have it – the thought of spending the money she'd earned when she should have been home with Mina made her feel physically sick. She was so behind with the payments, though, it would be a drop in the ocean and she didn't know when she'd be able to get any more. What was he doing here? He surely wouldn't come after her with the police in her flat? He was just standing. Looking. Was it some kind of message?

As they entered Nelson House, Dad shepherded them towards the lift quickly, past the dark patch on the concrete floor. Mum seemed to be holding her breath while they waited for the doors to open. This was a long way from Epsom – manicured lawns, shiny saloon cars, no dog mess in the street or overflowing bins. *Welcome to my world,* Sandy thought.

Jodie had told her that the lad who had been stabbed claimed to have seen Mina running in here on Wednesday. She took a deep breath, hoping to catch a fragment, a particle, the slightest note hanging in the air left behind by her daughter, but all she got was the sharp, chemical pine-scented twang of the stuff they used to wipe away the blood.

In the lift, Mum cleared her throat and said, 'Dad and I have been talking. We wondered if you'd like to come home for a few days.'

Home. What a loaded word. Sandy could feel her hackles rising.

'Leave here? When Mina's still missing?'

'The police would keep in touch. We could bring you back whenever you needed.'

They didn't think Mina was coming back, did they? They thought she was dead.

'I have to be here. I wasn't here on Wednesday. I have to be here now.'

'It's this place, though.' Mum sniffed disapprovingly. 'We don't like to think of you waiting here on your own.'

Sandy gave an ironic little laugh. 'I'm never on my own – I've got my minders, sorry, liaison officers.'

'That's not the same as family.'

Family. Another loaded word. She left it suspended between them as the lift reached the third floor and the doors opened.

Naz had gone up the stairs and arrived at the walkway at the same time as them.

'After you,' he said, holding one arm out.

They filed along towards number seven. Outside, Sandy hesitated.

'I'll just check on Kath. It's not like her to miss out on the fun. She didn't look well earlier.'

Mum nodded and Sandy could tell she was pleased to see signs of neighbourliness in her.

She rang Kath's bell, but there was no response. She knocked on the door, then bent down to the letter box. 'Kath? You all right?'

After a little while she heard Kath's voice. 'Sandy? Is there any news?'

'No, just back from the press thing. You okay?'

She expected her to open the door, but she didn't.

'I'm fine. Just tired. I'm going to have a little nod in my chair. I'll see you later.'

Sandy straightened up, then found her keys and opened her own front door.

228

'Do you think she is all right?' Mum said when they were inside and having a cup of tea in the lounge.

'I dunno. Must've got a nasty shock yesterday. She was the one who found . . . you know, the boy downstairs.'

'Oh, how awful. She was very kind to us yesterday. She's a lovely woman. Shame she's on her own.'

'She's got family, Mum. They're in Australia.'

'Oh yes, she said. No photos, though, of her grandchildren. Only a really old photo of her husband and daughter at the seaside.'

'God, Mum, you don't miss much, do you? We're not all like you – photos in silver frames. I haven't got any . . .' She scanned round the room and realised how sad it looked, how much nicer it would have been with some pictures up. Another thing to fix if Mina came home. If. When. Oh God, four days without a trace of her.

Day Four

Den

'Sundays are always quiet, Dad.'

'Not this bloody quiet.'

Den could tell his mood was darkening as the afternoon drew to a close. A plastic bag blew against the front window.

'The whole estate is in shock,' he said gently. 'No one's going out, having dinner or a cheeky cake. It'll get better.'

Den wasn't sure if he was even listening. They both looked up as the bell pinged and the street cleaner came in and walked wearily up towards them.

'That's it. I'm done for the day. Bloody hate working on Sundays.'

'What can I get you?' said Den.

'Tea and a bacon sarnie, please. Plenty of brown sauce.'

Dad retreated to the kitchen and Den could hear the sizzle as the bacon hit the hot plate. The man plonked himself down at the nearest table, obviously open to a chat.

'You don't work seven days, do you?' Den said, handing him his tea.

'No, five-day shifts.'

'More to come back to after your day off, though, eh?'

The guy took a slurp of tea and added another spoonful of sugar, stirring it so vigorously that it slopped over the edge.

'Nah, mate. The days I'm not here, Harry does it. About my age, hair in a poncy ponytail. Fancies himself.'

'Oh yeah, I've seen him.'

'You after a job with the council, are you?'

Den snorted. 'Might be better for everyone. I'm not sure I'm good for this place. Think I put customers off their food.'

'Don't worry about it. People have short memories. They'll be back.'

Dad came through from the kitchen carrying a plate with a doorstop sandwich, bacon wobbling out of it on every side. He walked round and put it on the table.

'Blimey, that's a good 'un.'

'You deserve it, mate, cleaning up everyone's shit. Anyway, I'm going to close up now. You're our last customer today, so you get to use up the bacon. Don't want it going to waste.'

The guy took a big bite, lurching forward over his plate to try to catch the drips of brown sauce. He made an appreciative grunt, as he wrestled to get through the crust. Den started giving the other tables a final wipe-down.

Dad went to stand near the front window, looking out.

'You must have been here twenty years or so,' the cleaner said. 'I remember the woman who had it before you, it was a pie and mash place then. Before that it was a newsagent.'

Dad turned round. 'You lived here a long time, then?'

'All my life.' He wiped a dribble of sauce from his chin with a paper serviette.

'Seen a few changes then.'

'Yes and no. Shops come and go. Not so many of them selling proper stuff – butchers, bakers, greengrocers – more phone shops and charity shops and God knows what. They bought in parking meters and double yellow lines all over the place. And put that crossing in down the road after a kiddie got knocked down there. It's still the same place, though. I wouldn't live anywhere else. My missus wants to move to the south coast but it's not going to happen.'

'Not a bad idea. Sell up. Start again somewhere. Bit of sea air.'

The man used the last bit of bread to mop up the sauce off his plate. Then he sat back and drained his mug of tea.

'No, mate. It's full of oldies down there. You'd die of boredom. There's always something going on here.' He scraped his chair back. 'Anyway, that was the business. Thanks, mate. See you tomorrow.'

Dad let him out and then turned the Open sign around. 'That's it,' he said. 'That's enough.'

Den was by the till. 'Here, Dad.' He took the bunch of keys and swung his arm back ready to throw them across the café.

'It's all right. I won't lock it for a minute. Your mum's going out. She's going to her knitting thing – knit and natter or whatever.'

'Stitch and bitch,' said Mum, appearing from the stairs, bundled up in her coat and carrying a zipped-up stripy cloth bag.

'That's what I said, wasn't it? I don't want you walking to the community centre on your own, though. Not with a kid with a knife on the loose.'

Mum shook her head. 'There's always a kid running round with a knife, Tony. We all know what it's like round here.'

'Yeah, and you know what I mean. It feels different at the moment. Den'll walk you over, won't you, son?'

Den had switched off a little, lost in his own thoughts. He came to when he heard his name mentioned. 'What?'

'Wake up, soft lad. You'll walk your mum to the community centre, won't you?'

'Sure.'

'Here, take that plate of cakes with you, Linda. There's another plate there for Kath and Sandy. Den can take that round on his way back.'

The resurgence of Dad's bossiness was almost welcome. It was better than subdued moodiness anyway.

'Can I just fetch my coat? It's brass monkeys out there.'

'Okay.' Dad waited as Den went upstairs and then came back again.

Dad slapped him on the back as he went out of the door. 'Good lad,' he said. 'I'll sweep up down here. It'll all be done in a minute. You keep your eyes open and look after your mum.'

Den thought he heard something else. Had Dad added, 'Love you,' on the end? It didn't seem likely.

'What?' he said, turning to look at Dad.

'Nothing. Go on, she's miles ahead. Off you go. Piss off.'

It wasn't far to the community centre, but Den was happy enough to walk Mum over there. The yellow ribbons on the lampposts were already looking tatty and sad. He wondered how long it would be before people took them down. What if Mina was never found?

As they passed the church and approached the crumbling mishmash of buildings that made up the community centre, Mum said, 'You know, I remembered where I'd seen that man, the one at the vigil.'

'Marlon? Yeah?'

'It was here. They run a family contact session in one of the other rooms while our stitch and bitch is on. It's where estranged parents can see their kids in a supervised place. He was kicked out. I don't know what he'd done but we all saw him escorted from the building. They told him he couldn't come back.'

'I don't like the guy, but that's got to hurt.'

'Mm. You never know what people are carrying around with them, do you?'

Day Four

Kath

It had only been four days but I felt like I couldn't take any more. My nerves were shredded and I was breaking down physically too; my blood numbers were completely up the creek. I put a nice film on in the afternoon, but my eyes weren't the best and my heart wasn't in it. I nodded off several times and kept waking with a start, remembering the boy. I fancied I could smell blood in my nostrils, taste the metallic tang of it on my tongue. It was all my fault – I couldn't stop thinking about it.

I felt like keeping my door shut and hiding away from the world forever, but being a hermit is never a good idea, particularly if you're feeling a bit down. Den saying that the lift was working again was such a boost. I could get a little fresh air and stretch my legs without having to face those wretched stairs again. I'd take my trolley and maybe pick up a pint or two of milk or something different for tea. It was starting to get dark. *Come on, Kath. Stir your stumps.*

I got myself up and squeezed my poor swollen feet into my shoes, put my coat on and checked round the flat. Nice and tidy, just how I liked it. I looked at the urn on the mantelpiece. 'Bye, love,' I said. Old habits die hard.

I heaved the trolley out behind me and then shut the door. My knees hurt even walking along the flat walkway. It's no fun getting old. I wouldn't let it put me off, though. I called the lift and felt a surge of relief to see the numbers changing – 0, 1, 2, 3. That was better. I manoeuvred the trolley inside and pressed 0 for the ground floor. Just as the door was closing, a hand grabbed the edge of it and braced, causing it to open again. There was Danno, grinning at me.

'Nearly missed it,' he said, stepping smartly in.

My first thought was to get straight out, go to number seven and tell Jodie or Naz or whoever was there, but he planted himself between me and the door. It was obvious he wouldn't let me go. The door closed again and my stomach lurched as we started going down.

I might have said before that I wasn't scared of lads like him, but I was. I knew what he could do. Now he was looming over me, staring at me like a wolf. My Ray always used to tell me to pretend to be braver or more confident or whatever. Act the part. *'Fake it till you make it, Kath.'* He knew all about that. Easier said than done, though, but that's what I needed to do now.

'There are people looking for you,' I said.

'I know this estate better than anyone. They won't find me.'

3 . . . 2 . . .

I'm bigger than everyone. I'm better than everyone. I'd met his sort before.

'Where've you sprung from now?'

He tapped the side of his nose. 'I got friends,' he said. 'I was waiting for you. Watching.'

My heart started fluttering. I tried to keep calm but it was difficult to get my breath. I only needed to keep him talking – keep things civil – for another few seconds and then we'd be at the ground.

1 . . . 0.

We bumped down onto the ground floor. Thank God, I thought, it's over.

Then he pressed 'hold' and the doors stayed closed.

'What are you doing?'

'We need to have a little chat.'

'I don't think we've got anything to talk about.'

'The thing is, I don't like cops and I don't like grasses.'

He had one hand on the lift button and the other in his pocket. Was that where he kept his knife? I tried to back away from him, but there was nowhere to go.

'I know what you did to that poor boy.'

He shook his head. 'That wasn't me. I didn't go anywhere near him.'

'Didn't want to get your hands dirty,' I said. 'Why would you when you've got others to do it for you?'

The grin was back. 'Not as daft as you look, Miss Marple.'

'All right,' I said, 'so what if I told the police what Sam told me. It was because of the girl. Everyone's worried about her. It's been days now.'

'Yeah, and I didn't do a thing to her.'

'No?'

'No! I swear! I chased her, just for fun, like. That's all. I stopped at the bottom of the stairs. I heard her run all the way up. She was crying.'

There wasn't an ounce of regret in his voice. I tell you, if I'd been the one with a knife in my pocket, I'd have stabbed him there and then. What a nasty piece of work.

'She was alive. I told the cops. That's why they let me go. But I didn't appreciate being there in the first place. Like I said, I don't like grasses.'

He'd brought his face close to mine now. I could smell his breath – stale food and cigarette smoke.

We both started when there was a bang on the door behind him. Someone had kicked or thumped it.

This was my chance. Summoning up as much puff as I could, I shouted, 'Help! We're stuck in here!'

At the same time, I jabbed at the top of his foot with my walking stick, digging down hard.

Everything combined to startle him. He let go of the button momentarily and the door started to open. Den was waiting outside.

'Mrs C!' he exclaimed. 'Are you okay? Oh!'

Danno barged past him, sending a plate of cakes or something flying into the air, and legged it out of the stairwell. 'Go after him!' I gasped. Then my legs started to go and I slid gently down the metal wall of the lift.

Day Four

Den

Den's first thought when he saw Kath collapse was that she'd been stabbed. There was no way he could leave her. He crouched next to her on the floor.

'Are you okay, Mrs C? Did he hurt you?'

'He didn't touch me. I'm fine. It's just my legs, not used to going in this lift. I've lost my sea legs.'

He'd heard that people sometimes didn't realise they'd been stabbed, didn't feel the pain until later. He checked the front of her coat but couldn't see any blood.

'It's probably the shock. I need to call the cops, quickly, before he disappears again. Then maybe an ambulance.'

'I don't need an ambulance. I'll be fine if you help me up.'

The lift door closed.

'Oh Gawd, where are we going now?'

They stayed where they were. Den tried his mobile but couldn't get a signal.

'I'll need to go outside to ring. Do you want to get up, or stay here and I'll take you home as soon as I've rung?'

Kath looked confused. Too many questions. She didn't answer.

'Okay. Stay there for one minute.' He pressed the button to open the door again and dashed outside, picking his way through the bits of shattered china and splattered cakes. He reported the sighting and darted back to the lift. The door had closed again. He pressed the up button and it opened. Kath was still on the floor but was now making efforts to stand up. Den supported her elbow and handed her the walking stick, which had been lying next to her. After a bit of a struggle, they managed to get her upright.

'Let's get you home.'

They went up to the third floor. Kath was quiet. Her breathing was very rapid. It seemed to Den that however hard she tried to get air into her lungs, it didn't seem to be enough. He held on to her elbow with one hand and pulled her trolley, which was surprisingly heavy, with the other as they walked along to her front door.

'Have you got your keys?'

'What, love?'

'Your keys.'

He wondered if she had her hearing aids in. He mimed turning a key in a lock as he spoke to her.

'Oh yes.' She started fumbling in her pocket and produced the keys. She handed them to him and he opened the door and let them in. He parked the trolley in the hall and led her into the lounge. There he helped her take her coat off, put it over the back of the chair and watched as she sank onto the sofa.

'It's all right now. You're home,' he said. 'Listen, I'll put the kettle on and we can sit quietly until the police get here.'

'Police? I don't want them here, Den! I don't want them!' She was surprisingly agitated. Den watched as she gasped for breath and then clutched her chest. He should have called that ambulance.

'It's okay, Mrs C. It's all right. I'll stay here with you.'

'They should be out looking for him, not bothering me! Tell them to go away, Den!'

'They're not even here yet.'

'Don't leave me, Den. Just sit here for a minute.'

He did as he was told. They sat quietly together. Den could hear the breath rasping in and out of her. Two big shocks in as many days. That would be enough to rattle anyone.

'It's my fault, Ray. I'm so sorry,' she said after a while, so softly he almost didn't hear it. Ray? That was her husband's name, wasn't it? He took her hand in his.

'It's really not, Mrs C. You mustn't think like that. You did the right thing.'

She turned to look at him and it was almost like she was waking up. Her eyes seemed to focus and her face brightened. 'Oh Den, it's you.'

'Yes, Mrs C. It's me. You've had a bit of a shock, but you're all right now.'

She patted his hand.

'You're a good boy, aren't you?'

The ring of the doorbell pierced the stuffy air. Kath looked panicked again.

'They've come to get me. Don't let them in.'

Den didn't know whether she was joking or not, but one look at her face told him she wasn't. Poor Mrs C. She was losing her grip on reality.

'It's all right. I'll go and talk to them.' Den leaped to his feet and went into the hall.

It was Naz, the police officer who'd had the chips at lunchtime. Behind him sirens were wailing, the sound swirling up to the third floor, bouncing off the walls of the blocks around the courtyard. They must have caught up with Danno. Maybe this was all going to be over soon.

'Are you here to interview Mrs C?' Den asked.

There was a flicker in Naz's eyes which startled Den.

'No, I heard you were here. Den, you need to go home. It's just come through on my radio. The café's on fire.'

Day Four

Sandy

She heard the news on Naz's radio. It had been crackling and buzzing with messages for the past half-hour. There'd been a sighting of the lad they were looking for: Danno. It sounded like he'd been here, in Nelson House.

'What's going on?'

'Sit tight, Sandy. Mrs Cartright saw Danno in the lift. We'll get him now.'

She felt a sharp stab of hope – would she, could she see Mina again soon?

There were footsteps outside and Kath's door opened and closed. Then the sirens started up. It was eerie. There was something in the air. After waiting for four days, stuck here with no news, things were ramping up. Things were happening.

She wanted to be out there, doing something. Just sitting here with the walls closing in was unbearable. She got up and Naz mirrored her.

'You really should stay here,' he said.

'I need a fag, some air.'

She went out onto the walkway. A couple of men were running across the courtyard – she wondered if they were plain-clothes cops. The sirens were coming from outside the estate. Had they got him yet? She was surprised to find that her hands were shaking as she tried to light her cigarette. It felt like this was it, whatever it was. She didn't know if she could face it alone. She wished she had somebody with her – not a babysitting copper – somebody who cared. Should she text Brett? Ring her parents? They'd all take the best part of an hour to reach here, even if they dropped everything. She was going to have to do this on her own.

The air above the rank of shops was cloudy in the darkness. She watched as the yellow streetlights illuminated the bottom of a patch of mist. No, not mist. Smoke. She could smell it now. A different note to her cigarette smoke. Something was going up.

She stepped into her doorway. 'Naz?' she said. 'Look at this.'

He came out to join her. 'It's just come through on the radio. It's the café.'

'Shit.'

She was sorely tempted to go and look, but then Naz said, 'Den's next door with Kath. I need to tell him.'

Sandy watched as he knocked on the door of number eight. He was clearly nervous, pulling at the hem of his jacket. The door opened and Den peered out. As Naz broke the news, Den put his hand up to his face and breathed, 'No!'

He looked over his shoulder, then caught sight of Sandy watching him.

'Sandy,' he said, 'I've got to go but Mrs C's not right. She was in the lift with that lad. She's had a fright and is a bit confused. Can you sit with her?'

'Yeah, sure. You go. Go on.'

He sped off along the walkway. Sandy waited for a minute to see him shoot out of the bottom of the stairwell and across the yard. There was more of a glow over the rank of shops now. It wasn't just streetlight – there were flames. It was mesmerising.

'Jesus Christ,' she muttered, and turned to go in to see Kath. Perhaps she'd like to come out and watch with her. Take her mind off whatever she'd been through earlier. They could wait together.

Day Four

Den

You idiot! It was all Den could think as he sped across the courtyard. He couldn't believe Dad had gone through with his stupid plan. He should have smelled a rat when Dad sent him out with Mum.

He'd have to try to control himself when he saw Dad, so he didn't give the game away, but it would be so difficult not to shake him until his teeth rattled. For fuck's sake. Their home! Their business!

He turned the corner and was met with a battery of fire engines. Police were trying to get the crowd, faces lit up by the glow from the fire, to stand back. Den barged his way to the front. A uniformed officer put his arm across Den's front.

'Stand back! You can't go any nearer!'

'I live here!' Den shouted. 'I live over the café. It's my family's business!'

The officer rested his hand on Den's shoulder. 'Okay, okay. Stay here, please.' He took his radio out of its holster, turned away slightly and spoke into it. 'Yup. Okay. Sir, just stay with me for a minute. Someone's coming over.'

Den looked along the front of the crowd, trying to locate Dad. He couldn't see him. Maybe he was lying low somewhere. He got his mobile out and rang Dad's number, scanning the crowd again. The phone rang out.

A fire officer approached them. 'I understand you live here. Can I take your details, please? Do you know if anyone's in there?'

'No, I don't think so. There's three of us. Mum's gone out. Dad was locking up. I don't where he is—' Den stopped. He was covered in sweat from running here and from the heat given off by the fire, but now he shivered. 'I don't know where he is.'

Orange flames were rolling around the inside of the café. Black smoke was pouring out of one of the windows of the flat, billowing up into the night sky.

'Have you been in there?' said Den. 'Has anyone checked it out?'

'Not yet. The heat's too intense. We'll get it under control first. Do you think your dad's still in there?'

'I don't know. I don't know.'

Den rang Dad's number again. No reply. He killed the call and rang Mum. She picked up after several rings. Den could hear voices and laughter in the background.

'Mum?' Words suddenly failed him. He didn't know how to tell her. 'Mum, the café, the flat. I'm outside now. I'm sorry, there's a fire.'

Day Four

Sandy

She called out, 'Knock, knock,' as she breezed into Kath's flat, walking straight through to the lounge. Kath was sitting on the sofa. She turned her head as Sandy came into the room and it looked very much like Sandy had startled her awake.

'Knock, knock,' Kath echoed, then worked her mouth like she was chewing on something or trying to get her teeth into the right place. 'That's it, Mina. Knock, knock.'

Sandy frowned at her. Mina? What was she talking about?

She sat opposite Kath and leaned forward. 'It's me, Kath. Sandy.'

Her mouth was still working, her eyes travelling round the room, not settling on anything. She finally looked at Sandy's face.

'Sandy. Oh, Sandy, just like your daughter. Knock, knock.'

'What are you talking about, Kath?'

The old woman looked troubled. 'Nothing. It's nothing,' she said. She flapped one of her hands in the air like she was batting something away. 'I don't want to get her into trouble.'

'You're worrying me now, Kath. What trouble? What's going on?'

Kath shifted in her chair, grunting as she tried to move a cushion behind her. 'She wasn't allowed to talk to me, was she? You had rules for her. Straight home. Don't talk to anyone.'

'Yeah, that's right.'

'Well, she did talk to me once, or rather I talked to her. I heard her come home and I talked to her through the letter box. She wouldn't open the door – she was a good girl. After that, we were friends. She used to knock on the wall, let me know she was home safe and sound.' She paused and blinked rapidly and Sandy felt her heart breaking, just a little. 'Please don't be cross with me.'

'Kath, I'm not cross. I'm . . . I'm glad she did that. I'm glad she had you here.'

Kath seemed to relax a little. 'She's a good girl, Sandy.'

'Yes, Kath, she is.'

Sandy had a tight feeling at the back of her throat, a ball of grief trying to get out. She'd left the front door open and the wailing sound of the sirens swirled into the flat along with the smell of smoke. The feeling of doom she'd had earlier, of things coming to a head, hadn't gone away.

'Kath, the café's on fire.'

'Is that why Den left?'

'Yeah.'

'The poor love. That's his home.'

'I know. It's really going up. You can see it from here. Do you want to look?'

'I don't know, love. I'm tired. You go and look and then come back and tell me about it.'

She really did look done in.

'It's okay,' Sandy said. 'I'll sit with you.'

Kath waved her hand again. 'No, you don't want to miss all the excitement. Take a picture on your phone to show me.'

Sandy didn't need telling twice. Anxiety was flushing through her body. It was too hard to sit still while the world was burning outside. She jumped up. 'I'll be back in a minute.'

She joined Naz, who was outside her flat. It seemed like everyone was on the walkways now. Sandy could see people dotted along the balconies on every level of every block. It was like a community happening – a weird sort of event drawing them all together with horrified fascination. A column of black smoke was billowing up from the shops. Fragments of ash were being carried in the air, dancing delicately like black snowflakes. Sandy brushed some away from the edge of the balcony before she leaned her forearms there and looked down into the yard.

People were streaming across, all heading towards the café to get a better look. Idiots, she thought, you got the best view from up here, rather than at the back of a crowd at ground level. She scanned around again. Amazing how you can live in a place and not even know what your neighbours looked like. She hardly recognised anyone.

Hearing a noise behind her, she turned round. Kath was emerging from her front door. She had her coat on and was trundling her trolley.

'Come to join me?' Sandy said.

'I want to go and see if Den and his family are all right. They've been very good to me.'

'Kath, there's hundreds of people there now. It'll be chaos. Someone will be looking after Den. I'd leave it if I were you.'

'It's important, Sandy. I owe him.'

'I'll come with you then.'

'I'd rather you stayed here, Sandy.' This was Naz. She'd almost forgotten about him. 'There's a lot going on. It's better if you're here.'

Her stomach lurched. She wasn't the only one expecting more news, then.

'Is there—? Have you—?' She couldn't get the words out.

'There's nothing I can tell you yet,' he said. 'It's still a waiting game. I'd rather you waited here.'

'Okay.' She turned around. 'Kath, will you wait with me?'

But Kath had gone. Sandy looked along the walkway and saw her disappearing into the stairwell. She felt a pang of guilt. Den had asked her to keep an eye on Kath and, to be honest, she did seem a bit confused. Should she go after her? She hesitated for a little longer, watching the smoke rise over the rooftops and the increasing activity on the ground.

Her eye was caught by Kath and her red tartan trolley emerging from the building. She was walking very slowly, leaning heavily on her stick. She looked around and then, instead of heading towards the café, she turned and disappeared into the estate. *Oh no*, thought Sandy, *she's wandering off. She really is in a state. I'll go and bring her back.* Then there was a loud bang and an accompanying roar from the crowd, as something inside the café exploded.

Day Four

Den

Den could only stand and watch like everyone else. Except, of course, he wasn't like everyone else. This wasn't an event, something to be filmed and tweeted, the neighbourhood's own personal Bonfire Night. This was his home. This was everything. And it was going up in flames.

It didn't take long for Mum to get there. Her stitch and bitch friends came with her, a supportive cluster of women, flanking her like a guard of honour. Mum made a beeline for Den. They hugged and then she asked the obvious question, 'Where's your dad?'

Dad. The idiot behind all this. The fool who couldn't see that setting fire to your life wasn't a good solution.

Dad. The man who had taken him to football when he was little, who'd fetched him home when everything had gone wrong at uni, who'd made tough love into an art form.

'I don't know, Mum.'

She clutched his arms and stared into his face. The light from the fire was dancing in her agonised eyes. Then she opened her phone and stabbed at it. It was no use Den telling her he'd already done that. After a minute, she held it away from her ear and shook her head.

'Are the Singhs out?'

'Yeah, they're over there.'

'And David next door?'

'Yeah, he's with them. Look.'

Den pointed to a group further along. She squinted in that direction, then nodded.

They both turned to face the fire and watched wordlessly. There were flames inside the café – licking round the tables and chairs, consuming them. It was unreal. There was such beauty and power mixed up with the horror of it.

'If he'd finished cleaning, he'd have gone upstairs, put the telly on.' They both looked to the first-floor windows. They were open, with smoke billowing out. If he'd been up there, Den thought, he'd be at the window, wouldn't he? They could get a ladder to him. It would be okay.

'Did you know about this?' Mum's question caught him off guard.

'About what, Mum?'

She nodded towards the fire. 'It's not a very original way out of your problems, is it?'

'Mum, what are you saying?'

'I'm just saying that I do the books. I know how bad things are. And I know how daft your dad can be.'

Den looked behind them, checking that no one could overhear. 'Shh,' he said. 'We can't even talk about this.'

Surely with this many people fighting it, they'd get it under control soon, be able to get inside and find out if Dad really was in there.

The explosion seemed to come from nowhere – shaking the ground, blasting out the café windows, sending out a shower of glass. Instinctively, the whole crowd shrank back even though they were out of range. The fire officers retreated too, walking backwards while still directing torrents of water at the blaze.

Day Four

Sandy

She should go after her, Sandy thought. She was obviously not right. It would be easy to catch up with her and bring her back.

'Naz, I'm just going to fetch Kath back. I think she's confused.'

'I'll come with you,' Naz said.

'There's no need . . .'

Then she saw in his expression that he was acting under instructions – to stick to her like glue. She couldn't be bothered to argue with him.

'Okay, I'll just fetch my bag and keys.'

She turned to go into her own flat and saw that Kath's door was open. As far as Sandy knew, Kath had never left it open before, even when she'd been popping next door. More evidence that she wasn't with it.

She had better check inside, see if she could find Kath's keys and then close up for her.

She walked into number eight. It was just how it had been when she'd visited to use Kath's bathroom. Everything spick and span, the heating up too high for comfort, every surface occupied by

252

an ornament or knick-knack. She checked the kitchen, including the top couple of drawers, the most likely places to keep keys. Nothing there. A drawing on the fridge caught her eye. A rainbow and some writing. 'Thank You.' Oh Mina. Kath was right. She was a good girl.

Sandy went into the lounge, hoping to find a handbag or maybe a purse with keys attached on a ring. There wasn't anything on the floor. The TV remote was on the arm of the sofa. Some magazines were in a neat pile on the coffee table. The framed photo of Kath's husband and daughter at the seaside was on the mantelpiece. That photo. Why was it odd? Then she remembered what her mum had said. There was only that picture of Kath's daughter. There weren't any of her as an older child or as an adult, and there were no photos of the grandchildren in Australia either. Sandy looked at the shelves in the alcoves either side of the fireplace, at the array of little animals and figures. No kangaroos or koala bears. No snow globes with Sydney Opera House inside.

She turned back to the mantelpiece. There was something missing. She remembered how Kath had made her jump when she touched the urn. 'My Ray's in there.' Now there was a gap, just an empty plinth where the urn had been. There was something on the side of the plinth facing the wall. Sandy picked it up and turned it round in her hands. It was a plaque, a shiny brass one, with letters engraved into it:

Elizabeth Violet Cartright, 1965–1980

'Our Evie'

Day Four

Den

He tried Dad's number one more time. Nothing. The fire crews were training their hoses through the first-floor windows now, trying to quench the flames from above. The café and the flat were gone, but Den hoped to God they could stop it spreading to either side.

Someone tapped him on the shoulder. He spun round. It was Marlon in his high-vis jacket.

'I'm so sorry about the café, man.'

Den looked at him. Those words. They could be sympathy or apology. Den searched the other man's face for clues. What was going on here?

'Are you?' he said. 'Sorry?'

Marlon looked surprised. 'Yeah . . . 'course.'

'Well, just keep it to yourself.'

'Den, that's enough,' Mum said.

Marlon held his hands up. 'Hey, mate, just being a good neighbour.'

'You're not welcome here.' Den repeated Marlon's words back to him.

'Den!'

Marlon started walking away, saying, 'It's okay. It's cool.' He was almost out of earshot when Den heard the stinger: 'Hell of a way to get rid of evidence, though.'

Den narrowed his eyes. He could feel Mum's hand on his arm but nothing would stop him now.

'What did you say?'

Marlon turned his head. A little smile was flickering at the corner of his mouth. He was laughing at him. A red surge of fury ripped through Den. All the frustration and anger and hurt of the past few days crystallised in this moment. He barged at Marlon with both hands out and shoved him hard in the middle of his ribcage. Caught off guard, Marlon staggered sideways, lost his footing and fell to the ground.

Den stood over him, fighting the urge to kick his head and keep kicking. The man was sprawled out at an awkward angle. Den looked down at Marlon's work boots. They were spattered with paint. Nothing unusual there, he supposed, except that in the glow of the fire it looked as if it was red. Red paint. Like the stuff that had been daubed across their shutters, that was now, no doubt, blistering against the metal as it twisted and buckled.

Red paint. Dog mess. Their tormentor had been a grown man, not a bunch of kids. Did he hate them enough to set fire to the café? What if Marlon had wanted to get rid of the CCTV footage? Could this really be his work and not Dad's after all?

'Did you do this? Was this you?' Den shouted, his outstretched arm indicating the burning building.

Marlon held his arm across his forehead, shielding himself. 'No, mate. You've got me all wrong.'

Den pulled his foot back, ready to aim a kick.

Mum grabbed his arm. 'Den, what are you doing?'

'This guy,' he said. 'He's the one harassing us – the paint and everything. He was talking to Mina a few days before she disappeared. It was on our CCTV. I reckon it was him hanging about the school too.'

People were gathering round now. A uniformed police officer had joined them. Den recognised her as Jodie, one of the ones liaising with Sandy.

'You need to search the building site in Sycamore Road,' he said. 'I think that's where he's got her. He's in and out there seven days a week.'

Marlon was sitting up now, holding his hands up as if in surrender. 'Whoa, whoa, whoa – I might have sprayed a bit of paint around, but I never took that little girl. Yeah, I spoke to her, but she's in my daughter's class; I wanted her to give Rosa a message. I'm in and out of the site because I live there. I've had nowhere else to go since my wife kicked me out.'

Jodie stepped forward. 'I need you to come with me, sir. I'm arresting you on suspicion of criminal damage.' That'll do for starters, Den thought. There were jeers coming from the crowd as Marlon got to his feet, some of them aimed at Jodie, others at Marlon.

'Leave him. He hasn't done anything! That's harassment. This is the guy that attacked him!' one of Marlon's mates shouted, gesturing at Den.

But others had Mina uppermost in their minds. 'They've got him!' someone shouted. 'He's the one!'

People were starting to push and shove. There was an edge to it all, like things could really kick off. Den could see that Jodie was determined but there was a glint of uncertainty in her eyes, even fear. She radioed for help, as she was jostled in the back and nearly lost her footing.

Marlon, towering over her, put his hand under her elbow to support her. Then he looked around at the crowd. 'Hey, it's all cool. I'm going. It's fine. Everyone calm down.' It seemed he wasn't ready to relinquish his community leader status yet and his words had some effect on the people nearest to them.

The crowd parted and Den watched as Marlon let himself be led towards a squad car.

Was this nearly tied up now? Was Marlon telling the truth or would a search of the site finally find Mina? Den looked towards the wreckage of his home and a thought that had been niggling him earlier, before he went to see Kath, was back again.

Now he remembered what he'd wanted to ask her. The umbrella. Mina had it with her, tucked into her bag on Wednesday. If she had dumped it when leaving the café, Harry, the relief cleaner, would have picked it up when he was doing the bins on Thursday morning. So it must have appeared sometime on Thursday. If Mina had left it there, she would have been seen. Someone else had put it there. Someone had *planted* it.

Thursday was the day that more evidence had turned up in the form of Mina's scrunchie, too. He or Dad swept the floor every night after closing. They never went upstairs without leaving the café spick and span. How, then, had Kath spotted it on the floor by a table on Thursday afternoon? Kath, with her glasses as thick as bottle ends, her wheezy chest and dodgy knees. She'd somehow seen the scrunchie, which was right next to her, and made great efforts to lean down and pick it up. He could see it now, and in his mind's eye he zoomed in on her hand. It would be so easy to pretend to pick up something *that you were already holding*.

A squad car was moving slowly off now, light flashing, siren going, but Den headed in the opposite direction, shoving his way through the crowd until he broke free and started running, faster than he'd ever run in his life before, towards Nelson House.

Day Four

Sandy

Sandy stared at the plaque for a while, reading the words a couple of times more, taking them in. There was no daughter in Australia. All that was left of her was in the urn. It had been all along.

Kath had been – what exactly? – spinning lies, telling tales, imagining the life she wished her daughter had had? No grandchildren, then. No phone calls. No letters or cards. Poor Kath. How terribly lonely she must have been.

Sandy replaced the plinth on the mantelpiece, plaque facing the wall as before. It wasn't her place to change things. Maybe Kath herself would turn it the right way round after Sandy had had a chance to talk to her about Elizabeth Violet – Kath's Evie.

She took a last look round for the door keys, thinking that the likeliest thing was that Kath had taken them with her. Perhaps a quick look in the rest of the flat. She walked out of the lounge and went into Kath's bedroom. It was exactly how she imagined it would be. The bed was made immaculately. A lilac quilted coverlet lay on top of blankets and sheets. No duvet for Kath. The wardrobe, dressing table and chest of drawers were all made of the same dark wood. A cosy dressing gown hung on a hook on the back of the door. There was no sign of a handbag or keys.

She started wondering what to do. She didn't want to leave Kath's door open, but neither did she want to be responsible for locking her out. She walked out of Kath's bedroom and faced the door on the opposite side of the hall. The second bedroom. There was a small ceramic sign at eye level, decorated with flowers around the edges with words in the middle: 'Evie's Room'.

It felt wrong, very wrong, but Sandy couldn't resist. No one would know, would they, and she wasn't snooping, she was looking for Kath's keys. She reached for the handle and pushed.

It was like walking into the past – the room was frozen in the late 1970s. Bright wallpaper, patterned covers, the whole thing screamed of a period that Sandy only knew from old reruns of *Top of the Pops* and retro movies. It was amazing to see the reality of it preserved like this. There was something wonderful about it and something very chilling, because, of course, Kath had kept the room untouched since Evie's death. It wasn't just a bedroom. It was a shrine.

Sandy stepped further into the room. For the sake of her cover story, she scanned the surfaces for Kath's keys. They weren't there and Sandy turned to leave. Whatever she decided about the door, she should go after Kath before she wandered off too far.

As she walked past the end of the single bed, she saw the edge of something sticking out from under the duvet. It spoiled the lines of another perfectly made bed. Sandy went over and pulled back the duvet, expecting to find a 1970s nightdress or some little pyjamas.

There was a piece of cloth in the bed, sort of mangled up and grubby, chewed at the edges.

And now it felt like the walls were rushing in to crush her, the floor was dropping away, the whole world was spinning out of control. What was this doing here? How could it possibly be here? Because Sandy recognised the piece of cloth. It was Mina's favourite thing in the world. It was her cuggy.

Day Four

Den

He looked up as he ran towards entrance to the stairwell. Someone was sprinting along the third-floor walkway, really fast. He dived in through the door and started taking the steps in great leaps. Above him he could hear someone clattering down the stairs.

Halfway up, Sandy came swinging round a corner, almost colliding with him.

'Hey, Sandy. Do you know where—?'

'It was her! It was Kath!' she shouted.

She didn't stop, just barged past and carried on bombing down the stairs.

'But where—?'

She didn't answer. Den turned and plunged down after her. When he emerged out of the door, he could see her running off to the right, deeper into the estate. He followed her blindly, cursing the way he'd let his fitness lapse.

They ran between the blocks, along the network of concrete paths that dissected tired, grassy patches.

Eventually Sandy stopped and Den was able to catch up. She

was leaning forward, hands on knees, breathing heavily and crying at the same time. 'I let her go. God, I let her go.'

'Mrs C? Kath?' said Den, barely able to speak himself.

'Yes! I know you said to watch her, but I was talking to that cop and she slipped out. I saw her heading off this way.'

'On her own?'

'Yeah. She had her trolley with her.' They looked at each other. Den remembered the weight of it when he'd trundled it back to Mrs C's flat an hour or so ago. *Small for her age*, that's what all the police appeals kept saying.

'Oh God, Sandy. The trolley. You don't think—?'

Sandy's hands flew up to her mouth. She stared around wildly.

'It's okay,' said Den. 'She can't have gone far. There's two of us and one of her. Have you got your phone? Give me your number.'

She handed him her phone and he rang his. Then she took it back.

'Have you told the police?'

'I told Naz. He was getting on his radio.'

'Okay. Let's split up.' They went their separate ways. Den tried to think his way into Mrs C's head. She'd been so tired earlier – had that all been an act? He didn't think so. If she'd been walking for ten minutes or so, she'd be exhausted now, needing to rest.

A couple of women were walking towards him. He jogged up to them.

'Excuse me, have you seen an old woman with a shopping trolley, a bag on wheels?' They looked startled and he realised he was frightening them, puffing and panting, wild-eyed and standing too close. He backed off. 'If you see her, call the police!'

Ahead of him he saw the metal gates of Fincham park, still open. Plenty of places to sit there. He jogged through the gates. The park was mostly dark with paths picked out by streetlamps. The kids' play area was on the right in a fenced-off area. There were seats and swings to sit on and benches round the edge, but it was eerily empty. Where the hell could she be?

He jogged on further. The path sloped gently down the hill. He knew it led to a round pond with a little island and a duck house in the middle. Mum and Dad would bring him here when he was little and they'd feed the ducks with stale bread from the café. They were quite bold – he remembered tipping a bread bag up and emptying the contents and shrieking and running away from them as the hungry birds chased him.

There was only one light working on this section of path, sending out an eerie glow that melted into darkness towards the middle of the pond. As he got closer, he could just make out that the bench nearest the light was occupied. She had her back to him, but there was no mistaking the broad shoulders and padded coat.

He stopped for a moment. Mrs C was sitting dead still. No need to startle her. He quickly texted Sandy. *Found her. By the pond in the park.*

Then he walked towards the bench.

Day Four

Den

His heart was in his mouth as he approached the bench. The traffic noise and wailing sirens seemed very distant here, in this quiet, dark, lonely place. During the day, this would be busy with families and joggers, skateboarders and dog-walkers. Now it was just the two of them.

She was so still. When he was three or four metres away, not wanting to surprise her, he scuffed his feet a little on the tarmac. She didn't react, her figure motionless, slumped almost. The tartan trolley was parked next to her on the tarmac. He tried again and cleared his throat. No reaction. There was a low thudding sound now, getting louder. Out of the corner of his eye, he could see a light moving across the sky – a helicopter tracking across the estate where smoke was still billowing up. In his panic, he'd almost forgotten it – forgotten that his life was going up in flames. All that mattered in this moment was the woman in front of him and the secrets that she held.

He took another step towards her. And another.

'Mrs C,' he said. 'Kath.'

He drew level with the bench, then walked in front of her and crouched down.

Her eyes were open.

'Mrs C,' he said again and put a hand over hers.

She blinked.

Her mouth was working but no sound was coming out. Den leaned a little closer.

'I'm sorry,' she whispered. 'I'm so, so sorry.'

Day Four

Kath

I always knew they'd come for me. I'm glad it was Den, in the end, who found us.

When they searched the flat, I was panicking the whole time. I didn't want it to end like that, with them finding her in the hidey hole in the roof. I nearly had a heart attack when the officer asked about the loft space, and another when I spotted a fleck of paint on the duvet, left there from me chipping away the paint that had sealed the trapdoor for years, with my screwdriver. You'd only see it on Evie's lovely swirly duvet cover if you were looking for it, though. And he wasn't looking because who would suspect the little old lady next door? There are advantages to being old, invisible, overlooked.

She kept quiet while they were in the flat, good as gold. Quiet when her mum was there using the bathroom, too. She didn't want to go home, see? Not then. We'd been having the time of our lives. I cooked for her and read her stories. She did some drawing for me. We watched telly together, cuddled up on the sofa as happy as anything. It felt like it was meant to be.

She'd knocked on my door – cold, wet through, terrified because that little shit Danno had been chasing her – and I knew the moment I saw her that this was my chance. I missed Evie so much. I'd never stopped missing her. Now here was another little girl, sent from heaven. The second chance I'd waited a lifetime for.

When we nipped next door to fetch her cuggy, I couldn't believe my eyes. The state of the place. Leaving her all alone in that miserable flat – that's criminal in my eyes. I could do so much better. I could give her everything she'd been missing out on.

It was only later that she wanted to go home. I don't know what changed exactly, but she started getting whiny. I couldn't have that. Couldn't have her making noise. I turned the telly up louder, but even so it was getting risky.

That's when the sleeping pills came in handy. I had hundreds of them. They're a bit mean with them nowadays but in the past they doled them out like sweeties, those and antidepressants. I had a nice stock of them, too.

The only trouble was I couldn't have her anywhere in the flat all woozy. I wouldn't be able to get her up into our emergency hiding place if she was out of it, so I made it into a game. Got her up into the roof space while she was awake and then handed her up a little picnic – iced buns and a flask full of hot chocolate. That stuff's so sweet you'd never taste the crushed-up pills. I wasn't sure how many it would take – she's only a slip of a thing – but I needed to be sure she'd sleep. I needed to buy some thinking time.

I had a sleepless night wondering what to do next. I couldn't bear to take her home. The police had talked about child protection and social workers and that, but there were no guarantees that they wouldn't send her back into that flat with Sandy. I don't hate Sandy or anything. She's just not up to the job and that kiddie deserves better. But I couldn't keep her in my flat forever. I thought maybe we could get out, go somewhere where no one knew us, maybe the seaside or something, but who was I kidding? I could barely breathe walking along on the flat now. My legs were swollen something terrible and I was having trouble with my eyes. It was over, or it soon would be. Maybe one last adventure. We'd walk until I couldn't walk anymore. Me and my girl.

I made it as far as our special place. My eyes were shot, but I knew the path so well it didn't matter – a blurry river of lights leading the way through the darkness and down the hill, my trolley trundling along behind me. *Hold my hand, Evie, that's a good girl. Shall we feed the ducks today? Don't go near the edge, though. Stay back here, darling. Safe with me.*

Day Four

Den

'Is she . . . is she in there?'

He didn't wait for Kath to answer but shifted a little to the left and flipped open the top of the trolley. He wasn't sure what he was seeing to start with. The streetlamp was casting his shadow over the inside of the bag. He moved and brought the trolley into the light. It was surprisingly heavy. Oh God, he thought, then reached in. His fingers found a soft blanket. Please, please be all right, he prayed to himself. He gently moved the cloth and now he felt something cold and smooth. Not flesh, though, an object, hard and round. Puzzled, he cupped it between both hands and lifted it out. It was a dark pottery jar, about the size of a grapefruit. He felt a jolt of recognition.

There were footsteps on the pavement now and Sandy's voice: 'Have you got her? Is she there?'

'No, Sandy. It's not Mina. It's just this.'

Sandy was breathing heavily. She gaped when she saw the urn.

'That's her daughter,' she said. She walked up to Den and took the urn, then carried it over to the bench. She sat next to Kath and put the urn between them. 'This is Evie, isn't it? Elizabeth Violet. E. V. and this is her bench.'

Kath seemed to come to. She looked around her like she was waking up, even though she'd been sitting with her eyes open. She scrunched up her eyes behind her glasses, like she was trying to focus. Sandy touched her shoulder.

'Kath! Kath, look at me. This is your daughter in here, isn't it, Kath? Now tell me where mine is. Where's Mina?'

One Year Later

Kath

I don't get many visitors but I'm used to that. Years of solitary confinement in my little flat, which now I look back at it, wasn't all that different to my current cell with all mod cons. I was surprised to receive the request and not a little bit curious. I mean, I pleaded guilty and I was doing my time at Her Majesty's pleasure. I didn't know if there was really anything more to add, but I wasn't going to say no.

The young woman who walked into the visiting room was different from the one I'd last seen months ago. It wasn't just the hair colour, a sort of tawny blonde now instead of raven black. It was the way she carried herself. She looked a little unsure as she stood in the doorway, but as she walked towards me there was a lighter step. She looked like she was carrying less weight on her shoulders.

She came over to my table and stood there, opposite me.

'Sandy,' I said.

'Kath.'

She hesitated for a moment longer, then pulled out a chair

and sat down with the little table between us. She didn't seem in a hurry to talk, which was odd seeing as she was the one who'd wanted to come.

'Nice to see you,' I said, to try to break the ice.

She pulled a face, unable to say something pleasant back, kept looking at the floor, the table, her hands, anywhere but me. Gawd, I thought, talk about awkward. No point pussyfooting around things, though.

'How's Mina?'

She flinched like she'd been stung by a wasp.

'She's fine. She's doing really well, actually.'

That was a relief. I hadn't been able to find out much since my trial.

'Don't tell me you're still in that flat.'

'No, no, we've moved out of London. Started again. New school. New neighbourhood. New neighbours.'

I didn't miss that little dig. Couldn't blame her for it.

'I'm glad she's all right,' I said.

Sandy seemed to be wrestling with something, probably the urge to tell me to eff off, if she was anything like her old self, but she stayed silent. I couldn't think of anything else to say and time was ticking. I'd had to leave *Countdown* halfway through to come to the visiting room.

'Sandy, dear, why have you come here? If you wanted to see that I was safely locked away, well, you've seen me, but I could've sent you a selfie for that.'

She gathered herself together, sat up a bit taller in her chair. 'You're a cold old cow, aren't you? I came here because I want to understand what happened. I want to understand *why*. You owe me that.'

I wasn't sure about that. I understand now that I did something quite beyond normal behaviour; I crossed several lines and caused her a lot of pain and worry, but I did it for the best of reasons.

271

'I was looking after her, Sandy. Doing what you should have done.'

A flicker of pain showed in her face.

'She was cold and wet and scared. She'd been chased through the streets by a hooligan. She came to me for help. Refuge. So I took her in. I looked after her. Made her feel safe.'

She was clutching her hands together tightly, digging her fingers into the backs of them so hard she was making little marks. Not easy to hear the truth, I suppose.

'But why did you keep her? That wasn't right, Kath. And all the lies. All the time you were in my flat, pretending to be my friend. It was all lies, Kath. How could you do that?'

'There's lies and lies, though. I was protecting her. She was better off with me.'

'You can't say that. It wasn't your decision to make.'

I shrugged. I beg to differ, I thought, but it wouldn't help to say that.

'I don't know if you'll believe me,' she said, 'but I'll never forgive myself for not being there. I think about it every day. It wasn't easy, though, doing everything on my own.'

I shook my head. 'I know all about that. I know it's difficult being a single parent, but in lots of ways things are easier now than when I had my Evie. Nobody bats an eyelid about girls having a baby outside marriage now. It was different in my day. There was a word for a child like that – a nasty word. I heard it more than once.'

'But you were married, Kath. You had your Ray, at least to start with.'

She was looking at me now. Looking and listening. I had her full attention. Perhaps it was time for a bit of honesty. Maybe I did owe her that.

'He was never my Ray, love. And we were never married. He was married to someone else. We had a thing for a few years and then he moved on to a younger model. It was easier to call myself "Mrs". Not so much a lie, more like self-preservation.'

Her face had softened. 'Oh, Kath. Not so different after all. I wish I'd known. I wish . . .' She trailed off but I understood.

'I thought I could do better than you, Sandy. I thought I could do better than me the first time round.' My chest was starting to feel tight, so I had a little pause and tried to get my breath back. 'I was wrong, love. I was wrong and I'm sorry.'

She pressed her lips tightly together like she was trying not to cry. Her eyes were brighter, though, tears not far away.

'Thank you for saying that,' she said. We sat in silence for a while. 'Kath, what happened to Evie?'

'It was an accident. She ran into the road by the shops without looking. They put a crossing in after she died, but I don't think it would have made any difference.'

'How do you mean?'

'The thing was, we argued, me and her. She was upset. If she hadn't been upset, she wouldn't have run away from the flats and across the road like that.'

'You mustn't blame yourself. Everyone argues.'

Bless her, she didn't know any better. She couldn't possibly know how carrying guilt like that for nearly forty years can shape you, become so much a part of you that it's like the weather, or the air around you, or gravity pulling you down. It's always there. It always will be.

'This was . . . different. She kept going on about her dad, wanting to see him. Going on and on and on, so I told her he was dead. That was a lie. A wicked lie. She ran out crying. That was the last time I saw her alive.'

'I'm so sorry, Kath. I wouldn't wish that on anyone.'

'Will you do something for me, Sandy?'

She narrowed her eyes. 'Depends what it is.'

'Give Mina a big hug when you get home. Don't tell her you've seen me. It's better that she forgets about all that, but give her a hug and keep hugging her, even when she turns into a stroppy teenager. You've got your second chance now.'

'Shall I come and see you again?'

'It's up to you, love. You don't need to. I'm all right in here. It's warm and dry; I've got a nice little colour TV. Actually, if you don't mind, I'll get back now. I could catch the end of *Tenable*. Warwick will be waiting for me.'

One Year Later

Den

He'd been dreading this day. One year since Dad died. Since their home and business had gone up in flames. He hadn't wanted to travel back from college in Birmingham to join Mum at the cemetery. The funeral had been bad enough.

So he'd gone online and looked for a bouquet for Mum to put on the grave for him.

Say it with flowers. There weren't enough flowers in the world to express what he would like to say to Dad.

You're a dickhead.

You didn't need to do that.

I miss you.

In the end, he'd chosen a dozen white roses and asked them to put: 'Love you, Dad. Now and always. Den'. Bland, but adequate, and the best he could come up with.

He went for a walk at eleven when he knew Mum would be arriving at Fincham cemetery, leaving his student hall and strolling through the streets, going where his feet took him. He ended up walking along the canal towpath. It was cold and overcast when he set off, but after a while the clouds passed over and the sun came out, bright blue sky reflecting in the still surface of the water.

A year ago, everything had changed. His faith in human nature had been rocked. Not just Dad and his terrible final act, but Mrs C, too. How could such a nice old lady be capable of such a wicked thing? The neighbourhood thug, Danno, had been arrested, finally. Marlon had been cautioned for the harassment he'd carried out at the café. And Mina had been found, drugged but otherwise unharmed, in the roof space above Mrs C's spare room.

Nothing could ever be the same after that day, but maybe, in some ways, it was for the best.

By the time he got home, he was feeling better. It was just a day, like other days, no need to dread it. He had a tutorial this afternoon and then a five-a-side footie game with some of the others from his course. Just a knockabout – no one cared if you took a breather or fluffed a shot.

He let himself into the shared hallway. Today's post was on the mat. He picked it up and started allocating it to the pigeonholes for the other students. There was one with his name on in beautiful, neat handwriting, which he didn't recognise. He frowned.

There was only one page inside – a piece of A4 printer paper, folded in thirds. He opened it up and started smiling. It was a drawing of a girl and a dog in a flowery meadow. Arching over them were the words 'Thank You' drawn in rainbow colours and at the bottom right a signature: 'Love Mina. xx'

One Year Later

Mina

At half past three the streetlights were popping on. Mina was used to the walk home from her new school. She still didn't like the dark but it was okay now that she walked with Nirmala. She lived in the next street along from Grannie and Grandpa's, so they met in the morning and walked in together and waited for each other at the end of the day. It made all the difference.

Sometimes they stopped at the corner shop and bought some sweets or crisps. They talked about bands and boys and who'd said what at school. Nirmala had never asked her why she didn't live with her mum, and Mina hadn't told her. It had just never come up.

As she let herself into the house, Summer started barking and rushed into the hall. The little dog hurled herself at Mina, her front legs reaching up, tongue desperately seeking Mina's hands. She'd been Mina's birthday present in April, an amazing, wonderful surprise at the start of a perfect day.

'Okay, okay. Hello, hello.' Mina fussed the dog enough to make her calm down, then she hung up her coat, left her shoes by the front door and padded into the kitchen. The dog circled her, nearly tripping her up. Grannie was there, like she always was.

'Hello, darling. Did you have a nice day?'

'It was okay. I'm hungry.'

'Do you want some milk? There's flapjack in the tin.'

'Thanks.'

'Just one, though. I'm getting tea ready for five today. Have you remembered that Mum's coming?'

'Yeah.'

She saw her mum two or three times a week and every weekend. It had felt weird to start with, like everyone was on their best behaviour, but they'd settled into it. Mina had never gone back to Nelson House. After the Thing had happened, Grannie and Grandpa had taken her to their house and she'd stayed there.

She didn't quite know what had gone on but somehow Grannie and Grandpa had helped Mum to give up the flat and find a studio apartment near to them. She'd overheard a muttered conversation one evening with Mum saying she'd pay them back and Grandpa shushing her and saying something about wiping a slate clean, but she didn't know what that meant. Anyway, Mum was going to college during the day now and working in a pub in the evening. She was happier than she'd been for ages, and she'd even stopped smoking.

Mina washed her hands at the kitchen sink, then took the tin over to the kitchen table and selected the biggest piece of flapjack. The dog sat bolt upright at her feet, willing her to drop a crumb or two.

Grandpa wandered in. He had a half-day on Wednesdays. Mina liked it when he was home.

'Ooh, flapjack.'

'Not for you,' Grannie said, firmly. 'You'll spoil your tea.'

Grandpa pulled a face at Mina and mimed slapping his hand, then took a square anyway.

'I've got a joke for you. Knock, knock . . .'

Something stirred in the back of Mina's mind. She tried not to think about Nelson House, but sometimes she couldn't help it. She hadn't told anyone what had happened with Nana Kath. She remembered some of it but the rest was blank. She had nightmares, though – dreams where she was shut away in the dark and couldn't find the way out. They were getting less frequent but she still slept with the light on, and had her cuggy with her, even though she was twelve. Something else she probably wouldn't tell Nirmala.

'Mina?' Her Grandpa's voice brought her back into the room. 'Knock, knock. You've got to say, "Who's there?" Don't they teach you anything at school these days?'

'They don't teach us jokes.'

'Knock, knock,' he repeated.

She sighed and rolled her eyes. 'Who's there?'

'Little old lady.'

'Little old lady who?'

'I didn't know you could yodel!'

It was so bad, it was almost good. Despite herself, Mina started giggling.

'Oh, Mina,' Grannie scolded. 'Don't laugh. It only encourages him.'

A Letter from R.M. Ward

Thank you so much for choosing to read *Safe With You*. I hope you enjoyed it! If you did and would like to be the first to know about my new releases, click below to follow me on Twitter.

I loved writing this book and trying to get inside the heads of Kath, Sandy and Den. I hope you loved *Safe With You* and if you did, I would be so grateful if you would leave a review. I always love to hear what readers thought, and it helps new readers discover my books too.

Thanks,

R.M. Ward

@RachelWardbooks

Acknowledgements

I'd like to say thank you to everyone involved in bringing this book blinking into the light. My family are endlessly encouraging and always have been. I'm so lucky to have many writer friends who have supported me through the peaks and troughs of my writing life.

Thank you so much to everyone at HQ Digital, especially Cicely Aspinall who is a delight to work with and has brought much wisdom and insight to the book, Helena Newton for smoothing out the wrinkles in the copy edit, and to all involved in design, marketing and sales.

A huge thank you to my wonderful agent, Sarah Hornsley, who has worked so hard to help me make *Safe With You* the best it can be. Sarah is the sort of calm, smart, clear-headed person you would want by your side in a zombie apocalypse.

Rachel Ward, June 2022

Dear Reader,

We hope you enjoyed reading this book. If you did, we'd be so appreciative if you left a review. It really helps us and the author to bring more books like this to you.

Here at HQ Digital we are dedicated to publishing fiction that will keep you turning the pages into the early hours. Don't want to miss a thing? To find out more about our books, promotions, discover exclusive content and enter competitions you can keep in touch in the following ways:

JOIN OUR COMMUNITY:

Sign up to our new email newsletter:
http://smarturl.it/SignUpHQ

Read our new blog www.hqstories.co.uk

🐦 https://twitter.com/HQStories

📘 www.facebook.com/HQStories

BUDDING WRITER?

We're also looking for authors to join the HQ Digital family!
Find out more here:

https://www.hqstories.co.uk/want-to-write-for-us/

Thanks for reading, from the HQ Digital team

Safe With You

R.M. WARD

ONE PLACE. MANY STORIES

HQ
An imprint of HarperCollins*Publishers* Ltd
1 London Bridge Street
London SE1 9GF

www.harpercollins.co.uk

HarperCollins*Publishers*
1st Floor, Watermarque Building, Ringsend Road
Dublin 4, Ireland

This edition 2022

1

First published in Great Britain by
HQ, an imprint of HarperCollins*Publishers* Ltd 2022

ISBN: 978-0-00-856027-0

This book is produced from independently certified FSC™ paper
to ensure responsible forest management.

For more information visit: www.harpercollins.co.uk/green

Printed and bound in Great Britain by
CPI Group (UK) Ltd, Melksham, SN12 6TR

h... ... Surrey and now li...
hu...
wo...
Her ...
won m...
in twent...
has writte...
Living, set ...
first psychol... 2024

This item should be returned or renewed b... the last date stamped below.

Dychwelyd neu adnewyddu'r eitem erbyn Y... olaf sydd wedi'i stampio isod.

Newport
CITY COUNCIL
CYNGOR DINAS
Casnewydd

BETTWS